GIRL GIANT
AND THE
JADE WAR

ALSO BY VAN HOANG

Girl Giant and the Monkey King

GIRL GIANT
AND THE
JADE WAR

VAN HOANG

Illustrated by
Nguyen Quang and Kim Lien

ROARING BROOK PRESS
NEW YORK

Published by Roaring Brook Press
Roaring Brook Press is a division of Holtzbrinck Publishing Holdings
Limited Partnership
120 Broadway, New York, NY 10271 • mackids.com

Library of Congress Control Number: 2021907412
ISBN 978-1-250-24044-6

Our books may be purchased in bulk for promotional, educational,
or business use. Please contact your local bookseller or the Macmillan
Corporate and Premium Sales Department at (800) 221-7945 ext. 5442 or
by email at MacmillanSpecialMarkets@macmillan.com.

First edition, 2021 • Book design by Aurora Parlagreco
Printed in the United States of America by LSC Communications,
Harrisonburg, Virginia

1 3 5 7 9 10 8 6 4 2

For those of us still learning to embrace our strength

1

THOM NGHO HAD BEEN WRONG about many things lately, but there were four things she knew to be true.

One, the Monkey King had betrayed her, just when she thought she would finally achieve the one thing she had always wanted to do—get rid of her superstrength.

Two, she had changed her mind—she knew her power was a part of her she couldn't change. A part that came from her father, the Boy Giant, who had wanted to give her an opportunity to learn and train with him, one she now wished she hadn't turned down.

Three, the Monkey King had turned her mother into a cricket—which was why she needed to go after him.

And finally, Thom was pretty sure that she and Kha were in over their heads.

They crouched in their hiding spot behind a cluster of trees. As a dragon, Kha could turn invisible, but he'd changed into his human form now. From their perch on the hill, they had a perfect view of the tallest mountain on the island, the home of the demons where the Monkey King had taken her when they had still been friends. Before he had betrayed her.

Thom wondered if she and Kha were at the wrong spot—there were so many mountains on the island, and since they'd arrived, she hadn't seen anyone—not the demons or the Monkey King.

"It's so quiet," she whispered to Kha. "The Monkey King should be here. He had a head start."

After he'd turned her mother into a cricket, he had revealed that he was just a clone of his much stronger self, a version he was going to break free from under the Mountain of a Hundred Giants. Once the true Monkey King was released, he would be even more powerful than the clone that had tricked her.

Kha frowned and gazed out at the view. If they hadn't been on a dangerous mission to stop the demon-god from unleashing himself from his five-hundred-year prison sentence, it would have been a beautiful scene: the lush field at the base of the Mountain, the green canopy of trees growing along the slope, the expansive blue sky, and the ocean in the distance. But a heaviness weighed the air, a tense pause like something bad was about to happen.

"This is the right mountain, though, I'm sure of it," Kha said.

"How?"

"I can feel some sort of enchantment around here, like there's a spell keeping the Mountain intact so the real Monkey King can't break free."

Thom unstrapped her backpack. She reached inside and pulled out the mason jar containing the cricket—her mother. One antenna twitched like she was trying to reach out toward Thom.

"Hey, Ma," Thom whispered, feeling silly. Could Ma understand her while she was a cricket? The black beads of her eyes shone, and her antennae stilled as if she were listening intently.

"How's she doing?" Kha asked.

Thom held the jar up to him. "She's a cricket," she said dryly, like it was the worst thing in the world, because it *was* the worst thing in the world, at least to Ma.

Kha pouted sympathetically. "We'll catch the Monkey King, Thom. And we'll make him turn her back."

Thom tightened her jaw. Yes, they would. She was going to make the Monkey King pay for what he'd done.

Something rustled down below, then grew louder. The crunch of dried leaves and the snapping of twigs. The thundering of feet.

Demons.

As they marched into the field at the base of the Mountain, they looked scarier and bigger and stronger than what Thom had remembered them to be. The demon friends she'd met the last time she was on the island had been gentle giants. These demons, the ones gathering as if they were assembling an army, looked like they could snap her in half with a flick of their wrist. They were all some breed of predator—a chimera with the head of a boar and the body of a lion, a hyena with the head and neck of a giant snake, a wild boar with the muscular legs of a stallion.

And there were so many of them. Hundreds, maybe thousands, pouring in at the base of the Mountain, most on feet, some on wings. As they gathered, they grew louder like the crowd at a concert, a constant roar, but high-pitched and wild. Feral.

Thom stuffed the mason jar securely into her backpack, where her mom would be safe, and turned to Kha, whose horrified expression mirrored what she was thinking. How were they supposed to go up against that? Where had so many demons come from? She knew the Monkey King had friends, but the last time she was here, there had been twenty, maybe thirty of them.

"What do we do?" she asked.

Kha's chest moved up and down a few times, his eyes scanning the crowd below them. "We wait until they calm down, maybe later tonight, and then we sneak to the base of the Mountain and . . ."

"And what? Guard it? Wait for the Monkey King to show up?" Thom could take on the Monkey King; she could beat him if she really tried. Maybe with a bit of luck, she could steal back the cudgel, and then she and Kha would have a fighting chance. But the thing was, the Monkey King wasn't alone. He had an army now.

The demons roared. They were excited, jumping, shrieking, some tackling one another. Fights broke out in parts of the crowd, circles forming to make space as the violence spread.

Then they all quieted, something catching their attention.

The Monkey King.

He skipped through the air, twirling a wand like he was conducting a symphony—only it wasn't a wand at all. It was the iron cudgel. He'd shrunk it down, showing it off like a long-lost toy.

At the sight of him, Thom's fist clenched. If she could fly, she would have launched straight for him. But she could only stand at the top of the hill, hidden behind the trees, and watch as he flew above his followers, whirling his iron cudgel and changing it back to its staff-length size. The weapon that she had stolen from the heavens for him only so he could betray her.

"Brothers!" the Monkey King called in his giggly, singsong voice. "Some of you have traveled far to witness this momentous event. For four hundred and ninety-eight years, I have been stuck under this mountain!" He pointed the cudgel at the base of the incline behind him, and the demons roared, the air filling with their shrill excitement.

Thom stepped back, easing behind a tree, even though the demons were too far away to notice her. These guys were much bigger than the ones she'd arm-wrestled, their muscles bulging, their roars guttural, their teeth sharp as they growled at one another. No way could she take on a whole army, even if she was superstrong, even with Kha by her side.

"Now," the Monkey King continued, silencing the demons, who went still with anticipation, "is the time for my imprisonment to come to an end."

He dropped to the ground. The demons moved back to make space, bowing, some lowering to all fours as if to kiss his feet. A circle formed around him as he approached the base of the Mountain, holding his cudgel like a baseball bat.

"We have to stop him," Thom said, moving forward.

"Wait, Thom." Kha darted in front of her. "We're outnumbered. There's no way we can beat him and all those demons down there. Maybe if we had more time or more people on our side—"

"We don't, though. We have to try now, on our own!"

Thom tried to walk around him, but Kha transformed into a dragon so fast that she bumped against his scaly body. He circled her, but his coils remained loose, like he was protecting her instead of trapping her.

"Look at them," he said, jerking his head at the demon army. Their shrieks echoed across the mountainous terrain. The leaves quivered, the ground rumbled.

He was right. Thom and Kha were outnumbered, and the Monkey King would destroy them both. They had no plan—heroes always had a plan. Already, nothing was going how she'd expected. She'd thought she would find the Monkey King alone, that she could take him on by herself.

She stood helpless, watching as the Monkey King turned to his demon brothers one last time, gave them a smirk, and then flew at the Mountain. As he raised the cudgel, Kha's dragon body curled tighter around her, almost like he was afraid she would rush down toward the demon army on her own.

Then the Monkey King brought the cudgel crashing against the Mountain. The whole island shook as he slammed it at the ground again and again. Dust filled the air, swallowing his powerful form. The shaking grew stronger. The demons shrieked louder. Large chunks of rock and dirt cascaded all around them, blurring Thom's view of the Monkey King and the demon army.

Eventually, after what felt like hours of utter chaos, the rocks stopped falling. The demons quieted. The dust started to settle, and slowly the air cleared.

The Monkey King stepped forward from the foglike dust. But he wasn't alone. A second figure emerged, just as tall and lithe and powerful.

The *real* Monkey King.

2

HE LOOKED ALMOST EXACTLY LIKE the first one, the one she thought had been her friend, except that he seemed older somehow. It might have been the thick layer of dust coating his fur, making it look gray and aged, but there was something serious about his gaze as he peered out at his army, something mature and knowledgeable, the absence of the silliness she always associated with the Monkey King. With *her* Monkey King.

The demons bowed to the second Monkey King, all of them falling to their knees, some pressing their foreheads to the ground. He turned to the first Monkey King, the one who still held his cudgel. The real Monkey King held out his hand, and with a giggle, the clone handed it to him.

The weapon purred, hummed with pure happiness. A contented sigh went through the crowd, as if they could feel how right it was that the real Monkey King had been reunited with his cudgel.

Then, with a pop, the first Monkey King, the clone who had betrayed her, disappeared. A single golden hair floated where he had just been. The real Monkey King snatched it, rolled it between his fingers, and stuck the hair into his armpit.

Great. All this time, the Monkey King she'd thought was her friend had been nothing more than an armpit hair.

Then the real Monkey King turned to the crowd. He curled his wrists around the cudgel, lifted it up to his chest, tucked his chin down. And giggled. His grin spread wide across his face, his eyes crinkled, even his ears wiggled.

Everyone was enraptured. Even Thom felt drawn to his glee.

Then he threw his head back and cast his staccato laughter out over the crowd. It bounced across the army of demons until they were all roaring along with him.

That familiar sound sent a wave of longing through Thom. He was her friend, he had been her friend. If only things had been different. Why couldn't he have been good? Why couldn't he have told the truth?

Why did he have to turn her mom into a cricket?

At that thought, anger boiled through her veins. She moved forward, forgetting that Kha's dragon body was blocking her way.

"No, Thom," Kha said. He dragged her away from the edge and farther into the copse of trees they'd been hiding in. "Let's regroup. Think of a plan."

"What plan?" She tried to jerk free but only managed to get an *oomph* out of him. "He's out now, the real him. It's too late to come up with a plan. He's going to do something, something bad. We need to stop him!"

"Brothers!" the Monkey King called to the crowd.

Thom stopped fighting and strained to listen.

At his voice, the crowd died down, waiting with hushed expectation.

"I'm free!" he declared.

Again, cheers. Applause.

"Are we ready?" the Monkey King shouted at his army.

Screams and shouts of agreement. Thom's ears rang with the noise.

"Ready for what?" Thom asked.

"I don't know," Kha said.

The Monkey King grabbed a handful of fur from his shoulder, held his fist to his mouth, and blew. The tufts of hair spread out like dandelion seeds, floating across the crowd. One by one, each hair popped into a clone of the Monkey King. His giggles echoed as each clone grabbed a demon and launched into the sky. The demons who had wings could fly, but those who couldn't paired up with a clone. Thousands of demons and Monkey King clones burst up, until above her, a whole army of flying, shrieking monsters swarmed the sky like giant vultures.

Together, they flew up, becoming dots until they were

gone. And the real Monkey King led them, his demon army, toward the heavens.

◆ ◆ ◆

The silence that remained made Thom feel hollow and weak. Her knees were so wobbly that she would have fallen if Kha hadn't been holding her in place. The Monkey King and all the demons were gone, and she and Kha had just watched it happen. They hadn't done a thing to stop him.

"We need to go after him," Thom said. "Follow him and the demons and find out what their plans are."

A snap of a twig made them both jump.

It was Concao, the fox demon, the Monkey King's closest friend. Her white fur, usually so fluffy and pristine, was covered in dirt and something red and viscous. She crouched a few feet away, studying them with a guarded expression.

"Concao," Thom said, one hand braced on Kha's back. "Wh-what are you still doing here?" Thom didn't trust her. Why hadn't she gone with the army?

"Please," the fox demon said, coming closer on all fours. She was limping, her back left paw curled and hurt. "You must come. It's Shing-Rhe. I can't carry him, but you can, strong girl. You have to help me."

Shing-Rhe was hurt? Thom dug her fingers into the feathers along Kha's back.

"It could be a trap," he whispered.

"It's no trap!" Concao said, her voice desperate. "Please. I will explain, but Shing-Rhe is hurt. There's no time."

Thom let go of Kha.

"Thom," Kha whispered, a guttural sound vibrating in his throat.

"It's okay." Thom patted his back. "Show me," she said to Concao.

The fox demon didn't hesitate, turning and bounding away rather quickly for someone who was hurt. They raced after her into the forest, barely keeping up, until they came across a group of monkey brothers all slumped on the ground.

Even though the monkeys were technically demons, they didn't have the grisly, predatory look of the monsters that had joined the Monkey King's army. These guys had always been kind and gentle with Thom. They were peaceful, their faces adorably innocent, their hands reaching out when the fox demon sniffed at them. Thom covered her mouth. They were all injured in one way or another, clutching wounds or curled into balls.

"Did the Monkey King do this?" Thom asked.

"It was the others," Concao said.

For some reason, Thom was relieved, even though she knew the Monkey King might as well have hurt the monkey brothers himself if he hadn't stopped the others from doing so.

"Shing-Rhe!" Thom spotted the elder monkey against the roots of a tree. She knelt at his side. His eyes were barely open, and he groaned when she touched his shoulder. "Shing-Rhe, it's me, Thom."

He didn't respond, just closed his eyes.

Thom looked at Concao and Kha. "We need to get him and the others back to the cave behind the waterfall," she said. "The rainbow water there will heal them."

"I can carry some of them," Kha said.

But when they led the monkey brothers to the dragon, none of them had the strength to hang on to him.

"Wait." Thom dug through her backpack—peeking in at her mother the cricket to make sure Ma was okay—then pulled out the golden string the Boy Giant had given her when she'd met him in the heavens. As she twisted it in her fingers, she remembered how her father had looked as he had given it to her, nervous and awkward. A jolt of guilt made her pause. She hadn't known he was her father at the time, didn't understand why he was giving her a magical string. And when she'd found out who he really was, she hadn't exactly reacted . . . the way a good person would have. No, she had hit him with the cudgel she'd stolen and then left him there. She had to get back to the heavens, if not to stop the Monkey King, then to find her father and apologize for everything, for hurting him and not trusting him.

She grimaced with regret as she lengthened the golden string. Even though it was as thin as thread, it was unbreakable, and kept growing longer no matter how much she used.

And it could be loosened only by the person who tied it. With some maneuvering, she bound the monkey brothers to Kha's back, being extra careful with Shing-Rhe, until they were all secured.

"Can you take the weight?" she asked Kha.

He hovered experimentally. "Yes, but I don't know if I can carry the two of you."

"That's okay—we'll walk."

The fox demon nodded.

Kha couldn't go very fast or fly very high with so many monkeys on his back, but he needed Thom and Concao to show him the way to the cave anyway. It felt like hours by the time they reached it, each step reminding Thom that she was moving farther from stopping the Monkey King, wherever he was, whatever he was doing.

The monkey brothers were all unconscious by the time they made it to the rainbow stream. Concao and Thom both worked to help them from Kha's back. They filled several gourds with rainbow water and helped each of the brothers gulp it down. But then the monkeys fell unconscious again.

"There's nothing more we can do," Concao said. "They need to rest." She sank back carefully on her hind legs.

"You need some healing water, too," Thom said, filling an empty gourd. "What happened to your leg?"

"Ah this." Concao glanced back at her injured paw. "This, the Monkey King did do."

"But I thought he was your friend." Thom handed her the gourd.

The fox demon took it and gave Thom a funny look. "And I thought he was yours."

Thom looked away, keeping her face blank so Concao wouldn't see how much her words hurt. Kha had changed into his human form and was walking around the cave, studying everything in wonder. Thom remembered seeing the sanctuary for the first time, the light filtering through small holes in the cave ceiling, the sound of babbling water echoing across the walls. She wished they could stay here forever, but the longer they stayed, the farther the Monkey King got.

"I tried to stop him," the fox demon said in her soft, husky voice. "He wanted me to lead the army. But I said no. I tried to convince him that his plans would not work, that he was being ridiculous. Then, when he wouldn't listen to me, I thought Shing-Rhe might be able to talk some sense into him. I was wrong." Concao looked at the monkeys sleeping across the grass. "This was my fault. If I hadn't told Shing-Rhe about Sun Wukong's plans," she said, referring to the Monkey King by his name, "the monkey brothers would never have tried to stop him. I should never have involved them. They're not fighters. They didn't stand a chance against those monsters."

"It's not your fault," Thom said. "Shing-Rhe would never have agreed to the Monkey King's plans. He would have wanted you to tell him."

Concao fixed Thom with her frighteningly intense gaze. Her eyes were a blue so pale, they were nearly white, rimmed in a shadowlike shade of gray. They were almost frightening to look at, but Thom didn't turn away.

"What will you do?" Concao asked.

Kha came back and sat next to Thom. They both waited for her answer, but Thom had no idea. Stopping the Monkey King had seemed so easy when she first set out with Kha, as simple as tackling the Monkey King before he was able to break himself free and stealing back the cudgel. Then she and Kha would have raced back up to the heavens and returned the cudgel to the Forbidden Armory, and all would have been well.

But now that plan seemed naive. Of course it couldn't have been that easy. The Monkey King was so much stronger and smarter than her. And even if she had been able to return the cudgel to the heavens, she would have had to face the consequences of stealing it from them in the first place.

"It's too late to warn the heavens now," Concao said when Thom didn't respond. "Wukong planned to break in through the Bridge of Souls. He could be infiltrating the temples as we speak."

Thom's stomach twisted. "So we'll have to stop him and hope that we can save as many people in the heavens as possible before he does too much damage."

"No one has been able to stop the Monkey King before," Concao said.

"Yeah they have," Thom said. "Who put him under the Mountain in the first place?"

Concao looked down. "Yes, I suppose you're right. Buddha was the one who did it, but only after hundreds of gods and dragon soldiers, and even other demons, appealed to him for help. Wukong was uncontrollable back then, and he did whatever he wanted to whomever he wanted. He stole from gods and goddesses, harassed dragon kings, disturbed the order, made enemies of demons, and released other evil beings just for the fun of it. They had no choice but to ask Buddha to step in, and the only way Buddha could defeat him was by tricking him."

"How?" Thom asked.

"He made a deal with Wukong," Concao said. "He held Wukong in his palm and claimed that Wukong could not escape it. Wukong took the challenge and flew to what he thought was the end of the heavens, where he saw only five pillars. He marked those five pillars as evidence that he had won, and then flew back to Buddha, who then revealed that the five pillars had actually been his fingers and that Wukong had never left his hand."

"Buddha must have a giant hand," Thom said.

"He can become larger, the same way Wukong can," Concao said. "But Wukong had never imagined that anyone would be bigger or more powerful than him. It was his arrogance that defeated him."

"Okay," Thom said. "So we do that again. We can appeal to Buddha for help."

"Buddha may not want to step in again."

"Why not?" Thom asked. "This is the Monkey King. Last time, he destroyed half the heavens, right?"

"And ate the peaches of immortality," Kha said. "My mom told me about it. She and her fairies were so upset because they take such good care of the orchards, and he just stomped through their garden like it was a pile of trash."

"He stole the pills of immortality, too," Concao said.

"And drank the heavenly wine," Kha added. "Which also makes him immortal."

"So . . . how immortal does that make him?" Thom asked.

"Um," Kha said. "Very?"

Thom let out a breath. The more she learned about the Monkey King, the more she was starting to realize how impossible it would be to defeat him. But she had to try, not just to save the heavens—it was her fault for putting them in danger in the first place—but also for her mother's sake. Ma couldn't stay a cricket.

"Last time he was free, he nearly destroyed the world," Thom said. "What if he does that again? We have to get Buddha involved if he was the only one able to defeat the Monkey King."

"There is no saying what Buddha will or will not do," Concao said, "but it took many immortals and important beings to convince Buddha to step in. Unless you can get other gods on your side, that would be nearly impossible. Buddha doesn't like to concern himself in matters like this."

If Thom could get other immortals on her side, she might not even need Buddha's help. "Fine, but if Buddha defeated the Monkey King before, that means the Monkey King isn't as invincible as he says he is. That means we have a chance at stopping him."

The fox demon considered her logic. "If anyone knows how to stop Wukong, it would be Shing-Rhe. No one knows him better. We'll wait until he wakes up before we decide what to do next."

"We?" Thom asked, surprised.

"Wukong betrayed me." Concao stood, stretching her now-healed back leg. "You didn't think I'd let you have him all to yourself, did you?"

3

NIGHT FELL BEFORE ANY OF the monkey brothers stirred, the least injured among them waking up first. They tended to one another, bringing fruits and water, and making Shing-Rhe as comfortable as possible on a bed of plush leaves. Some came up to Thom and hugged her, nuzzling their faces against her hoodie. They surrounded Kha, practically burying him with treats, combing his hair, and patting his back in gratitude.

Thom sat by the stream and took the mason jar holding the cricket out of her backpack. She stared at the water. It was supposed to have healing properties. What if it healed Ma and made her human again?

She filled a gourd with water and uncapped the mason jar. Carefully, she tipped a few drops of the water inside, dotting the bottom of the glass. The cricket turned, her antennae twitching as if studying the water. Thom tipped the jar so that the cricket slid closer to a drop, but when the cricket's leg touched it, nothing happened. Maybe she had to drink the water in order to be healed. But how do you get a cricket to drink something?

Thom placed the jar by her side, waiting for the cricket to take a sip of the healing water. She didn't know how long she sat there, watching her mother and wishing she was her human self. Ma would probably know what to do.

When Shing-Rhe finally woke, Thom was getting ready to nod off herself. Kha was huddled in the corner while a monkey groomed his hair and another massaged his shoulders. He came back to Thom's side as she leaned over Shing-Rhe. The elder monkey looked like he hadn't slept in days, the fur droopy and rugged on his face.

"How do you feel?" Thom asked as he sat up. "Do you want more water?" She reached for a gourd.

"No," he said, waving a hand. "No, I'm all better."

"Shing-Rhe," Thom said, a knot forming in her throat. She pushed out all the words before she wouldn't be able to, afraid she would start crying if she stopped talking. "The Monkey King is gone—he took the whole demon army with him. I thought I could stop him, but there were too many of them. Now it's too late. He's probably in the heavens already, but I still need to find him. I need him to turn my mom back. He made her into a cricket and—"

"Hush, hush," Shing-Rhe said softly. "It's all right."

"But it's not all right. There must be some way to defeat

him. Can you think of anything? Or anyone? Concao says last time it was Buddha who stopped the Monkey King, but she thinks Buddha probably won't want to step in again. Maybe if we had more people on our side, maybe if we had an army of our own. Or if I had a weapon, like the cudgel." She thought of all the weapons in the Forbidden Armory in the heavens. If only she'd grabbed one of them along with the Monkey King's staff when she'd had the chance.

"Any god or goddess or being powerful enough to stop him would be in the heavens," Shing-Rhe said. "He will have barricaded the entrances by now. He planned to lay siege to the Jade Palace until the emperor named him the heavens' ruler."

Shing-Rhe paused to cough, his whole body shaking. Thom handed him the gourd, and this time he took a long swig from it.

"He wanted to take us with him, said that he would create a better world for us up there," Shing-Rhe continued. "But we are happy here in our sanctuary. What more could we want? That was when the others came, the demons. I suspect . . ." Shing-Rhe looked incredibly sad as he continued talking. "I suspect Wukong wanted to show us that our sanctuary would not remain our own for very long. He wanted to give us a reason to come with him to the heavens, and maybe we would agree if our home was destroyed. But the monkeys, our brothers, took the fight outside. We defended our home. And we almost died doing so."

"I'm so sorry," Thom said, not just for the physical injuries, but also for the Monkey King's betrayal. How could he just let the demons attack his peaceful brothers like that? "I'm going to find him and make him pay. For everything." She picked up the mason jar and brought it up to her face. The water droplets were gone, but the cricket was still a cricket.

Shing-Rhe touched Thom's hand. "Be careful, child. You are stronger than others, but you are still no match for Wukong. You are good and pure. He . . . he has lost his way. He will not be afraid to hurt you, the way he was not afraid to hurt his brothers."

The words stung, but she knew they were true. The Monkey King was still much stronger than her, even more now that he had his cudgel again. "Then I'll need help. Aren't there other gods and goddesses?" She turned to Kha. "Like the ones in charge of small areas of the earth. Wouldn't they be in this world?"

Kha nodded. "But they won't be a match for the Monkey King. Most of them will be too scared to challenge him, especially after what happened last time he was free."

There had to be a way. She and Kha and Concao couldn't be the only people willing to go up against the demon-god.

"What about the Four Immortals?" Thom asked. "I know the Boy Giant is . . . in the heavens." She gulped, still ashamed at what she'd done to her own father. "But what about the other three: the Mountain God, the Sage, and the Mother Goddess?"

No one said anything. Thom sat back, defeated.

"It might be possible," Shing-Rhe said. "Together, they could combine their powers and be strong enough."

"Then let's find them," Thom said, starting to get to her feet.

"But they may not want to," Shing-Rhe said. "They rid themselves of mortal affairs long ago."

"This isn't a mortal affair—this is war in the heavens!" Thom pointed out. How could beings so powerful, with gifts strong enough to save the world, just sit back and do nothing? "And once the Monkey King is done up there, who knows what he'll do? He'll want to start in on the mortal world next. Or the hells. What if he unleashes every being from there?"

"Even so," Shing-Rhe said, "Wukong doesn't need to be defeated. What he needs is someone to show him that he can be good. That he can *still* be good, despite all he's done."

"I don't care what the Monkey King *needs*," Thom said, her fists clenching. "He turned my mom into a cricket! And he's planning to hurt everyone in the heavens." Her father was up there. And so many others.

But Shing-Rhe shook his head, not listening. "The best thing you could do for him is find Guanyin. The Goddess of Mercy will show him compassion. She'll help him find his way back to who he really is."

Thom stared at Shing-Rhe in disbelief. After the way the Monkey King had allowed his demon friends to hurt his monkey brothers, after how he had injured his supposedly close friend Concao, after the way he had betrayed *her*—Thom— Shing-Rhe still believed the Monkey King was good.

"Guanyin's temple is in the heavens," Kha said when no one else spoke, "so we still need to figure out how to get back up there. Even if we do, though, her temple is higher than the Jade Palace. We wouldn't get to her in time."

"We have to find the other three immortals," Thom said, thankful that Kha had come up with the excuse she couldn't think of. "Do you know where they are?" she asked Shing-Rhe.

He hesitated, scrutinizing her face with his wise, old eyes. She tried to look innocent, to not think about how she planned to beat the Monkey King with his own cudgel when she caught up to him again.

"I do," the elder monkey said.

Thom held her breath.

"But you must promise that when you get into the heavens, you will find Guanyin first. You will ask her to have mercy on Wukong. Promise."

Thom breathed once. Twice. "I promise," she lied.

✦ ✦ ✦

The monkeys packed their bags with food, mostly bananas and nectarines and other snacks they had around the sanctuary.

They followed Thom, Kha, and Concao to the exit, patting them on their backs and legs affectionately, some clutching handfuls of their clothes as if trying to keep them in the cave where it was safe.

"Be careful, Thom," Shing-Rhe said, pulling her into a hug. "Find Wukong and bring him back to us."

Thom swallowed the lump in her throat. "I'll try."

She turned to leave, but one of the monkey brothers pulled on her sleeve.

"What is it? Oh."

The monkey handed her a few gourds and nodded, patting her hand when she wrapped it around the bottles. They were filled with the healing water from the brook.

"Thank you."

When she stuffed the gourds into her backpack, wedging them safely against her mom's jar, something sharp scratched the back of her hand. It must have been a bur or something that had gotten inside, but when she searched for it, she couldn't find anything.

Her heart was heavy as they walked through the tunnel. When

there was enough space, Kha transformed into a dragon so that she and the fox demon could climb onto his back.

As they flew away, Thom looked back at the waterfall blocking the entrance to the cave. She had no idea when she would see the monkey brothers again, no idea if she would ever be back. She wanted to believe that she could defeat the Monkey King, that she could find a way to stop him, but she also knew that he was much stronger than her. She pictured the way he wielded his cudgel, as if it weighed no more than a chopstick, when she had barely managed to lift the thing without shaking under its weight.

Not to mention all his other powers. He had mastered the Seventy-Two Transformations: He could become invisible, fly, transform into other shapes, clone himself, and do so much more, she couldn't remember it all. And he had the demon army. Sure, she might be able to get the Four Immortals on her side, and they were powerful beings. But would they be a match for an entire army of feral, angry demons? What about the Monkey King's endless supply of clones? Even if he ran out of hair—she shuddered at the image of a completely bald Monkey King—his clones could clone *their* hairs.

As Kha flew, following directions Shing-Rhe had given him to find the Mountain God, Sơn Tinh—the first of the Four Immortals they would seek—she slumped against his back. The wind wasn't that strong today, and Kha didn't fly as high as the Monkey King, so when the fox demon spoke behind her, Thom had no trouble hearing.

"What made you finally realize the truth," Concao asked, "about Wukong?"

Thom was grateful Concao couldn't see her face. "When he admitted that he'd always lied about taking my power away. I didn't want him to, not anymore. I don't hate my strength now." She'd learned that she needed her power, especially now that she would have to fix all the mistakes she'd made. But it was also a part of her she could never change. "And when he turned my mom into a cricket," she added.

"I'm sorry about that. When we catch him, we will make him turn her back. Or you might even ask one of the immortals to do it for you."

"Really? Do you think they could?"

"Perhaps. You are one of them—one of their daughters anyway. They will at least try."

"Did you always know?" Thom asked, remembering how Concao had whispered in the Monkey King's ear the first time she'd met the fox demon.

"I could smell it on you. Your blood is . . . sweet."

Thom shivered, tried not to find it horrifying that Concao could smell her blood. "Can all demons do that?"

"No. I'm different." The fox demon paused. "I wasn't always a demon."

Now Thom wished she could turn around to look at Concao's face. "How? I didn't know that was possible." Shing-Rhe had explained how the first demons were made, but that was eons ago. Concao couldn't be that old, could she?

"It's very rare," the fox demon said. "But I was once a fairy. I lived in the heavens and tended to the Forbidden Garden."

"What happened?" Thom wondered if it was rude, how much she was prying. "You don't have to tell me if you don't want."

"I do want to tell you," Concao said. "After all, lack of honesty is what usually gets us into messes like this. You didn't know the Monkey King's full story, so you believed his version. I will tell you mine."

Thom waited, and she knew Kha was listening intently, too, from the way his ears stretched back to catch their voices.

"I was a fairy, not a high-order goddess, but I lived in the heavens. I was respected. I had friends. I was one of them. My job was to tend to a particular orchard in the Forbidden Garden, where the peaches were not ripe yet. It was a simple job, but I felt like I was part of something bigger, like I was helping in my own way."

The wind gusted. Kha rode the crest and settled back into an easy glide.

"One day," Concao continued, "I was going about my

duties, checking on the peaches and pruning the dead ones, when I heard a giggle. It wasn't one of the other fairies. It sounded like . . ."

"The Monkey King," Thom said.

"Yes," Concao said. "Though I didn't know it at the time. He wasn't as famous back then. We all thought he was just some high-minded servant. A low-level immortal proclaiming to be more than he was. I'd heard about the Jade Emperor appointing a Master of the Horses, but I had never expected it to be a . . ."

"Demon?"

"A monkey."

This was when the Monkey King had only been appointed Master of the Horses? How old was the fox demon?

"He was dressed in armor," Concao continued.

Thom remembered the red-and-gold plating that she had seen inside the Forbidden Armory, the one the Monkey King had called glorified shackles.

"So I assumed he was someone special. He asked me for a peach. I said no, they were forbidden and only served during special occasions, but he said the Lotus Master had sent him there to fetch some for the student banquet. He was so convincing, and he knew so much about the Lotus Master and the Lotus Academy that I couldn't help but believe him. Everyone respected and feared the Lotus Master, you see. He sent his students on errands for him all the time. But never a monkey. I should have known."

"No," Thom protested. "He tricked you. It's not your fault."

"I'm glad you see it that way, but many others did not." Concao's voice was thick with regret. "I gave Wukong the peaches, and he made off with them. It wasn't long before the others found out what had happened—Wukong never liked to keep his own tricks a secret after he'd managed them. He was always a braggart. When the head fairy in charge of my orchard heard about what happened, she didn't give me a chance to explain. But then again, no explanation would have sufficed. As fairies, we all knew the rules. We all knew the peaches were under our protection. I had broken my own vows."

Concao fell quiet. They continued to fly peacefully through the sky, surrounded by fluffy clouds and a blue expanse ahead of them.

"They stripped me of my fairy abilities, but I was not mortal," Concao said, breaking the silence, "so they could not send me back to earth. My superior thought sending me to the hells would be too harsh."

"Of course it was harsh—it wasn't your fault," Thom said.

"So they banished me to the island to live among other demons."

"But . . . I mean, that's not fair, either."

"No," Concao agreed. "It isn't."

"You've been there ever since? But it must have been, like, at least five hundred years ago."

"Yes," Concao said.

"But . . . if the Monkey King betrayed you, why are you friends with him?"

"We weren't friends right away. After he learned that I was banished—and that it was his fault—he came to find me. I didn't trust him at all. But I didn't know how to be a demon, not at first. I wasn't . . . prepared for their viciousness, and the island was different back then. Nothing like what you see now."

"The Monkey King said he was the one who made it better."

"He was. That's why the demons respect him so much. He taught them how to keep order, how to live a life free of chaos. The thing is, Wukong isn't always a bad person. You saw that for yourself, Thom. He can be a good friend. He found me in my lowest moment, cared for me, taught me how to live on the island, how to survive among the demons, how to make friends. I didn't want to forgive him at first, but I had no one else, and he was . . . he can be . . . very kind."

Thom didn't want to admit it, but she knew what Concao meant. She was still too hurt by the Monkey King's betrayal to feel anything soft or affectionate toward him, but the image of him teaching the demons how to talk and be kind to one another reminded her of the times he had been surprisingly nice to her. All their moments on the soccer field. The way he'd taught her to control her kicks, to use a percentage of her strength to do what she loved. The Monkey King had been so nice to her, the only one who truly understood what she felt, the only one who could teach her how to accept herself without making her feel like she was doing anything wrong to begin with.

"But there is something else," Concao continued. "Something I have never told anyone before."

"What is it?" Thom asked.

"Even though Wukong and I became friends, I have never forgotten what he did to me. Not because I can't forgive him, but because I am all too aware that, given the chance, he would do it again. He will always look out for himself, and just as there is a side of him that is good, there is a side of him that will always be bad. So I made a deal with the heavens."

Thom waited.

"When the Monkey King was imprisoned under the Mountain of a Hundred Giants," Concao explained, "I agreed to guard him. Once the five hundred years were up and I had accomplished my task, I would get another chance to become a fairy again. I would be welcomed back into the heavens."

"But the Monkey King broke himself free." Because of Thom. Because she had helped him. "I'm so sorry, Concao."

"If I capture him again—if we help to defeat him—there is still a chance the heavens will honor the agreement."

"Do you think so?"

"I have to hope so. I do not think I can stand to live on that demon island for much longer."

"You want to go back to the heavens? After the way they banished you and treated you so unfairly?"

"It is my home," Concao said. "It is not perfect, but that's no excuse to abandon it. I still belong there. I can go back and maybe fix things from the inside. And I miss it."

Thom wanted to hug her. "It's my fault the Monkey King escaped. I'll take the blame for it all. They'll have to reward you—you were only two years short of your agreement."

"Let's hope so," Concao said with a sigh.

Kha suddenly jerked to the side as a gust of wind slammed into them.

Thom clutched his feathers, gritting her teeth. "What's happening?" she asked as the wind swiveled around them like a twister, sending Kha into a spiral.

"We're nearly to Tản Viên Mountain!" Kha shouted, the home of Sơn Tinh, the Mountain God.

"Why can't we land?" Thom asked.

"Because"—he struggled to remain flying—"it doesn't look like the Mountain God wants to be found."

4

THE WIND WAS SO STRONG that Kha lost control of the flight. He spun and flipped, the wind whipping and tossing them like they were flimsy leaves. Thom hung on, hoping she wasn't hurting him. She wondered if Concao was doing okay behind her.

"There it is!" Kha shouted.

Thom looked down at a huge mountain range.

"Which one is it?" she shouted to be heard. In the distance, a river—so wide Thom couldn't make out the other side of it—coursed aggressively and crashed against the walls where the land dropped away. The waves sounded almost angry as foam sprayed high above the ground.

"That one." Kha darted for a crest that looked like all the others to Thom, but he must have known what he was searching for. Each time they got close, the wind whipped them around again, like some force field protecting the mountain from intruders. Kha tried to go around to find a way in, but no matter where he flew, the wind blocked him from getting close enough. They couldn't even land far away and walk. Each time they lowered, a twister pushed them back up.

"It's impossible," Kha said, panting as they hovered above the wind. "I can't break through."

Thom looked around for some possible solution. The river roared, waves slamming over the rocky edges. The shield of wind kept the foam that burst into the air from getting too close. The twister around the mountain moved in such a powerful gust that it looked almost solid, like a dome of glass.

"Do you think *I* could break through?" Thom asked.

"What do you mean?" Kha asked. "How?"

"I could, like, punch my way through the wind."

"What? No—you're too little. It will just toss you around."

"It's too dangerous," the fox demon agreed. "The Mountain God really does not want to be disturbed. Shing-Rhe warned us of this. None of the Four want to get involved in mortal affairs."

Thom looked up at the heavens. Their only option was to get to Guanyin somehow, but that was a paradox. The Goddess of Mercy was up there, too, and they couldn't get into the heavens without the Four Immortals' help. She didn't see any other way.

Taking the magical golden string from her pocket, Thom came up with an idea. She wrapped one end around her waist and the other around Kha's body.

"Let's regroup!" Kha was saying, shouting to be heard over the wind and the river. "We could find the Sage next. He'll take us through his path into the heavens. My uncles might know where he is."

"How long will that take?" Thom asked.

"Another day, maybe?"

The longer they waited, the more damage the Monkey King would do in the heavens. What if, by the time they got up there, no one was left to save? She thought of her father. He was the Boy Giant, one of the most powerful beings in the world, and he had been knocked out cold by the cudgel. And it hadn't even been the Monkey King who had wielded it. It had been her, Thom, and she hadn't known how to use it properly. He wouldn't stand a chance against the Monkey King, who now wielded the cudgel and led a legion of demons. The rest of the heavens would certainly fall.

She looked desperately around her. Nothing was going the way she thought it would.

"We don't have the time," Thom said. Before the others could stop her, before she could consider how dangerous her plan really was, she slid off Kha's back.

Weightless, she realized what a terrible idea this was. She was in the wrong position, but now there was nothing to do about it. The dome of wind came closer. She thrust out a leg, ready to kick her way through the shield.

But as soon as her foot hit the wind, Thom was whipped sideways. She swung in an arc, tethered to Kha by the golden string. He shouted her name, but she was already swinging back, her world upside down. She couldn't right herself. She flailed her arms and legs just as the wind hit her again, and she swung in the opposite direction. Thom gasped for breath. It was like being caught in a riptide. Each time she came up for air, she got hit again.

"Thom, I'm going to pull you up!" Concao called.

Too breathless and whiplashed to respond, Thom couldn't decide whether she wanted to be pulled up or to keep trying. As she swung one last time, her body balanced itself, and she headed toward the dome of wind headfirst. She drew her elbow back, fist clenched, and just as the wind was about to shove her out of the way again, she punched as hard as she could.

Something snapped. It was as if the wind dome were a tight rubber band and she'd ripped right through it. She burst across the other side of the shield and, pulled along with the momentum, Kha and Concao followed. They shot toward the top of the mountain range, Kha barely managing to slow their descent before they crashed.

Thom stumbled onto the grass, rolling several times and finally coming to a stop with her bottom skidding painfully on the ground. Kha landed next to her. Concao climbed off his back and ran to Thom.

"That was the dumbest thing I've ever seen," the fox demon said, pulling Thom to her feet. "Are you hurt?"

"Just a bit scratched." Little rocks and twigs had dug into her palms, but her hoodie and jeans had protected the rest of her. She was never going to get the stain out of her clothes, though. Ma was going to be pretty upset.

Thom yanked her backpack off and pulled out the mason jar. The cricket hopped inside the glass frantically, but otherwise looked okay.

She untied the golden string from Kha and wrapped it around her wrist. "At least it worked."

"You could have gotten badly hurt," Kha said, changing back to his human form. "You're not a full goddess, Thom."

"I never . . ." Thom hadn't assumed that, being part immortal, she couldn't die. She had just done what she thought she needed to.

"And even if you were a full goddess, that wouldn't mean you can't get killed," he continued, tugging his shirt angrily into place. "You can't be so reckless—"

The mountain shook, ending Kha's lecture. The three of them stumbled, almost skidding down the steep hill to the right. Thom landed on her butt again and dug her feet into the dirt, but she couldn't stop. The mountain was deliberately shaking her off as if she were some sort of bug. Every time she moved, the earth crumbled beneath her, dirt and rocks rolling to loosen her grip.

The mountain was alive somehow. It didn't want them there. The Mountain God didn't want them there.

"Wait!" she begged. "Wait, please, we need your help."

It didn't work. Kha scrambled next to her, but the ground rolled beneath his hands and feet no matter where he tried to grab. The fox demon was the only one who didn't panic; lithe and quick, she hopped from a boulder to an upturned patch of dirt. But even she couldn't escape the downward slope.

"Please," Thom tried again, desperate. "I am the daughter of the Boy Giant! We're here to ask for your help. W-we need you!"

Nothing happened and they continued to fall.

Then the rumbling quieted. The ground stopped churning. They all slid to a stop, halfway down the mountain.

Thom breathed hard, looking left, right. Nothing at first. They were still alone. The wind dome was clearly visible from here, as if they were looking through a blurry round window. The river crashed even stronger against the rocks, the water spraying higher than before, lingering in the air like broken fingers. Above, clouds thickened and the world turned gray.

Then someone was directly in front of her. She bit back her shout of surprise.

It was a man. No, one of the Four Immortals. His skin glowed, a golden aura surrounding him like the one the Boy

Giant and the Jade Emperor had had. Surprisingly, he wasn't dressed in immaculate robes or armor. He wore a black T-shirt, jeans, and brown hiking boots.

"The Boy Giant has a daughter, huh?" He crossed his arms.

His skin had that leathery quality of someone who spent too much time in the sun—if they had seen him in public, Ma would have pointed him out and warned Thom that she'd end up like that if she didn't wear sunblock. Thom clutched the glass jar to her chest.

The immortal's eyes crinkled at the corners as he smiled. "I knew they weren't just 'friends.'" He held out a hand. "Come on, then, better get off the ground."

Thom took his calloused hand carefully so she wouldn't crush it and let him pull her up. She helped Kha up, too, and Concao bounded back to them, standing tall on her hind legs. The man observed all three of them with an amused squint.

"Well? How'd you get through my defenses?" he asked.

"You mean your wind dome?" Thom brushed the dirt off her jeans.

"Best thing I ever invented. Haven't had a single intruder for centuries, not even that jerk Thủy Tinh—I know he's always lurking around here somewhere." He whipped toward the river, as if whoever he was talking about was going to climb up the edge. Waves slammed into the riverbank, foam arching toward the sky, then curling toward them, beckoning, before dragging itself down to the sea. No one was climbing out of that river anytime soon.

"Um, who?" Thom asked.

"Thủy Tinh—the Lord of the Waters, my archnemesis. Always stalking about. Never gives me a moment's peace. Quick. Tell me. How'd you get past the wind? I can't risk letting him through."

Of course, Sơn Tinh, the Mountain God, and Thủy Tinh, the Water Lord, had been rivals for centuries, causing uproar in their lands, all over a princess. But in the end, the Mountain God was the one who had been made one of the Four Immortals because he had chosen peace over constant war with his rival.

"I punched through it," Thom said. Heat flooded her face. It sounded so silly when she said it like that.

"You . . . punched through it," the man repeated.

"I'm really strong." She held out her hands as if she could present her power to him like a gift. "I got it from my father, I guess."

"Right. Of course. Thánh Gióng's daughter. Well, you'd better come along. I'm starving, and my wife will kill me if I let the lunch go cold. I hope you like bún riêu."

At the mention of the crab noodle soup, Thom's stomach growled. Kha looked at her in happy surprise. They hadn't eaten since they'd left the monkeys' sanctuary that morning. The monkey brothers had packed them snacks and treats, but they weren't going to turn down a hot meal.

"Well?" the man said as they followed him. "What are your names, huh?"

"I'm Thom. This is my friend Kha. And—"

"Oh, I know you," the man said, bending down to study Kha's face. "The general's son, right? And Lady Cat's."

Kha grinned. "Yes, sir."

"Don't 'sir' me—I'm not your father. You can call me Sơn."

Sơn Tinh, the Mountain God. It really was him, then.

"And you?" he asked the fox demon, who eyed him shyly.

"Concao," she said with a dip of her chin.

"Concao? That's not a real name, that just means 'fox.' What's your real name—tell us."

"I don't . . . It was taken from me when I became a demon."

The Mountain God gave her a sympathetic look. "Never liked it when they did that. Here we are."

They weren't anywhere, though, still in the middle of the mountain. Sơn reached for what looked like a random boulder, and it popped open, a door swinging forward to reveal a tunnel.

"Come on in," Sơn said. When they hesitated, he stepped ahead of them. "I'll lead the way, then."

Thom, Kha, and Concao looked at one another. Was it really a good idea to follow this strange man through a pitch-black tunnel in the mountains? Ma would probably freak out if she knew what they were planning.

But Ma was a cricket—not that it was her fault—and they

had come too far to be afraid of the dark. Thom had punched through a wind dome. She couldn't turn back now, not after she almost died to get here.

She stepped inside, and the others came after her, following the dark shape of Sơn Tinh, the Mountain God.

5

THEY HADN'T WALKED FAR BEFORE the tunnel opened into a well-lit dining room with a round table and small kitchen filled with the smell of shrimp and jasmine rice noodles. A woman stood at the stove, ladling soup into a bowl. She was beautiful. Though her skin didn't glow like that of the Mountain God, there was an ethereal quality about her, the way she glided about the room, her movements graceful. Her silky black hair was tied back loosely from her face, her skin a golden complexion with cheekbones that caught the light as she turned to look at them.

"Why, you're just children," she said, setting the bowl down on the table. Thom and Kha both eyed it. Thom's mouth watered. She hadn't had vermicelli in so long, and this was joined by fried tofu, crab meat, and fish cake, steam rising from the soup's creamy orange surface. "When we saw that someone had broken through the shield, we thought you were much more dangerous."

"They *are* dangerous," Sơn said, kissing the woman on the top of her head. "But that doesn't mean we can't feed them."

"You must be starving after that battle with the wind," the lady said, placing three extra bowls on the table. "Please, join us."

Thom sat, too hungry to politely decline. She and Kha dug in, chopsticks in one hand and a big soup spoon in the other. The fox demon perched on the edge of her seat, sniffing at the bowl suspiciously. The broth filled Thom's stomach and made her warm, so she took off her hoodie and put it away in her backpack. She checked on the cricket, who had calmed down a bit and was now settled at the bottom of the glass. Something scratched her hand again, almost drawing blood this time, but when she checked, she couldn't find anything poking through the fabric of her backpack. Weird.

"This is my wife, Princess Mỵ Nương," Sơn said as they continued eating. He introduced Thom, Kha, and Concao.

By now, Thom should have been used to the fact that gods, fairies, and other mythological beings were real, but it was still so strange. Until recently, Princess Mỵ Nương was just a character in a story—the reason the Mountain God and the Lord of the Waters had fought for centuries. She had been a cutout Thom had made in her Culture Day art project with Kha. They had made a presentation about her and the Four Immortals to the bored faces of their classmates as if the princess were a character in a movie. But she was here, in front of them, a real, talking person.

"Well?" Sơn asked Thom, Kha, and Concao expectantly. "You must have come all this way for something. What is this thing you need help with?"

Concao and Kha both looked at Thom, waiting for her to speak for them. She blushed, feeling awkward and shy under the attention.

"It's the Monkey King," she said. She wished everyone would stop looking at her. Her face grew even hotter. Her whole body heated up actually, and she was pretty sure they could all tell, which made it even worse. "He's broken himself free of his prison—the Mountain of a Hundred Giants. And he raised a demon army and led them into the heavens to, um—" She glanced at Concao, and the fox demon nodded reassuringly. "To lay siege to the Jade Palace until the emperor names him the true ruler of the heavens."

She paused, waiting for the Mountain God and the princess to respond with horror and shock. But they blinked at her, their expressions unchanged, as if she'd just told them about her new shoes and not about the greatest disaster she'd ever witnessed.

"So we need your help to stop him," she finished lamely.

Sơn and Princess Mỵ Nương glanced at each other. Something in their interaction made Thom's stomach churn with nervousness, and she suddenly realized that things might not go exactly as she'd hoped. What if they said no? They couldn't do that, could they? The Boy Giant himself had said that those who had gifts and special abilities had the responsibility to help others who were weaker than them.

"He broke himself free?" Sơn asked eventually, scratching at the stubble on his chin. Golden sparkles flaked into the air.

"I mean"—Thom sank low in her seat—"I sort of helped him."

"He tricked her," Kha said, coming to her defense. "He convinced her that he was her friend and that he could help her take away her power."

"Why do you want your power taken away?" Sơn asked. "It's pretty useful, isn't it? Wish I had been born superstrong."

"But you love your land and your mountains," Princess Mỵ Nương said.

"True." Sơn nodded, patting her knee.

"I don't want my power taken away anymore," Thom said quickly. "I just thought I did. It doesn't matter anyway. It was a lie. I thought he was my friend. I didn't know he was a bad guy in the end. He tricked me."

"Of course he did," Princess Mỵ Nương said without a trace of sarcasm.

Thom sighed with relief. They were on her side, at least when it came to the Monkey King betraying her. It was something she knew not many would believe, and she wouldn't blame them. The evidence was stacked against her. She had befriended the Monkey King. She had released him from the temple where she'd found his hair. She'd stolen his cudgel from the heavens to give to him.

If she was able to defeat the Monkey King and his demon army, she would have to convince the Jade Emperor and the officials in the heavens of the same thing. Right now, everyone in the heavens probably thought she was on the Monkey King's side. But once they saw how hard she'd worked to correct her mistakes, they would have to believe she was on the heavens' side.

"I never wanted Sun Wukong under that mountain in the first place," Sơn said, slapping his palm on the table. "A sacrilege, it was. A disrespect to the hundred giants. And look what happened. I was right, wasn't I? Well."

Thom waited for him to say more, but after a moment, she realized he was done.

"So will you help us?" she asked. "We can't do it alone. Kha's a dragon, and Concao was the Monkey King's friend— she knows more about him than anyone. But we're still no match against him."

"No one is, cưng," Princess My Nương said, and the endearment—*sweetie*—reminded Thom so much of her mother that she took out the mason jar. She smiled at the cricket hopping around inside.

"Oh," Princess My Nương said, surprised. She started to reach for their almost-empty bowls of food, as if afraid the cricket would escape the jar and dive into their meals. Ma would have loved her.

"This is my mom," Thom explained. "The Monkey King turned her into a cricket when she tried to protect me."

"Oh dear." Princess My Nương gave Thom a sympathetic look.

Sơn also seemed very sad for her sake. But neither of them said anything more.

Neither of them offered to help.

Thom waited, but the more seconds ticked by, the lower her heart sank. She knew the answer, but she asked the question anyway. "Will you help us?"

Sơn at least looked ashamed, bowing his head. "No. We vowed long ago not to get mixed up in these matters."

"But the heavens—"

"Those who live in the heavens have survived long enough without us."

"But—" Thom's voice cracked.

"Besides," Sơn added, "I've been at war for almost all of my existence. This is my first chance at any sort of peace."

"But this is the heavens," Thom said. "We can't just abandon them."

"You know, when I was made one of the Four Immortals, I petitioned them to let Princess My Nương join me in the heavens, ascend with me as one of the Four. But they said no. She could be a goddess, yes, but not one of the great ones. She would not get her own path into the heavens. She would not get her own realm. She was welcome in my realm, they said, but she had done nothing to deserve ascension." He shrugged. "So why should we help them?"

Because . . . But Thom couldn't think of a good reason Sơn and his wife should want to help. He made a good point. If Thom were Princess Mỵ Nương, she wouldn't want to help the heavens, either.

"That's why we live here, instead," Sơn said. "Constantly plagued by the idea that the Lord of the Waters could attack at any time, we have to set up barriers and be extra careful with where we go. The heavens never once offered to help us, never once offered to provide a safer space where we can be together. So we created it ourselves, a home where we're equally respected."

Thom looked down at the mason jar in her lap. When she'd been studying the Four Immortals for her school project, she had asked Kha the same thing: How come Princess Mỵ Nương hadn't been made a great immortal with a capital *I*, too?

"You must understand, cưng," the princess said, "that all of the Four Immortals have vowed not to involve themselves in mortal or heavenly affairs. They will not involve themselves, not after what we've already been through."

"But the Boy Giant is doing something," Thom said. "He's in the heavens. He's training the Lotus Students. He . . . he tried to help me." It hurt her to say the words, because then she was reminded of how she'd turned him down, chosen the Monkey King over her own father. What if she made it to the heavens and he refused to forgive her?

"Well," Sơn said with a cough. "He's not really on earth or helping the immortals. He's just training Lotus Students to become soldiers of the Jade Army. Besides, you can't really compare us with him, hah? We were made higher immortals because of our love for one another. He was made one because he sacrificed himself for an entire village. It's in his blood to help, hah?"

Thom didn't think that was very logical at all. She tried to think of an argument but couldn't find one that might make sense to them.

A slurp interrupted the silence. Concao had finally given in, tasting the noodle soup experimentally. She licked her lips, then practically plunged her whole face into the bowl.

"Can you—will you—" Thom cleared her throat and tried again. "Will you turn my mom back into a human?"

Princess My Nương looked at Sơn sadly. He leaned down and squinted at the cricket, who waved her antennae as if she were scrutinizing him back.

"I'm afraid the magic on this cricket can only be reversed by the one who placed it," Sơn said. "You'd have to get the Monkey King to do it."

So they weren't going to help at all. She and Kha and Concao had come all this way for nothing. Had put themselves in danger for nothing.

Well, not nothing. Concao slurped noisily until she scraped the bottom of the bowl. At least they had gotten a free lunch out of it. Thom couldn't remember the last time Ma had cooked bún riêu, or anything except warmed-up frozen dinner trays. But it didn't matter what Ma made for them to eat next. Thom just wanted her back.

As if she could read Thom's thoughts, Princess My Nương placed a hand on her husband's arm. "We can't send them away empty-handed."

"But what—" He stopped. "Oh."

"What?" Thom asked. "What is it?"

Sơn got up from the table without answering. He came back with a long, large parcel in both hands. As he unwrapped it, they all leaned forward.

"Oh my God," Kha said, speaking for the first time since they'd sat down. "Is that really . . ."

"The Sword of Heaven's Will," Princess My Nương finished for him.

It was a huge sword, almost as long as Thom was tall. When Sơn held it like a walking stick, it came up to her shoulder. The blade was flat and wide, curved and sharp on one edge, blunt and straight on the other, engraved with ancient characters over the shining metal. The hilt was as thick as Thom's forearm, made with a black stone material that shimmered colorfully when light touched it.

"The Sword of Heaven's Will?" Thom asked, resisting the urge to reach out for it.

"Yes, Thuận Thiên," Sơn said. "It belonged to the past kings of Vietnam. Whoever found the sword and was able to master it was said to be the heavens' chosen ruler."

"Wow," Thom breathed. "It's like . . . a Vietnamese Excalibur."

They all gave her uncomprehending looks.

"It's basically the same," Thom tried to explain. "Excalibur is, like, this sword that's stuck in stone, and whoever is strong enough to pull it out becomes the rightful king."

They blinked.

"Never mind."

"But anyone could be strong enough to pull a sword out of stone," Sơn said. "I mean, *you* are, first of all. The Monkey King could do it, also. The Boy Giant when he was just a baby."

"Well, the stone would only release it to someone who was worthy," Thom said. "It's not really about strength."

Sơn looked unconvinced. "Even demons are strong enough to pull the sword out. Imagine them being king—"

"Hush. She said never mind." Princess Mỵ Nương cut him off. She gave Thom a kind smile. "They are very similar, aren't they? But the difference with Thuận Thiên is that it was lost for many centuries between rulers. The one who finds it becomes the rightful king."

Maybe Sơn had a point, but Thom didn't see how being good at hide-and-seek was a better requirement for becoming a king than being strong was.

"It's not just a matter of who finds it," Sơn said. "They must also be able to master it."

"Which only the most worthy can," Princess My Nương agreed.

Thom remembered something, a secret the Monkey King had told her. But she didn't voice it aloud, mostly because he had made her promise not to tell anyone, but also because she no longer knew whether what he said was lie or truth. He had once told her that the secret to controlling a weapon—or at least, the cudgel—was to use its name, because all magical objects deserved to be treated with respect.

"I thought it was lost," Kha said. He looked like he wanted to touch the sword, too, but he settled for ogling it. "Or buried with the last king who had it."

"Well, things buried in mountains are basically mine to keep," Sơn said.

"Um, I don't think—" Kha started to say, but Thom nudged his foot under the table.

"If you found it," Thom asked Sơn, "does that mean you're the next king of Vietnam?"

"Goodness, no." The Mountain God let go of the sword as if it burned him.

Instinctively, Thom reached out and caught it. The hilt

had looked beautiful, yet it was uncomfortable to the touch. Bulky. The engravings bit into her flesh. But the longer she held it, the more her fingers sank into the stone as if it had been molded to fit her.

"I don't want to be king," Sơn was saying as Thom held the sword up. "I just like shiny things. But you can have it. You need it more than I do."

"You want us to take it?" Thom asked, even though she'd been hoping Sơn would say that. This was exactly what she needed. The Monkey King had his cudgel. Now she would have a weapon of her own—it was only fair.

"Whoever wields the sword will have ten thousand times their normal strength," Sơn said. "Not bad, hah? Can't say we didn't help after all."

"It will also make the wielder taller," Princess My Nương added.

Thom smiled. She had no idea how to use a sword, but how hard could it be? She had been able to use the cudgel without any experience. The sword looked like it would be heavy, but it weighed no more than a pencil, at least to her. Could this really be a challenge for the Monkey King's staff?

"Do you feel taller?" Kha asked, eyeing the sword.

"Do I look taller?" Thom asked.

He tilted his head. "Maybe? By like an inch or two?"

"Well then, you're not using it properly," Sơn said. "You must wield it in battle against your enemy! That's how it was meant to be used."

Thom placed the sword back on the table. It was better than nothing, but she wished that Sơn and Princess Mỵ Nương had offered to come with them. Or at least to take them up to the heavens. "Thank you for your help," she said, trying not to sound too disappointed. "But we should probably go."

"What will you do next?" Princess Mỵ Nương asked.

"We plan to ask the other three of the Four Immortals," Thom said. "Maybe find a different way into the heavens."

"But we told you," the princess said. "They won't want to be involved."

Thom tried to stuff the sword into her backpack next to the cricket's mason jar. The hilt stuck out between the open zipper, so she used her golden string to strap it to her back instead. "We have to try."

6

OUTSIDE, THE DAY WAS GOING by fast, the sun about to set. Thom, Kha, and Concao walked away from the mountain with heavy footsteps. Sơn had said he would leave a pocket in the wind dome for them to walk through before he brought his defenses back up.

"Well, that was a waste of time," Kha said as they headed toward the river, the smell of salt spraying the air.

"Not completely," Concao said, licking her lips where traces of bún riêu lingered on her white fur. "We have a sword now."

"That's true," Thom said, reaching up to pat the hilt where it poked out behind her head. "Still, though, why won't they help us when they can? We're just kids. They're grown-ups. They should do something."

Concao made a funny noise.

"What, you don't think so?" Thom asked, a bit hurt.

"You mortals always think that everyone should come to your beck and call."

"But it's not as if I want something selfish. I'm not asking for, like, a video game or something. We're trying to defeat the Monkey King—"

"Who you set free."

"—and save the heavens."

"Which *you* put in danger."

Thom frowned. She thought the fox demon was her friend.

"I only meant to say," Concao added, seeing the look on Thom's face, "that they have their own lives. They are not simply going to drop everything just to help you. They barely know you, even if you are the daughter of a friend."

Okay, fine. When she put it like that, it made sense. But Thom still felt bitterly disappointed.

They paused as they reached the edge of the wind dome. First, Kha slipped through the pocket where the air remained calm and still. Thom and Concao followed him, and the three of them walked farther away so that Kha could transform without getting sucked back into the twister.

They neared the river, angry waves crashing up as if the water meant to attack them. It seemed like no one and nothing was on their side. They were alone, standing there, just the three of them. Two kids and a fox. The sun hid behind darkened storm clouds, the river roared like it was ready to murder them, and everything was doomed.

Concao was right. The Mountain God and Princess My Nương had no reason to help them. Not everyone wanted to be a hero. And Thom couldn't blame them. The heavens hadn't exactly treated the couple like they deserved to be treated.

"Cheer up, Thom," Kha said, facing her. The water sprayed into the air, framing his figure as he started to transform. "We can still convince the other two immortals to help us."

As his body lengthened, another wave crashed the rocky shores, the foam growing thicker in the air. Water droplets fused together until a wall of water hovered over them.

That couldn't be normal.

Those waves were not normal waves.

"Um, Kha . . ." Thom started to say.

Concao dropped to all fours and eased backward.

"What?" Kha, now a dragon, turned just as the wave crashed down on them. He darted into the air, rising above the water just in time, then toward Thom. Thom and Concao grabbed hold of his back as he flew up.

Not fast enough.

The wave crashed over them, pulling at Thom's clothes and hair. The cold knocked the breath from her lungs. She clung to Kha as hard as she could. Concao got caught in the current. Thom tried to reach for her, but their fingers only grazed before the fox demon whirled away, limbs flailing.

The wave receded back into the river, pulling them with it. Buoyed by the water, Thom slipped off Kha's back. She gripped his feathers but could barely hang on as the water churned and he rolled, pulling her under. Salt filled her mouth and rushed up her nostrils, sending a piercing shock through her forehead. Her face broke the surface. Her legs kicked, trying to find the ground, but the water was way too deep, and she tumbled as it rolled over her. Kha tried to lift off, but every time he came close, another wave slammed him down. The river pulled at them, dragged them between rocks and fallen branches.

Thom managed to grab on to a log that had fallen in the water, trapped between two large boulders. She wrapped an arm around Kha's body and tried to keep them still against the current. But it was no use. The wood was too wet and slippery, the water too strong, and she was dragged along with him, gasping for breath, eyes and nostrils burning from the salt water, fingers numb from the freezing temperature.

Kha thrashed, tried to lift up, but he only managed to drag them farther out into the river.

And then they dropped as the river gave way to a small waterfall. Thom took one last gulp of air before she was engulfed, still clinging to Kha. She had no idea where Concao had gone, and as she tumbled, the water falling from above pushing her deeper into the river's depths, she had no idea where up or down was. The water, which was white with foam at first, turned darker blue, then violet, then black. Her lungs burned. Was she still hanging on to Kha? She couldn't see, couldn't feel, couldn't hear.

And then, eyes. Big, bulbous eyes the size of her body blinked at her. A face formed in the darkness. A giant man, made of shadows.

No. He was made of water, his outline barely visible in the dark abyss.

"Who are you?" he asked.

His voice thundered so that the vibrations echoed in every fiber of Thom's being. She couldn't help it. She opened her mouth and screamed.

Whatever precious breath she'd been holding escaped. She tried not to breathe the salty water in, but she couldn't stop herself. Her mouth and lungs filled with liquid. She choked and made it worse.

The eyes blinked, observing her cruelly, and then the giant sea monster opened his mouth and blew out a pocket of air, like a bubble-gum bubble. It moved toward her, bouncing against Thom's feet until it swallowed her, and she fell straight through to the bottom. She gasped and gasped, spitting and choking.

"Who are you?" the sea monster repeated, his voice not as loud from inside the bubble.

"Th-Thom."

"What is a Th-Thom?"

"That's my name," she sobbed, wiping her nose.

"What were you doing on Tản Viên Mountain?"

Thom's wet clothes clung to her skin. She started to shiver, out of cold or fear she didn't know. Only the monster's face was visible in the darkness, his bulging eyes and red mouth, but she imagined that the rest of him was just as big and mean. What did he want with her? Where were Kha and Concao? Were they safe? She felt so small, tiny compared to this monstrous being holding her captive.

"What were you doing?" the monster screamed when she didn't answer. The bubble wavered. Water dripped down on all sides, splashing Thom like a downpour of rain.

"Trying to get help!" she shouted.

The angrier he got, the more likely she was to drown. She couldn't see anything beyond him, the river dark and scary and infinite. Growing up near a beach, she had never been afraid of the ocean, but she'd also respected it for the dangerous and mysterious place that it was. Now she desperately wished she was on land with solid ground beneath her feet.

"Help?" the giant repeated with derision. "What kind of help could that useless cheat offer you?" His expression changed for a second, his eyes not so cruel but curious, maybe even a little hurt. "Did you see the princess?"

Thom realized who he was. The Lord of the Waters, Thủy Tinh. The Mountain God's rival. Of course—Sơn had said he was always lurking around, and he was right. Was the Water Lord still pining for the princess after all these years?

"Yes, I saw her," Thom said. "Princess Mỵ Nương. She was very kind to us."

"Of course she was. She is kind to everyone." His sharp pupils fixed on her. "They sent you away?"

Thom considered how to answer. Maybe if she complained about Sơn, the Water Lord would take their side, or at least let her go safely to the surface. But as she thought about what to do, something moved in the darkness behind the monster, a snakelike figure getting larger and larger.

It was Kha. She didn't recognize him at first—he looked different in the water, his scales reflecting the darkness, his feathers like fins. He opened his mouth, and a bright light blinded her, attracting the Water Lord's attention. The monster turned just as Kha shot an orb of fire straight at him.

The Water Lord ducked, and the ball slammed into Thom's bubble instead. Water rushed in. She took a breath before she was completely submerged, immediately kicking for the surface.

"Thom!" Kha called, his voice bubbly. He swam toward her, but giant flaky fingers wrapped around him, making him look like a tiny garden snake in comparison. The Water Lord swung Kha aside.

The monster came for Thom next. Kha screamed, a screeching dragon roar that reverberated through the river.

He sounded like a very angry whale. He did it again and again until the Water Lord turned away from Thom to stop him.

Thom couldn't hold her breath for much longer, and she had no idea how far away the surface was. She kept kicking and kicking . . .

But she got nowhere. The water continued to drag her down. The current was too strong. Her legs were tired. It was pointless, and her lungs burned, begging to take in a breath.

Something wrapped around her leg. The Water Lord, his mouth stretching into a rotten-toothed grin. Thom kicked him with her free foot, and he released her immediately, his face registering shock. He hadn't thought she would be strong enough to inflict any pain.

His face tightened with anger, the folds of his scaly skin fusing together, pieces breaking off in flakes.

The water around her gushed downward, pulling her no matter how hard she kicked. The Water Lord's face loomed until he was next to her. His fingers wrapped around her entire body. Thom's vision went dark around the corners. She needed air. And he was crushing it out of her. His hands grew tighter. She struggled in his grip, managing to free one arm. She pounded down on his hand, making him grunt, but not hard enough to release her. As she raised her fist again, her fingers brushed against something behind her head.

The Sword of Heaven's Will.

She grabbed it and swung. Still sheathed, the sword hit

the side of the Water Lord's head. His eyes rolled back. His fingers loosened.

Thom kicked free, and then upward. But she was tired, so tired. She could barely hang on to the sword. She wanted to breathe so bad. Her vision grew darker . . . darker. Was she still kicking? She was so cold and sleepy . . .

She closed her eyes.

"Come on, Thom-Thom," a voice whispered, familiar but far away. Her eyes burned from the salt water.

In the darkness, a familiar figure emerged, floating in front of her. But it couldn't be, could it?

"Hang on." The Monkey King's voice was bubbly.

It couldn't be him. He couldn't be here. She must have passed out. She tried to wake up, but it was so hard. Her eyelids were so heavy, and she was exhausted and cold.

Just before she closed her eyes again, she thought she saw him move closer. His hands gripped her arms and pulled her upward.

She burst through the surface, gasping for air, salt burning her throat and eyes. Something was holding her up, trying to haul her out of the tumultuous waves, but every time they got high enough, a huge crash dragged them back down.

Thom thrashed, feeling helpless and trapped against whoever it was who held her. She felt fur—was it Concao? But when she looked down, the fur was golden. Not white, like the fox demon's.

She turned and screamed and thrashed harder to break away.

"Don't!" the Monkey King shouted. "I'm trying to save you!"

"Let go of me!" This couldn't be real. She was hallucinating. She had held her breath for too long and damaged her brain or something.

A wave slammed into her, rolling her under the water. The Monkey King was ripped away, and Thom tumbled, her heavy backpack dragging her down, the sword still gripped tight in one hand. Ma was in the backpack. What if she'd drowned? Thom gasped when her face broke across the surface, only for another wave to pull her back under the water.

"It's okay, Thom-Thom!" she heard distantly, her ears muffled.

Then the Monkey King's arms looped under hers, hooking around her armpits, and pulled her up and out of the water. Thom was too exhausted to fight back, too grateful to be out of the cold river. She focused on not letting go of the sword as the Monkey King flew them up and back over the shore, landing far away from the river.

When she was back on dry, solid ground, she collapsed onto her hands and knees and coughed, spitting up water, her throat stinging, her nostrils burning. Her fingers were stiff as she unzipped her backpack. Somehow, miraculously, the contents weren't soaking, just damp. Only a few drops of water had slipped through the small holes she'd made in the mason jar lid. Her mom the cricket was safe.

Thom slumped, her limbs heavy. Her head throbbed. Everything tasted salty and bitter. Her hair hung in wet lumps all around her face.

"Are you okay?" the Monkey King asked, slapping a hand on her back.

She jerked away from him. She grappled for the sword and held it up. "What are you doing here?" she demanded.

The Monkey King looked confused but then giggled nervously, the familiar sound making her want to laugh and cry at the same time. "Is that any way to greet a friend?"

She breathed hard, resisting the urge to cough some more. He looked . . . the same. Not like the real Monkey King, but the one she remembered. And he didn't have his cudgel with him, while she still held the sword in her hand.

"You said we weren't friends," she snapped.

"Did I?"

"Yes. When you took the cudgel and betrayed me," she said through gritted teeth.

He stopped giggling. "The last time I saw you, we were about to leave the heavens."

She narrowed her eyes at him. "I'm not stupid. You betrayed me—you lied to me. I'm not going to keep falling for it."

He scratched his chin. "You almost drowned. I saved you. You should thank me, you know."

"Thank you? I—"

What was really happening? Was she even awake? Had she passed out in the river, drowned, died? She ached too much, her limbs tired from the cold, her wet clothes clinging and dragging her down.

Or maybe she really was hallucinating. Lack of oxygen or whatever. Maybe he wasn't even here.

To test that theory, she shoved him, hard. Taken by surprise, the Monkey King stumbled back. Anyone else would have fallen, but he sprang into the air, limbs spread like an acrobat finishing a flip and showing off.

Thom got to her feet. Pushing him had felt good. She wanted to do it again. She would have lunged at him just to hurt him, if she hadn't been so battered and cold. Her limbs felt heavy and numb.

"You're getting better at this," the Monkey King said.

She wished she could ignore him, wished she no longer needed his approval or his praise, but she couldn't help it. "At what?"

"At fighting. At hurting people."

She blinked. Her fist unclenched. The sword hung limp at her side.

"Oh, don't stop," he said, sounding disappointed. "I wanted to have fun."

"Fun?" she nearly shouted. "That's all this is to you—a joke, isn't it? You thought you could play with me, like I'm a little human toy you found. But it's not fun. I'm going to go after you." She pointed the sword at him. "I'm going to *destroy* you."

His eyes shone with hurt confusion. "But why? I don't get it. I thought we were friends."

"Friends don't lie to each other! Friends don't turn friends' moms into crickets!" She pointed at the glass jar sitting next to her backpack.

"When did I do that?" the Monkey King asked.

She swung the sword even though he was too far away to reach. It made a satisfying, metallic swishing noise. "Stop pretending like you don't remember."

"I don't, I truly don't. I'm—I—" He touched down, approaching her slowly as if *she* were the wild demon. Thom pressed the point of the sword against his collarbone, but he didn't seem to notice or care. "I'm just a clone. You know that now. I'm not the true me."

She blinked. That's right. He wasn't lying about that.

"You're a hair," she said. She remembered all the scratches on her hand when she'd reached inside her backpack. Was that him? Had it been the Monkey King's hair all this time?

"Yes, the hair my other self gave to you before you entered the heavens."

Of course. A clone of a clone that she'd snuck into the heavens, where he had only been able to transform into a tiny, thumb-sized version of himself. She had never given it back to him. She'd been too busy getting betrayed. By another clone.

Her head throbbed.

"I don't remember anything after I turned back into a hair," he said. "I tried to reveal myself, but you were never alone, so I hid in your backpack."

Thom pressed a finger to her temples. An itchy heat blossomed in her throat. She wanted to believe him. His earnest eyes, his pleading voice. She wanted him on her side. Especially after the day they'd had, especially when no one else wanted to help them. If they had the Monkey King, they would be unstoppable. They would get to the heavens in no time and defeat . . . his true self.

It was impossible. Even if he was telling the truth, she knew better now than to hope that it could be so easy.

"I don't believe you," she said.

"But it's true. I promise."

"Even if it's true, I don't trust you."

He whimpered. He sounded genuinely hurt. "But—" He stopped. His ears twitched, and he glanced sideways right before he disappeared with a pop. A thin, golden hair floated in front of her, drifting down. A breeze blew it toward her, making it stick to the sleeve of her wet hoodie. Thom picked it off, thought about ripping it into tiny pieces, chopping it up with the sword, stomping on it, digging it into the ground, tossing its broken pieces back into the river.

But when she heard footsteps, she panicked and stuffed it into her pocket.

A second later, Concao ran up to her. She was wet and dirty, but otherwise unhurt. "Are you all right?"

"Are *you* all right?" Thom asked.

"What happened?" they both asked at the same time.

"The water pushed me all the way back to the wind dome," Concao said. "I got sucked into the twister. It took forever to get back out, but I finally managed it." She sounded breathless and exhausted. "What happened to the two of you?"

Thom was about to explain when a dragon burst out of the river. Kha wasn't alone. Another huge serpentine creature was with him. He had blue feathers down his back, like Kha, but his scales were black and reflective, and Thom was sure that if she had been in the water, she wouldn't have been able to see him at all.

Kha floated down in front of them. "Climb on!" he shouted, right as a huge wave crashed against the shores, the foam forming into claws reaching for them.

Thom and Concao didn't hesitate, clambering onto his back.

Kha took off before the Water Lord could strike again.

7

THOM DIDN'T REMEMBER MUCH OF the journey they took next, only that another dragon was with them, and that they headed high into the air. She was too tired to shout above the wind. She rested her head on Kha's back but couldn't relax enough to fall asleep, always scared she would fall off.

Still, she must have dozed, because she woke up later in a bed, and she was dry. She was also alone.

Ma.

Thom dug through her things—her backpack still slightly damp—but the mason jar was gone. The cricket was gone. Her mother . . .

She scrambled out of bed, taking in her surroundings. She was in some sort of temple. The stone floor was cool against her bare feet, and she was dressed in black robes and pants, similar to a karate uniform but made of soft, silky fabric. Someone must have taken her clothes.

But . . . the Monkey King's hair. She had put it in the pocket of her hoodie. What would happen to it?

Maybe it was for the best if he was lost. She couldn't trust him anyway. What if he reported back everything he saw to the real Monkey King?

Still, a sinking disappointment dragged her down. He was gone. Again.

She needed to find the others. Around her were little shrines with incense burning, although there weren't any statues, so she had no idea who the temple belonged to. The room was minimally furnished, the bed she'd been lying on a square slab on the floor, the chairs wooden and bare. Even Ma would have said it needed some cushions or something.

Thom left the room and stepped into an outdoor corridor, the awning above her scalloped at the edges, the pillars painted red with carvings of dragons curled around the surface.

And all of it was on a cloud.

Was she in the heavens? Had she died after all? Or had the Mountain God decided to help them get up here?

She stepped to the edge of the platform and peered at the tuft of cloud beneath her. It could have been cotton candy. She pushed her foot down anyway, careful to grab on to a pillar in case she slipped. But the cloud was solid, her foot sinking through soft mist before hitting a sandlike bottom.

"Whoa, whoa, whoa, what are you doing?" shouted a boy

not much older than she was and dressed in similar black robes. He ran toward her. "Don't jump!"

"I wasn't going to jump." Thom stepped back, planting her feet firmly on the stone.

"What were you doing, then?" The boy narrowed his eyes. He looked familiar, his nose small and round, giving his face a pixielike appearance. A sheen coated his cheekbones, sort of like Kha's when he got angry about something. He must be a dragon, too.

"Just seeing if it was a magic cloud or a real cloud," Thom said.

"What's a 'real' cloud?" the boy asked.

"Um, one that you'd just, you know . . ." She made her hand drop through the air to mimic falling.

His eyes widened. "You're Kha's friend, the half-mortal girl."

Thom started to answer, but footsteps behind her cut her off. She turned to see Kha, also wearing silky black robes, holding a stack of clothes as he walked toward them.

"Hey, you're up," he said. "And you met my cousin Miko."

"Did you know she can't fly?" Miko asked Kha.

Kha turned and went back into the temple. "Yes, Miko, I knew."

"But that's so *weird*. If she trips, she could fall and die." The corners of his mouth pulled downward into a dramatic grimace.

"Well, let's hope that doesn't happen." Kha rolled his eyes at Thom.

"Kha, my mom's gone," Thom said as she and Miko followed him. "Her jar must have fallen out of my backpack. We need to go back—"

"She's fine," Kha said. "She got a bit wet, so I took her to where she could dry off. They're trying to see if they can change her back."

"Is that possible? Can they do that?" Whoever *they* were. "The Mountain God said that only the Monkey King can turn her back."

"They want to study the enchantment he used," Kha said, not stopping.

"Um, where are we?" Thom asked as they went back to the room she'd just left. Kha placed the stack of clothes on the bed, and she recognized the hoodie and jeans she'd worn earlier.

"The Dragon King of the North's temple," Kha said.

Thom grabbed her hoodie and put it on. Everything had been washed and dried.

"We saved you!" Miko bounced up and down. The sheen on his face sparkled. "We heard Kha calling for help, so my dad came flying through the water and brought me with him! You would have died if it weren't for us."

"Oh." She grew uneasy under the pressure of his excitement. "Thank you?"

"You were out cold," Kha said.

"You almost drowned!" Miko said.

"I thought you did," Kha said, scratching the back of his neck and giving her a confused look. "You were under the water for so long."

"The Water Lord put me in this bubble thing," Thom said.

"And you were able to drag yourself out of the river," Kha said. "Which was pretty impressive."

Thom cleared her throat. She should tell Kha about the Monkey King's hair. She dug through her hoodie to see if it was still there, and something flew from the pocket, bouncing a few times on the floor before rolling to a stop. Thom picked it up. Guilt made her stomach roll.

"It's Jae's ring," she said. "The key to the Forbidden Armory." She'd brought it with her when they left, hoping she could return it to Jae—the daughter of the Jade Emperor—when everything was over.

Kha held out a hand, and she reluctantly dropped the ring onto it. "This isn't just a key into the armory, it's a master key for the heavens," Kha said, and showed her the jade-leaf engraving in the green stone. "Only, like, three people have one of these—Jae, the emperor, and Buddha."

"So if we found another gate, could we get in?" Thom asked.

"No, it opens the doors *inside* the heavens. There are only two ways to enter the heavens from the mortal world—the Judgment Veil, which you broke—" He coughed. "I mean, which . . . is destroyed." He didn't meet her eyes.

An uneasiness settled in her stomach. Kha had told her to destroy the Judgment Veil, though. She wouldn't have done it if he hadn't suggested it.

"And the Bridge of Souls," Kha said, "where mortals go when they die, to be weighed for their sins, which is where the Monkey King took the demon army."

Kha handed her the ring, and Thom pocketed it, relieved to have it back. Maybe if she returned it, she could prove to Jae and her father that she was a good person, that she was trying to do what was right. What must Jae and everyone in the heavens think of her now? That she was a traitor, probably—and who could blame them? But Thom hadn't known what the Monkey King had planned to do with the cudgel. She had only wanted to get rid of her strength, wanted it gone so bad that she had been blinded to everything else.

Even when the Boy Giant had tried to tell her the truth, she hadn't believed him. Her own father. Would he even want to see her again? Would he be willing to help her earn back the heavens' forgiveness once she defeated the Monkey King?

Her hand brushed against something sharp inside her pocket, but when she turned it out, there was nothing else in there. Maybe she'd imagined it, hoping so much that the Monkey King's hair had somehow managed to survive the wash. But it was really gone.

"What is it?" Kha asked.

Thom couldn't stand the concern in his eyes. Kha was

her real friend, someone she could trust, unlike the Monkey King, who had abandoned her more than once. But there was no need to tell him about the hair, not now that it was lost forever.

"Where's Concao?" Thom asked. "Is she okay?"

"Your fox friend?" Miko asked. "She's talking to my father, the Dragon King."

But wasn't Kha the son of the Dragon King? So how could his cousin also be the son of the Dragon King? She shook her head. She couldn't focus on that now.

"When she heard they were going to study the enchantment on your mom, Concao also wanted to see what it looked like," Kha said.

"I want to see my mom." Thom started for the door, even though she had no idea which way to go. Luckily, Kha and his cousin came with her, Kha leading the way.

"They're just looking at the enchantment, Thom," Kha said. "So don't get your hopes up too much."

"Yes, but this is the Dragon King," Thom said. "He's pretty powerful, right?"

"Yeah!" Miko said. "My dad can fix anything."

"He's *a* dragon king," Kha said. "And if one of the Four Immortals can't change your mom back, I doubt he can."

Thom's heart sank, but she tried not to let it show. "How many dragon kings are there?"

"Four—East, West, North, and South," Kha answered.

"Miko's father is East, the one who fought off the Water Lord and rescued us, but his temple is underwater, so we couldn't stay there. We're in North's temple now."

"The Dragon King of the East rescued us? And I slept through my chance to meet him?" He was supposed to be the great sea serpent that ruled the oceans.

"He's here, too," Kha said. "You'll still get to meet him."

"What about your father?" Thom said. "Didn't you say he was a Dragon King, too?"

"Yeah, he's the Dragon King of the West, but he's in the heavens right now, leading the Jade Army. Or at least, he was when we left."

They came to a spacious room with ornate chairs that would have belonged better in a museum. At the front, two officious-looking men stood together, both wearing áo dài of thick brocade and those black hats that had a plating across the back, indicating the men were very important. Their hats kept knocking together as the two bent close to each other, whispering furiously.

"No, not that, that won't work, we tried that earlier," one whispered.

"You think of a better idea, then."

"How about we place another spell, instead of undoing the first one?"

"Are you a shrimpleton? That's too much magic on her poor mortal soul."

"It's 'simpleton,' you simpleton. Maybe try coming out of the ocean once in a while and meeting somebody who isn't a seafood, hmm?"

The other man bristled. "The poor woman will be lucky if she remembers who she is if we try that."

"Face it, we've been beat."

"It can't be. I refuse to be bested by a monkey."

"Again, you mean? Bested by the same monkey. Again?"

"How dare you! We vowed never to speak of that. I was tricked, a victim of a heinous trickery—"

"Uncles?" Kha asked.

The two men whirled around so fast, one of them almost

dropped the mason jar that held Ma the cricket, bouncing it back and forth between his hands like a hot potato. He finally caught it securely, two circles of pink appearing like stamps across his cheeks.

Thom took the mason jar from him and held it close to her chest. The cricket hopped up and down, looking rather happy to see her. But then, maybe that was just how crickets acted. Thom had no clue.

"Oh, you're awake," the other man said, clapping his hands together. His thick black mustache wiggled, and his eyes crinkled. "You were quite drowned, you know. Almost dead."

"Yeah, we saved you," Miko said. "Didn't we, Dad?"

The mustached man put an arm around the boy. The gold embroidery on his silky black áo dài made circular patterns across the sleeves and hem. "We can't take the full credit. You had somehow managed to kick your way to the surface," the man told Thom. "And back onto land! How odd. How miraculous. People who fall into that river usually don't survive. The Lord of the Waters is not known for his mercy."

Again, an unease passed through Thom. But when she opened her mouth to explain about the Monkey King, nothing came out.

"She can't fly—she told me so," Miko said.

Thom laughed. It came out louder than she expected. "No, I can't. I have no idea how I did it. Maybe the waves crashed so high that it carried me back up." She felt Kha's gaze on her and paid special attention to the cricket.

"Thom," Kha said slowly, "this is my uncle, the Dragon King of the East." He gestured to the mustached man, who was also Miko's father.

"Pleased to meet you, Kha's friend," East said with a bounce. He hugged his son tighter.

Thom bowed.

"And the Dragon King of the North," Kha said, gesturing to the other man, who smiled at her from behind his round glasses and thick gray beard.

"Hullo there, ground-dweller," he said.

"They saved us," Kha added.

"You called half the sea to your aid," East said. "Of course we had to come."

"Thank you," Thom said, bowing again. "Thank you for rescuing us and bringing us here—and for everything." She looked down at the cricket. "I couldn't help overhearing—you don't know how to change my mom back?"

"The monkey's enchantment is such that only he can remove it," North said, confirming what Sơn Tinh had said. "If we strip away the magic, we risk harming your mother—at least, all the parts of her that make her who she is."

At Thom's crestfallen face, East patted her shoulder. "Don't worry, Thom dear. It's not the first time the Monkey

King has done something like this. We'll get him." He held up a fist.

"Oh really," North said flatly. "Like how you 'got' him after he stole your cudgel?"

East turned his stony expression on his brother. "We *vowed* never to *speak* of that," he hissed.

"Yes, but that was before the demon escaped, wasn't it? If you hadn't let him take the cudgel, none of this would be happening."

East sputtered, his face growing crimson. Even Miko looked indignant on his father's behalf. Thom jumped in before the two dragon kings could keep bickering.

"It was my fault," she said. "I released him—or a clone of him. Then I helped him steal the cudgel back from the heavens . . ." Her voice trailed off as everyone turned to study her. No one said anything. She grew hotter and more awkward under the weight of their judgment.

"Well then," a female voice said from the door. Concao leaned against the wall, her white fur almost blinding in the sunlight. "I guess you're in good company." She moved farther into the room.

"I am?" Thom asked.

"Yes. Every one of us has been tricked by the Monkey King in some way. He stole the iron cudgel from the Dragon King of the East." She nodded at the black-mustached man, who huffed, throwing his hands behind his back as if offended at the idea of being called out by a demon. "And Wukong convinced *me* to give him the forbidden peaches of immortality. Almost everyone in this room has been tricked by the Monkey King. But that's not what's important here."

North took off his glasses to wipe them with his sleeve. "And what is that, fox?"

"What's important," Concao said, "is how we can trick him back."

8

THEY DISCUSSED MUCH OF THAT over dinner, a rather extravagant spread of traditional spring rolls. A whole, deep-fried fish dominated the table, surrounded by platters of lettuce, cucumbers, raw plantains, carrots, herbs, and vermicelli noodles cooked to the right amount of chewiness. Everyone dipped their own rice paper in bowls of warm water before filling them with their favorite toppings and wrapping them into perfect rolls. Or, in Thom's case, a barely contained mass of ingredients she had to eat as quickly as possible before the whole thing fell apart.

"The problem simply is," East said, "that the monkey has no weakness."

"Especially after you let him have the cudgel," North said.

"How many times must I tell you—I didn't *let* him have it," East said. "He stole it. There's a difference."

"He swam out of the sea without anyone trying to stop him. No one even lifted a sword." North met Thom's gaze. "He just waltzed right out of there like he owned the thing."

"He was a dangerous and powerful demon!" East protested. "Even before he was famous, we all knew not to mess with him. Besides, no one had any idea that the cudgel would turn out to be so . . . versatile. It was just a chunk of iron no one wanted, so they tossed it into the sea like they do with all of their other junk." He bit his spring roll and chewed angrily, his black mustache wiggling.

Following the two dragon kings' conversation was like watching a Ping-Pong game. They barely paused to breathe as they spoke.

"But . . . I thought the cudgel was an ancient weapon that helped calm the ocean tides," Thom said. "In the stories, they said it was even used to create the world."

East huffed. "As if the ocean could be calmed. That's just what they tell you now, because they don't want to admit that they knew nothing about it. No one did. No one even knew it was a weapon or how to wield it. It was the size of a building, one of those ugly skyscrapers you see all over the place now. It was almost as tall as the sea was deep. They gave it to me to keep in the ocean because they had no idea where to put it, like they do with all the other things they have no idea where to put. We honestly all thought it was a useless piece of metal. Until the monkey came along."

"Loss of a great and magnificent weapon," North said with a sigh.

"It's just as well," East said. "No one else knows how to wield it."

But Thom did know the secret to controlling the cudgel, Ruyi Jingu Bang. She almost spoke up, but then she had promised the Monkey King she would never reveal his secret. But did she really need to keep that promise if he had broken his?

"Which is why, once they got it back," North said, "they locked it away."

"South confirmed it already," East said.

"South is my other uncle," Kha said to Thom.

She nodded. "What did he confirm?"

"That the monkey has blocked the Bridge of Souls," North said. "With the Judgment Veil down, the only other way into the heavens is through the Four Immortals. A path was created for each of them when they ascended. You were smart to go to them. No other being in the mortal world would be willing to join you against the Monkey King."

"No," East agreed. "They all remember what happened last time they tried."

"We already asked Sơn Tinh," Thom said. "He doesn't want to get involved."

"Of course he doesn't. Can't blame him. Deserves his peace, and living next to the Water Lord—well, you saw what he's like."

"Yes, and the Boy Giant is already in the heavens," East said.

"That leaves Princess Liễu Hạnh, the emperor's fourteenth daughter," North continued. "But no one has seen her since her last reincarnation."

"She's the one who broke the emperor's favorite cup," Thom said, remembering their research from the art project. "And got sent down to live among the mortals."

"She loved it so much, she insisted on returning to the mortal world each time she died," North said. "Mortals call her the Mother Goddess because she helped them grow crops and food during multiple famines and saved thousands of lives."

"Usually, we find her pretty quick," East added. "It's always some mortal girl who turns sixteen and develops some sort of superpower and spawns an entire series of teen novels."

"But it's been at least twenty years now," North continued. "And no sign of her."

"Maybe she didn't reincarnate this time," East said, stuffing a spring roll to bursting with fried fish skin. He licked his fingers one by one. "Maybe she stayed in the heavens."

"Ridiculous—she loves the mortals," North said. "Always finds an excuse to be with them. That's what got her into the mess of reincarnation in the first place. She could just stay a normal goddess like the rest of them, but she chooses to die every few decades. It's beyond me, let me tell you."

"If she loves mortals, she'll be the one most likely to help us," Thom said.

"Not necessarily," East said. "She might consider it a heavenly affair and refuse."

"But that doesn't make sense—that's why Sơn turned us down. He doesn't want to get involved in mortal affairs."

"Sơn doesn't want to get involved at all—doesn't matter what sort of affair it is," East said. "He's been battling the Lord of the Waters for most of his existence. The two have been enemies for so long, no one really remembers why they hate each other so much. I mean, obviously there's Princess My Nương, but there's got to be more to it than that. Anyway, I don't blame Sơn for wanting a bit of peace and quiet for once in his life. The heavens haven't exactly gone out of their way to help him and his wife."

Thom supposed he was right. "So that leaves . . ." She turned to Kha.

"The Sage," they said together.

"Where can we find him?" Thom asked the two dragon kings. Though even if they did find him, would he want to help them?

◆ ◆ ◆

Later that night, Kha and Concao joined Thom in her room as they prepared for their departure the next day to search for the Sage. Once again, their backpacks were stuffed with snacks for the journey, water bottles, flashlights, and a compass that North thought they might need.

As Thom tried to stuff the Sword of Heaven's Will down as far as it would go, she couldn't get rid of the nagging thought that it might all be hopeless anyway. If Sơn Tinh and Princess Mỵ Nương didn't want to help them, why would the Sage be any different? She was so used to grown-ups stepping in to help them—they were just kids. Ma always did everything she could for Thom, and teachers helped them find the answers to their problems. So why wouldn't these immortals offer their help? Especially when Thom was trying to save their own world, the heavens, from whatever the Monkey King planned to do with it.

Thom zipped up her backpack, leaving it gaping open around the hilt of the sword. Concao was right, though. The Mountain God had no reason to get involved. What did it matter to him what happened in the heavens when he was safely tucked away with his wife, the person he'd fought so hard to be with for centuries? Especially when the heavens had refused to offer her a place as well? Why *should* he help them?

Maybe the Sage would feel the same. Maybe it was all hopeless.

"Do you even know how to use that thing?" Kha asked as Thom plunked her backpack down on the ground. He nodded at the sword sticking out of her backpack.

"How hard is it?" she asked. "I didn't know how to use the

cudgel, but I was able to beat a bunch of Jade Army soldiers with it."

"Yeah, but the cudgel is destructive just by existing. A sword needs more skill than that."

"I'll just whack the Monkey King and take him out."

"I don't know, Thom," Kha said skeptically. "You might want to think of a better plan."

"Who's going to teach me?" she said jokingly. "You?"

"I mean, I would. If you asked." He looked almost hurt.

Thom grabbed the hilt and pulled the sword out of her backpack. "You know how to fight with this thing?"

Kha picked at his nails. "Of course I do." He sounded annoyed. "I'm the general's son. That's the first weapon we learn."

"Oh." How had she forgotten? Kha just seemed so . . . not the fighting type. He was more the "discussing things peacefully and knowing what hair product to use and what shoes to wear" type. "Okay, then. Can you teach me?"

Kha got up from his seat with a bounce in his step. "First, your stance is all wrong."

She looked down at her feet. "What's wrong with my stance?"

"You'll get knocked over for sure. You have to put your right foot back a little—yeah, that's right. And swivel it a bit. Bend your knees so you can absorb any hits; otherwise, you'll just fall."

She followed his instructions, feeling awkward and shy, holding the sword up with both hands.

"Keep your elbows tucked in," Kha said, "to protect your ribs. Now give it a try."

She swung the sword like a baseball bat.

"No, you're moving it too far from your body," Kha said.

"Isn't that the point? I don't want my, um, opponent to get too close."

"You still need to protect yourself. Here." He reached for the sword, but it slammed to the ground as soon as Thom let go. "Whoa. It's heavy."

"Not as heavy as the cudgel," Thom said, taking the sword back.

"I'll go see if my uncles have anything I can practice with," Kha said, leaving the room.

Concao uncurled from her cushion on the floor, tail swishing back and forth. She watched as Thom lowered into the stance Kha had taught her, right foot back, holding the sword up but keeping her elbows against her ribs. It wasn't so hard, but other than jabbing the sword forward and swinging, she had no idea what else to do.

Kha came back a few minutes later with a lighter sword and spent the next half hour teaching Thom how to use hers. Concao watched them with amused judgment but offered no opinions or advice.

"Don't raise your sword too high," Kha said. "Raising it

will give you more power, but less control. Plus, your vital areas will be exposed."

"Vital . . . areas . . . ?" Thom repeated.

"Yeah, like your guts and heart."

She gulped. This was starting to feel a bit too real. What if she got into a real fight? What if she faced off with a demon instead of the Monkey King?

But she was strong, and with the sword she could defeat the Monkey King easily. No need to worry about all that, especially now that Kha was teaching her how to take the Monkey King down efficiently.

"Want to try sparring?" Kha asked.

"Okay," Thom said, nervous but eager to practice her new skills. Concao's watchful ice-blue eyes followed them like a cat's.

Thom and Kha faced each other, knees bent, swords out. Kha nodded to make sure Thom was ready, and then he advanced, sword jabbing forward. His smaller blade looked like a needle next to her huge one, but he used it so skillfully that Thom couldn't help feeling jealous of how light and stealthy he was.

"I had no idea you knew how to fight like this," Thom said. "Do all dragons?"

"Only those who will become dragon kings," he said, grinning. "My uncles and my dad were all born into it. We're all expected to learn to fight and defend the realms and stuff."

"Wait, if your father is a dragon king, then"—Thom parried one of his jabs and moved aside—"does that make you a dragon *prince*?"

Kha ducked. "Technically, yeah."

"But isn't your mother a fairy?"

Kha followed, his foot movements opposite hers, like they were dancing. "Yeah. The head fairy of the Forbidden Garden of the Peaches of Immortality."

"So that means you're part fairy, too, doesn't it? Shouldn't you have a choice between becoming a dragon king or a fairy? You can follow your mother instead. Or do what you want, really."

"That's not how it works in the heavens. We follow after our parents."

"But your mother is a fairy," Thom repeated.

"Yeah, but I'm a boy. So I have to become a dragon king."

Thom was grateful it wasn't like that with her own culture. She loved what Ma did, but she didn't think she'd want to be an academic librarian. Besides, she knew Ma wouldn't allow it. There were only three choices for Thom, and Ma had offered them already: doctor, lawyer, or dentist.

His next blow was overhand, not too high, arms still protecting himself.

Thom blocked it, holding her sword horizontally. Even with the smaller blade, Kha bore down on her enough to make her arms ache.

"Is that what you want, though?" she asked. She angled her sword down, letting his blade slide off before attacking again with her own. "To be a dragon king?"

He blocked, stepped back, jabbed. "I don't know. Maybe. I'm good at it. I like being a dragon. I like flying and exploring, but . . . I also like nicer things. You know, like tea parties, and I like taking care of the trees and stuff. I don't always wake up wanting to battle my friends. But—" He shrugged, then ducked her swing. "I don't hate it, either."

Thom blocked. "Maybe you can be a dragon sometimes and a fairy other times. You don't have to be one or the other."

"You don't know my dad. He's a general. No son of his is going to be a fairy."

"But you *are* a fairy," Thom pointed out.

"I'm my parents' only son. My father wants me to be like him. Strong. Tough. A *man*. I just don't see the point in it, though. Even when I've done my best and think he'll finally be proud of me, he never is. It just feels so meaningless sometimes. Why bother when it's never going to be good enough for him?"

Thom smiled sympathetically. "You're always good enough, Kha."

Kha didn't answer, but his next swing was hard enough to make Thom step back.

"I bet your mother thinks you're good enough," Thom said.

Kha's face brightened at the mention of her. "She thinks everything is lovely, though. Everything. The world is a happier place with her around. Everyone loves her. You will, too. Maybe you'll get to meet her."

"That would be great!" Thom imagined walking in the Forbidden Garden. She could practically smell the peaches of immortality, see the glow of the fruits against the leaves. "You really think so?"

Kha's smile froze. He tried to hide it, ducking as she advanced on him. "Yeah. I think so. I'm sure the Jade Emperor will forgive you. You're trying to save the heavens from the Monkey King, so he'll have to."

Something flipped in Thom's stomach. That niggling doubt. She had been trying to tell herself that as long as she defeated the Monkey King and corrected her mistakes, she would be forgiven. But she had also thought Sơn Tinh would help her, had been so convinced that all immortals would want to jump to their aid. She had been wrong about that. What if she was wrong about the heavens forgiving her, too?

As Kha moved back, Thom saw her chance to attack. She swung sideways. Kha blocked in time, but their blades collided with a loud clang.

His sword snapped in two.

The broken metal whipped across the room and landed with a *thunk* in the wall. Concao darted to the other side of the room so fast that she was a blur, even though the blade hadn't gone near her.

"Whoa," Kha said, staring at the Sword of Heaven's Will. "That's a pretty awesome weapon."

Thom twirled the hilt. "You think I have a chance against the cudgel with this thing?"

Kha went to the wall and tried to pry the blade out. "You have a better chance than without it, that's for sure."

9

THOM, KHA, AND CONCAO LEFT early the next morning, flying straight to a city in Vietnam called Na Dang, where the dragon kings said the Sage had been living for years. When the East and North had told them this was where the Sage was hiding, Thom thought she'd heard them wrong. Ma used to talk about going to Da Nang, another city in Vietnam with a similar name, but maybe the dragon kings knew the country better than she did. As they reached the bustling area, the buildings in different sizes and colors created a quirky backdrop that looked like it had come straight out of a tourism guide.

Thom pictured what it would have been like to come here for a different reason. Ma had taken her to Vietnam once, and while the scenery was beautiful with the mountains and coasts, Thom had always found it too hot and humid to appreciate. She had just wanted to go back home to her friends.

Now, looking down at the crowded city, surrounded by rocky green mountains, she wished she were here with Ma instead—well, when Ma was human—just the two of them on vacation. She wished she had tried to be happier the last time they were together. She wished Ma knew how much she regretted their last fight. She wished her mother weren't a cricket.

The Sage was rumored to be located inside the caves of the Five Mountains, which sounded like an isolated life, except that these caves were a popular tourist destination. People could hike up to the cave sites from a trailhead inside a large regional park. Kha landed in a secluded spot outside the entrance, hiding behind some trees to change into his human form.

Thom inspected the rugged hiking trail close by while Concao fixed a scarf around her neck and up to cover her pointed ears. If anyone looked closely, they would definitely see a fuzzy white fox face, but hidden under the light cloth, Concao looked like almost every other tourist hiding from the sun. She reminded Thom of Ma and her phobia of becoming too tanned.

"Ready?" Thom asked as Kha brushed off his knees.

He was back in jeans and a striped T-shirt, which he immediately grabbed the front of and flapped up and down. "It's so hot here," he said.

Thom had changed out of the silky black robes and back

into her jeans and T-shirt, but now she took off her hoodie. Something scratched her hand as she folded it to stuff in her backpack. She inspected the pocket, flipping it inside out several times, sure that this time she hadn't imagined it. But there was nothing there. The Monkey King's hair wasn't hiding in the folds of lint. Maybe a bur had gotten inside the pocket or something—it wasn't the first time—but she would have to look for it later.

They followed the hiking trail until they reached the main road and joined the throng of tourists. The entrance was a tall, domed arch. The top of it might have been a bridge, except that it was wild and covered in rocks and vines, and way too high for a human to use. On the ledge at the top of the gateway, a statue stood vigil, head bent underneath a conical straw hat, leaning on a cane.

"Kha," Thom said, nudging him. "Is that a statue of the Sage?"

"I think so," Kha said. "Mortals here still pray to the Four, and this is his favorite spot on earth. Now we know why."

"How will we know if we find him?" Thom asked. "There are so many people here."

"Immortals glow to you, don't they? They can hide it from mortals, but not to other immortals, and you're half."

It was true. The Boy Giant and the Mountain God had glowing skin, and so did the Jade Emperor. And after her decaying skin in the heavens had flaked off, Thom had glowed a bit, too.

Still, the crowd pressed in on her. There were so many people, and the place was so big. They passed the gateway, pressing shoulders with strangers. There was no way they were going to find one dude out of this whole crowd, glowing skin or not, if he even wanted to be found. Where would they start?

Because no one else had any clue where to look for the Sage, either, they joined a tour led by a woman who spoke in Vietnamese. Even though Thom was technically fluent—Ma had enrolled her in private Vietnamese classes on the weekends up until she'd started middle school—she had trouble keeping up with the guide's fast speech and was always a few seconds behind with the translation in her head.

"Over here, we have the Five Mountains—named after the five elements of metal, water, wood, fire, and earth," the woman said. "If you hike up these mountains, you'll find caves and numerous tunnels, but only one is accessible through the first mountain here." She gestured at the hiking trail they passed. "The others are all closed due to how dangerous they are. In the past, some hikers got lost in the tunnels and weren't found for days."

Something tugged on Thom's backpack, which then became much lighter. Thom whirled around at the boy now holding the Sword of Heaven's Will. Or rather, dragging it on the ground. He could barely lift it.

"That's mine," Thom said, snatching the sword back.

"Why do you have a sword?" the kid asked in perfect English. He must have been an American tourist, like her.

"It's just a toy. See?" Thom swung it a few times, making it look as light as cheap plastic.

"Timmy!" an older woman called out to the boy. She shot the sword a worried look, grabbed the kid, and dragged him away.

"You can't just carry that thing around," Kha said.

"Where am I supposed to put it?" Thom asked, holding the sword like a walking stick instead of putting it back in her backpack.

"Maybe we can hide it," Concao said. "In those trees."

"No way." Thom gripped the hilt, as if either of her companions could take it away, though they couldn't lift it even if they tried. "Someone will find it." She finally had a weapon of her own—there was no way she'd let it out of her sight. If it really multiplied her strength ten thousand times, then she might actually be a challenge for the Monkey King.

But even as she walked with the thing, she couldn't help noticing how much lighter it was than the cudgel. It was almost fragile in comparison.

It was still a magical weapon, though. And she would get it to listen to her, the way she'd gotten the Ruyi Jingu Bang to.

By the time the tour was over, Thom's clothes were sticking to her skin. She wasn't the only one affected by the heat. Sweat dripped down Kha's face, his hair a wavy mess that barely resembled the sweeping style he usually wore. Even Concao looked hunched, face hidden beneath her wilting scarf.

No one said anything, but their stomachs all growled. They were hot and irritable, so they just sat on a giant boulder on the outskirts of the picnic area to eat the lunch North had packed for them—Spam musubi, a slice of Spam on top of a rice patty, all wrapped in seaweed—and debated what to do next.

"Where do you think he's hiding?" Thom asked. She set her sword by her feet and checked on the cricket. Half the carrot shavings Thom had put in the jar were gone, and Ma looked drowsy, her antennae waving more slowly than usual. It was hard to concentrate when it was so hot, difficult to decide on anything. The humidity made them even more sluggish. The air was thick and muggy. A gnat landed on Thom's arm and stuck to her sweaty skin. She wiped it off and almost wished she was back at the river near Tản Viên Mountain. She might even consider facing the Water Lord again, if only to get some relief from the crushing heat.

"In one of those caves?" Kha asked, his voice heavy with exhaustion. "Maybe?"

"Maybe," Thom said. "Your uncles said he was living in the Five Mountains, so it makes sense."

"We should search up there, then."

Concao sniffed at the air. "People are starting to leave."

She was right. The crowd, which had been shoulder to shoulder earlier, was thinning out.

"The park is closing soon," Thom said. "They'll probably kick us out."

"Where will we sleep?" Kha's voice was suddenly alert with panic, which immediately jolted Thom upright as well. She usually never had to worry about things like that. There was always a hotel to return to—or a relative's house. A grown-up to look after them. Now that grown-up was a cricket.

They looked at one another. Then up at the caves. Or rather, in the direction of the mountains, where the caves were located.

"Which one did the tour guide say people could hike up to?" Thom asked.

"The Water Mountain," Concao said.

Thom got to her feet, grabbing the sword. "Come on, we can still make it before they close the trailhead."

They wove through the crowd to get to the mountain in time. A park ranger in khaki shorts and a brown button-up eyed them with a bored expression.

"Trail's closing soon," he said, his Vietnamese laced with a regional accent Thom had trouble understanding.

"Um, my mom," Thom said, gesturing at the caves. "Up there already." She was embarrassingly aware of how incompetent she sounded in Vietnamese. Was this how Ma felt when she spoke English? "We had to use . . . toilet."

The ranger sighed. "American, huh?"

She nodded and gave her most innocent smile, eyes wide.

"Fine, then. Better hurry. Once the sun goes down, it will be cold and dark. Lots of night bugs and wild animals. You're sure your mom is up there?" The ranger gave her a hard look, then over at Kha and Concao. His eyes lingered on the fox demon a bit too long.

Thom nodded. "We'll be back as soon as we find her."

He waved them through but looked uncertain, so she climbed as fast as she could, glancing back a few times to be sure the others stayed close. The first part of the trail was steep, each step almost as high as Thom's knees so that they were practically lunging up the side of the mountain. Thom was used to vigorous exercise from being on the soccer team, and the fox demon bounded up the steps on all fours, now that there wasn't anyone around to see. But Kha, used to flying easily and not hiking up a steep hill in the heat, sounded like he might faint. His breaths came out in wheezes, and he pushed a hand off his knee with each step.

"You okay?" Thom asked.

Concao darted past her and up the steps, clearly done with waiting for her slower human companions.

"Oh yeah." Kha's hair was a wet mop on his head. "Great! Excellent!"

She wasn't sure if he was being sarcastic or just toxically positive, but the way he scowled and wiped angrily at his forehead wasn't a good sign.

"Want some water?" she asked hesitantly.

He shook his head. "Why can't we just fly up there?"

Thom glanced around. The sun hadn't set yet, casting the landscape in a beautiful golden glow that she was too sweaty to appreciate. "There are still people around who could see you transform."

"Concao just sprinted up the hill." He gestured dramatically after the fox demon, who was already out of sight.

"Yeah, but she could be mistaken for a really active kid. A fast runner is one thing—a boy changing into a dragon is another."

Kha heaved a sigh but continued dragging himself up the trail. Thom slowed their pace but tried not to be too obvious about it, stopping to tie her shoelaces or sip water. When they caught up with Concao, the sun was setting, the shadows of the trees and bushes around them elongating like claws stretching over the mountain. Buzzes filled the air. Thom slapped at a sudden sting on her elbow, trying not to picture all the bugs waiting to eat them alive.

On their way up, they had passed only a family of five returning to the trailhead, and now Thom, Kha, and Concao were on their own. Below them, the park was emptying as rangers ushered tourists back through the gateway.

As it got darker, a heaviness fell over Thom and she began to realize how truly alone they were, not just on the mountain, but on the quest to defeat the Monkey King. If they couldn't even find the Sage in a tourist park, how were they going to hunt down a demon-god laying siege on the heavens?

"The cave is not far from here," Concao said. She'd taken off her scarf and now looked radiant, in her element out among the trees, the wind fluffing up her hair.

Thom nodded. Kha had sat down on a boulder, staring intently at the sun as it dipped behind the peak of a mountain. It was almost frightening how quickly the day was suddenly cast in darkness. They were so far away from the city that the streetlamps didn't reach them, and there was no moon.

"Finally," Kha said as the shadows settled around them. He glanced around to make sure they were really alone before he transformed. Once he was a dragon, he let out a gravelly groan, the kind Thom gave when she finally got to sit down after a two-hour-long soccer practice full of passing drills and bleacher sprints. He stretched his long dragon body along a good section of the hiking trail, growling softly like a cat purring.

"Feel better?" Thom asked, laughing.

He hopped up and down. "Yes. I've been waiting to do that all day."

"How did you manage to pretend to be human for so long? You went all day at school without complaining once."

"Oh. I still went flying every night. That's how I saw you and the Monkey King one night when he took you to see his friends."

"Yeah, I thought you were a stalker back then." Thom climbed onto his back with Concao behind her.

"Hmph," he growled. "That's because the Monkey King lied to you and convinced you I wasn't your friend." His tone did nothing to hide his dislike for the Monkey King, and that funny twist sharpened in her belly again. She was glad she didn't have the Monkey King's hair anymore, and even gladder she'd never told Kha about him saving her from the Water Lord, especially now that the Monkey King was gone.

They took off and covered ground much faster than they had when they'd been walking. Thom was glad they were flying, especially now that she could barely see in the darkness. Who knew what animals or insects they would have encountered on foot?

The moonless night meant that when they got to the cave, it was pitch-dark. Luckily, Thom had packed some flashlights, which she retrieved from her backpack. Ma the cricket waved her antennae encouragingly—or at least Thom thought it was encouraging. Maybe Ma was actually scolding her on the danger she was putting herself in.

"I'm doing this for you, Ma," Thom whispered, zipping the backpack before the cricket could protest.

With the sword in one hand and the flashlight in the other, she led her friends forward into the cave.

10

IT WAS EMPTY. AT FIRST, it was too dark to tell, but when Thom shone her flashlight in every corner, it became clear that they weren't going to find anything. It wasn't a very deep cave, more like a large opening in the mountain, so it didn't take long for them to explore each inch and understand that they had come all this way for nothing.

Not for the first time, Thom felt a sinking disappointment after a long, tough day.

"Are you sure this is the right cave?" Thom asked.

Concao sniffed the air. "There are others deeper in the mountains."

"The tourist guide said this is the only one people are allowed to hike to," Thom said.

"If I were the Sage, I wouldn't hide here, then," Kha said.

"But he loves people. Mortals," Thom added. "That's why he decided to live in these mountains."

"Yeah, but he's still kind of a hermit, isn't he?" Kha asked.

"We should go farther," Concao said. "He might be hiding in one of the other caves."

Because they didn't have any better ideas, they flew up the mountain, stopping at every place that could possibly be a hiding spot for the Sage. Each cavern was empty.

By midnight, they were exhausted. Even Concao, usually full of energy, looked like she needed a nap.

"We need to sleep," Thom said. "We're not going to find him like this."

"Should we go to the city?" Kha asked.

"No." Thom thought about how grown-ups would react to two kids and a fox traveling in a foreign country by themselves. "We can camp in one of the caves. The first one didn't seem too bad."

When they returned to the very first one they'd explored, Thom hoped briefly that the Sage would be waiting for them after all. But it was still empty.

They hadn't packed any sleeping bags or blankets, so they had to lie on the hard floor. Concao was deep asleep within seconds, the cavern filling with her heavy breathing. She must have been used to sleeping out in the wilderness, living on the Mountain of a Hundred Giants.

Thom, on the other hand, couldn't get comfortable. She usually slept on her side, but the ground dug into her hips. She'd bunched up her hood into a makeshift pillow, but it was a poor substitute. She missed her bed and her fuzzy blanket and the knowledge that her mom was sleeping peacefully just down the hall. Instead, she had to comfort herself with the mason jar, which she placed next to her shoulder. The cricket was quiet.

"Do you think we're ever going to find the Sage?" Kha whispered.

Thom didn't want to consider the possibility that this would turn out to be another fruitless quest. "We have to," she said.

"What if we don't?"

A stab of annoyance—because she had been wondering the same thing all day and still didn't know the answer. "Then we'll have to find a different way into the heavens."

Kha grew quiet. She thought he'd fallen asleep when he spoke again. "If only you hadn't broken the Judgment Veil."

Shame rose up and left a terrible taste in her mouth. He had almost let it slip last time, too, but had caught it in time. Now he was outright blaming her.

She propped herself up on her elbow, but it was too dark for them to see each other. She glared at him anyway. "You told me to do it."

"Yeah, but I panicked. I didn't think—"

"What? That I actually would?"

"That you *could*. I didn't think it would break so easily. I thought we might, I don't know, make it stop working a bit, slow the guards down. But you *destroyed* that thing."

Her heart beat faster. A roaring filled her ears. Anger and hurt and confusion all warred with one another. Did Kha blame her? He had wanted to help her. He said he was her friend. Why was he bringing this up now? Was he having doubts?

Fine, then. Maybe she didn't need him. Maybe she could do this on her own. She would have to anyway; she'd always known she would. She needed to show the heavens that she was the one who could save them so that they would forgive her. She didn't need Kha, did she? Her fists clenched. Her face heated.

It wasn't true, though, that she could defeat the Monkey King on her own, which was what made the situation even more annoying. She wished she could do this alone, but of course she needed Kha, and the fact that he was the only one willing to help her made her even angrier. Well, Concao was with her, too, but the fox demon was in it purely for the revenge. No one else cared about the heavens, not about the Monkey King or the demons, and certainly not about her.

"Do you want to change your mind?" she asked, her voice quavering. "About helping me?"

"No." Kha sounded confused. "Why?"

"Because it's like you're having doubts or something."

He didn't answer for a long time. When he did, his words did nothing to make her feel better. "I just hope we find a way to fix this. I can't imagine failing. My father would be so disappointed."

"Yeah," Thom said, swallowing a lump in her throat. "Yeah, that would be a disaster. Your father's disappointment. Not, like, the heavens getting destroyed or anything."

Something rustled, like Kha was sitting up. "Okay, but, like, *you're* the reason it would be getting destroyed."

"I *know*." Thom took a deep breath. She hadn't meant for that to come out so loud and high-pitched. Concao had said the same thing as they'd left the Mountain God's hiding place. So it hadn't been Thom's imagination after all. Had they been talking about her? Did Kha and Concao agree that she was the one to blame? If so, they were absolutely right. All of this was her fault. If she hadn't been tricked by the Monkey King and if she hadn't helped him, they wouldn't be in this situation. "That's why I'm trying to fix it."

"And I'm trying to help you," Kha snapped.

Thom sat up, breathing hard. "Yeah, I know that, too. I'm grateful."

"Really? Because it doesn't sound like it."

"What do you want me to do? Do you want me to bow down to you, like you're a real dragon king, is that it?" Kha wanted to be like his father so much, and he wanted the dragon general's approval *so much*. That's what this was all about. Kha wasn't really here to help her, no matter how much he claimed to be her friend. He was here only to prove to his father that he could be a real dragon, to finish the job he'd been assigned.

"No, that's not—" Kha broke off. His voice sounded like it had cracked a bit. "Look, I think we're both exhausted. I'm hot—I'm not used to these conditions. The heavens are never like this, I swear. It's always— Anyway, I'm sticky. I want a shower. I'm . . . I . . . It's been a long day."

"Yeah, it has." Thom breathed through her nose, quick and deep, trying not to say something she would regret. She was sure Concao had woken up at the sound of their argument. The fox demon probably agreed with Kha, probably thought Thom was at fault for everything.

Thom suddenly felt very alone. She wished there were an easier way out of this. She wished she didn't need anyone's help, that she could do this alone, that she could single-handedly fix everything, that she could prove to them that she could be the hero, the good guy, in the end. She stuffed her fists into her pockets, and something sharp scratched her knuckle. "Ow!"

"You okay?"

"Yeah." Thom studied the back of her hand, pinpricks of blood lining the cut along her skin. She got up, too agitated now to attempt to sleep.

"Where are you going?" Kha asked as she got to her feet. "Thom—"

"I think someone needs to keep watch." She didn't meet

his eyes. "It's what they do in movies and stuff when they're on adventures like this. I'll go first."

"Oh, okay." Uncertainty strained his voice. "I can go next, if you want."

She didn't say anything, just dug through her backpack for her flashlight.

"You'll wake me when it's my turn?" Kha asked.

She nodded and left the cave before she said something mean, holding the flashlight in one hand and the cricket's jar in the other. It was dark and too scary to venture far, so she sat at the entrance and stared out at the scenery. In the distance, beyond the black void of trees and wilderness, little dots of light punctuated the night, evidence of a city, of life and people who had no idea of the danger they were all in. Because if the heavens were at war, Thom knew, there would soon be hell on earth.

The cricket hopped in the jar, which Thom held gently on her knees. She could make out Ma's beady eyes, and it was almost like Ma could tell how Thom was feeling and wanted to make it better.

"I know it's my fault," Thom whispered to her, wishing Ma were really here, as a human, so she wouldn't be so alone. "You know that, right? But I didn't mean to do it. I was tricked."

Thom imagined what Ma would say in return. *That just an excuse! You knew the Monkey King a bad guy—why you listen to him?*

"Yeah, but he wasn't like that. He was my friend." And

Thom hadn't had many of those, which made sense that she was sitting by herself in the dark talking to a cricket.

Ma pressed harder against the glass like she was getting closer to Thom. Or maybe the cricket was just trying to escape the jar.

"He told me it would be easy to get into the heavens and steal the cudgel," Thom tried to explain. She needed Ma on her side, but if Ma were human right now, she wouldn't be able to explain it all. Ma would ground her for life and scold her until Thom begged for the heavens' punishment. "He didn't tell me that it was, like, an unforgivable sin and that I would get sent to the hells if I got caught. And I had no idea . . . about the Boy Giant, about . . . Ba. So when he told me the truth about why I'm so strong, I freaked out, and then the Jade Army came after us and . . . oh my God, I hit him. I hit my own dad. In the head. With a really heavy magical weapon." She could still picture his eyes rolling back, his body falling.

The cricket hopped, making soft clinks against the glass.

"Yeah, he's a god, technically, but he was out cold." Thom traced the embossed design on the surface of the jar. The cricket's antennae twitched, as if she wanted to press her hand against Thom's. "What if he's still hurt? What if the Monkey King or the demons hurt him now that he's injured? I need to get back up there and make sure he's okay." Her heart sank. "If he'll even want to see me. He probably hates me now."

The cricket hopped a few times.

"I would hate me, too," Thom said quietly.

Ma didn't respond. Of course she didn't—she was a cricket. Thom sighed and hugged the jar against her chest.

She didn't know how long she sat there, fighting the urge to sleep. It was cold and lonely, but going back inside only to feel Kha's seething regret and Concao's silent judgment made her stay up longer than she probably should have. Her eyelids started drooping. Her chin nodded, and she jerked upright. But sleep was too tempting, rest just a bit out of reach. She wouldn't take long. Just a few seconds to herself.

Fingers freezing, she placed the jar next to her, and pushed her hand into her pocket. Again, something sharp grazed her skin. She absentmindedly ran her hands through the inner lining of the fleece, feeling for a thin, sharp piece of something familiar. She tried to remember, to figure out why she suddenly felt both scared and happy at the memory of a coarse pin between her fingers, but darkness enveloped her, and she sank into a deep, drowning sleep.

◆ ◆ ◆

Giggle.

Soft at first, as if he was trying to be quiet. Then a bit louder. Something brushed the side of her head, fingers combing through her hair. A staccato laugh.

Thom jerked awake. Her heart nearly stopped.

They both went very still. The Monkey King sat next to

her, cross-legged, pink toes up, looking very zen, as if it were perfectly normal for him to show up out of nowhere. His wide brown eyes blinked, reflecting the little light in the black wilderness.

"You're still here," Thom said. "I thought I lost your hair."

"Ooh-ooh," he murmured. "I hid in the seam of your jacket."

No wonder she hadn't been able to find it, though she always got scratched when she reached inside her pocket. She frowned, not knowing how to feel that he wasn't gone. Earlier, it had been a relief that she wouldn't have to decide what to do with him, that she wouldn't have to tell Kha and Concao that she still had a hair of his.

But now . . . now, after the argument with Kha, it was somewhat comforting not to be alone. Even though he had betrayed her. Or a part of him had. A different version of him that wasn't here. The only Monkey King here was one who was smiling at her as if he had missed her, as if he was actually happy to see her. It was all so confusing.

"What are you doing here?" Thom asked.

He tilted his head. "You still don't trust me."

"I don't have a reason to trust you."

"I saved you, remember? From drowning."

"Kha would have gotten to me eventually."

"Not before the Water Lord crushed you in his fingers." The Monkey King curled his hand into a fist. "I know that guy. He's not nice. Even the meanest of my friends don't like him."

"What do you want, Wukong?" Thom asked. She was tired of playing this game with him, every conversation like a riddle, never getting to the truth. "Why are you here?"

He pouted. "To keep you safe."

"If you really want to keep me safe, you should take yourself and your demon army out of the heavens."

He looped one leg up and over his head, like a half-twisted pretzel. "I don't know anything about that. All I know is that when I was cloned, I was given the task to protect you. So I shall do that." He gave a definitive nod.

He sounded so earnest, she almost believed him. Maybe he was telling the truth—maybe he didn't remember betraying her. Maybe he was different from the real Monkey King she had seen released from the Mountain of a Hundred Giants. She didn't want to, and she hated herself for it, but she missed the old Monkey King, the one who had taught her to play soccer and who had convinced her to accept her superstrength.

"Can you turn my mom back into a human?" she asked hopefully.

He scratched inside his ear with his big toe, then sniffed his foot. "I need my full powers for that. I need my true self and the use of my cudgel."

She let out a breath and turned away. "Then I don't want anything to do with you."

"You need my protection—"

"No I don't!" Her voice rose too high. She glanced behind her, but neither Kha nor Concao came out of the cave. "I can protect myself. I'm strong—you taught me that. I have a weapon of my own now. And I'm coming for you."

"But why, Thom-Thom? What have I done? We were working together. You helped me get my staff back. We were friends. We *are* friends."

She tried to ignore him, but everywhere she turned, he appeared in front of her, his lower lip sticking out, his brown eyes wide and shining. She crossed her arms. He sat in front of her, flipped upside down, crossed legs above his head, his nose almost touching hers.

"What are you doing in the heavens anyway?" she asked, exasperated. "What do you hope to gain by raging war on them? Why do you want to be ruler of the heavens so bad?"

He considered her questions with a pucker between his brows. "All I want is for the immortals to give my demon brothers and me the same rights that they have."

"What does that mean?"

His body turned sideways. He pressed his palms together and rested his face on his hands. "The fairies and gods and goddesses sit in the heavens eating peaches and looking down upon us demons, who are banned to an island or sent to the hells for no reason other than being what we are. Why?"

Thom shrugged. "Because that's the way of things. Because they're the good guys and you're the bad guys."

"*Good.*" He huffed. "*Bad.* I don't believe in those labels."

Despite not wanting to agree with him, despite her anger toward him and her determination to think of him as the enemy, she couldn't help but consider what he said. The demons lived on a peaceful island now, but no matter how beautiful the Mountain of a Hundred Giants was, it was nothing compared to the heavens, where the sweet smell of peaches filled the air, you could fly at will, and everything was so pretty and majestic and just plain beautiful.

"I want my brothers to have the same things as the fairies and immortals do," the Monkey King said. "Is that so bad?"

"No, it's not. But you can't attack the heavens to get it. You can't just steal what doesn't belong to you. Maybe you can earn it somehow. Maybe the demons can make a deal with the gods the way Concao did—"

"Yes. Concao made a deal with the heavens to become a fairy. And look where it got her."

Thom let out a sigh. "Waging war isn't the way to get what you want."

"Believe me, I have tried everything else."

She gave him a skeptical look.

"I have," he insisted, dropping his feet to the ground and standing up straight. "I tried to earn my place there." He pretended to hop onto a tall step. "They made me Master of the Horses, remember?" He hopped onto the next step. "I tried my best, too. I tended the horses." Another step. "I talked to them." Higher. "Took them out to exercise." He looked down at her. "Fed them." He mimed each movement, pretending to pet an invisible animal in front of him, rubbing his face against its neck, nuzzling its nose. "But that turned out to be a cruel joke." The Monkey King flopped onto his back, floated in the air, pretended to do a backstroke toward her. "And they call *me* a trickster."

"Okay, but . . ." She couldn't think of an actual argument. It did seem like a cruel thing to do, offering the Monkey King what he wanted—a real job, a way to earn their respect—only to laugh behind his back, and then to his face, about it.

"And then I tried to reason with them. I begged them to save my friends' lives and not send them to the hells," he said. "They wouldn't listen. All those fairies and immortals get to stay in the heavens, no matter what they've done. You should hear some of the stories I could tell about these fairies. Concao could tell you. But nothing bad ever happens to them. They are never punished, no matter how mean they are. Even mortals are weighed for their sins on the Bridge of Souls. But if a demon is defeated, he has no choice. Straight to the hells he goes. He never had an ounce of a chance."

"Is that when you struck your friends' names off the Book of the Hells?" Thom asked.

"I didn't see what choice I had."

"But that's wrong . . . I mean, those systems are in place for a reason."

"Imagine if Shing-Rhe was sent to the hells," the Monkey King said, flipping over and staring at her straight in the eyes. "Picture all the monkey brothers being tortured. No one has taught you about the different circles, have they? That's why they're called the hells. There are layers and layers, levels of torture, kingdoms and realms and dimensions, filled with various ways to torment souls forever and ever and ever. An eternity of torture. Those rulers of hell have had many centuries to conjure up even more ways to inflict pain. Would you want that for Shing-Rhe? Would you want that for my brothers? Simply because they are born the way they are?"

"No," Thom said. "Of course I don't. They're sweet and wonderful. They wouldn't deserve that."

The Monkey King smiled, a most satisfied smile, as if she had given him the greatest gift. "So you see? I am right."

Thom couldn't think of anything else to say. It made sense. She almost agreed with him. But the rulers in the heavens were not the bad guys—they couldn't be. There was a reason they were in charge. There was a reason everything worked the way it did. Wasn't there?

A clinking sound caught her attention, and Thom looked down, remembering that she'd brought the cricket out with her. She scooped up the jar. Ma bounced around inside, agitated. Was it because the Monkey King was here?

"Thom?" Kha's voice called out behind them.

The Monkey King disappeared. The tiny sliver of hair floated down, down. Instinctively, Thom caught it.

"You okay?" Kha asked. Footsteps coming closer. "Where are you? It's so dark."

She clicked on the flashlight.

"Oh." Kha breathed a sigh. "I thought . . . Were you talking to someone?"

Thom shook her head. "No. I was, um, talking in my sleep probably. I think I fell asleep and had a nightmare."

Kha smiled sympathetically. He looked like he wanted to say something else. He opened his mouth two or three more times, but eventually just scratched the back of his head. "If you're tired, I'll take the watch for now."

Thom nodded, even though she wasn't the least bit sleepy.

As she walked back to the cave, she felt Kha's eyes watching her, and she almost stopped and turned to him. Kha lived in the heavens. He'd been born there. Maybe he would have the answers to the questions Thom now had after her talk with the Monkey King.

But then she thought of the way Kha had blamed her earlier for the Judgment Veil, and she kept walking. He was the one who had told her to do it—or at least, she thought he had. Now she wasn't sure. Doubt skewed her memory. It had been such a stressful moment—escaping from the Jade Soldiers right after she'd stolen the cudgel, reeling from the fact that she'd attacked her own father. She had done so many wrong things. What if destroying the Veil was just one thing to add to the list? Had she justified her action by convincing herself he had told her to do it?

And she had thought all this time he was on her side. What else did he blame her for?

Besides, of course he was on the heavens' side. That's where his father and mother lived, where he would return, where he belonged. Even if the Monkey King had made some valid points, there was no way Kha would agree with any of them.

The Monkey King's hair was still in her palm. She should throw it away, stomp it into the dirt. But she couldn't do it. She had too many questions. She could use him. Maybe he was reporting back to his true self. She could feed him lies or find out what the real Monkey King was up to. Anyway, if she let the hair go, who knew what other havoc he could wreak? At least this way, she could keep an eye on him.

She repeated that excuse over and over like a mantra until it lulled her to sleep.

11

IN THE MORNING, THE FIRST thing she did was make sure the hair was in her pocket, poked several times through the inseam. No wonder she'd gotten so many scratches but hadn't been able to find it. Even dormant, the Monkey King was dangerous.

Ma the cricket needed more food, so Thom tore up some lettuce scraps from their dwindling lunches to add to the carrot shavings. She wished she had a banana—Ma loved them.

The others got ready also, but there was an unease in the air between them, a big giant question no one knew how to ask: Now what?

Kha wouldn't meet her eyes, and Thom was secretly glad. She didn't know what to say to him. She had no idea how to make things better, and she wasn't even sure who had been right. She was grateful for Kha's help, but what if he still blamed her for everything?

They had searched the mountain yesterday. With Kha flying, it had been easy to reach all the caves where the Sage could possibly be hiding, and yet he had been nowhere. Either he didn't want to be found, or they had the wrong place.

"But North said he was here," Kha said when Thom voiced her doubts out loud. They hiked down the trail together, Concao back in her human disguise. Below them, the park once again filled with crowds of tourists.

"Maybe he was wrong," Thom said. "Maybe the Sage had already left."

"We would have heard," Kha said. "It's the dragon kings' job to patrol the land and to make sure that everything is peaceful. They would know if the Sage had left to go somewhere else."

"I don't know, Kha. I think maybe . . ." But Thom had no idea how to finish that thought. She had no idea where else to look. If the dragon kings had been wrong, how would they be able to find the Sage? Who else would know where he was? How else were they going to get up to the heavens? He was their only remaining path . . . unless they somehow found Princess Liễu Hạnh. But that was impossible. She hadn't been seen for over twenty years.

They spent the day roaming the park for lack of a better plan, but even if the Sage was hiding among the mortals, there was no way he would appear in front of so many tourists.

As the sun started to set, Thom knew they couldn't spend another night in the cave. Her body was sore from sleeping on the ground, the little sleep she had gotten still left her exhausted, and even though no one wanted to say it, they were all starting to stink a little. She and Kha hadn't packed any extra clothes.

Plus, they were running low on the food the dragon kings had packed for them. She didn't have much cash on her. She hadn't thought they would be traveling the world. When she'd first embarked to follow the Monkey King, she had naively thought she could take him down easily and quickly.

"They're going to kick us out soon," Thom said as the park started to empty of the lucky people on vacation with comfortable hotel rooms to return to, people who had no idea the Monkey King really existed or what he was doing to their world.

"Maybe we can search again tonight," Kha said.

All three of them looked up at the mountains. Thom thought about their fruitless search last night, the empty caves, and the dark, scary tunnels that looked like no one had been there for centuries.

"No," Concao said, echoing what Thom was thinking. "He's not up there."

Kha looked down. "What do we do, then?"

No one had an answer.

"Are we just going to give up?" he asked. He looked at Thom for the first time all day, yearning for a solution.

She was too tired to think of one. She felt dizzy and sleepy, and a bit feverish. Every time she tried to think too hard, her head hurt.

"We need a better place to sleep," she said. "And then we can come back."

"He's here," Kha said as the three of them walked toward the exit. "I know he is. The dragon kings said he would be here, and they would know. They travel the world. They keep the order. They would have told us if the Sage left." Desperate to convince them, he let his voice get a bit too high.

Thom turned around to tell him that she believed him. Of course the dragon kings were trying to help—but maybe they were wrong.

Something caught her eye. They had passed the exit and stood on the other side of the gateway. The statue that had guarded the top of the arch was still there, but something looked . . . off. Different. She could have sworn that when they'd arrived yesterday, the figure had been holding a cane and wearing a conical straw hat on his head. But now he was holding the hat in his hand, a few inches above his head, almost as if he was greeting them. Or saying goodbye.

Kha was still talking. "They might have given us the wrong address. Maybe the wrong place. What if we're supposed to go to Da Nang instead of Na Dang? There are similar mountains there and—"

Thom waved a hand for his attention.

"What is it?" he asked, then followed her gaze to the statue.

"He looks different," Thom said.

"Who?"

"The statue."

"How?"

"You don't see it?" She waved at her head. "The hat."

Kha squinted. "No."

Thom looked at Concao. "Am I crazy?"

The fox demon shrugged. "I wasn't paying attention."

"I swear it's moved," Thom said.

"So?" Kha said.

"So? I think it's important."

"How?"

"I . . . don't know."

"Okay . . ." Kha shifted his weight. "So now what?"

"Can we get up there somehow?"

"What, to the statue?"

Thom resisted the urge to roll her eyes, only because Kha was finally looking at her directly again. "Well, yeah."

"And do what?"

"I don't know." Why were they both being so weird about this? "I'll see when I get up there."

Kha crossed his arms, his expression impatient and frustrated, and while a part of Thom understood why, another part couldn't help thinking that if the Monkey King were here, he wouldn't hesitate to fly up to the statue, if only because he thought it would be fun.

"I just want to see it. Up close," Thom added. "Maybe once it gets dark again, we can fly up there."

Kha exchanged a weird, knowing glance with Concao. It reminded her of Bethany Anderson and Sarah Mazel, the two bullies on her soccer team, the way they would make fun of her. But this was worse. Kha and Concao were supposed to be her friends, or at least on her side, and the look they now shared sent shooting pains straight into her belly. They *had* been talking about her behind her back. Maybe last night, after Thom and Kha's argument, or maybe all along. Maybe they had doubted her this whole time, only now they were expressing their questions out in the open, right in front of her.

They were right, if that was the case. She had no idea what she was doing. She was just trying to find the answer as she went along.

And right now, she knew she had to get to that statue. She couldn't ignore the feeling that it was very important.

"Come on, what else are we going to do?" she pointed out.

"We could fly back to North's palace," Kha said. "Maybe he'll have a better idea."

"Okay." She thought about it. "But how about we check out that statue first, while we're here. And if nothing happens, then we'll go back?"

Kha and Concao looked at each other again, in that way that made Thom feel incredibly alone, which was an odd feeling since lots of people were moving all around them, practically shoving them aside in their hurry to leave the park.

"Okay, fine," Kha said eventually. "We'll wait until dark. But then we'll go back to my uncle's and figure out a different plan."

Thom nodded, relieved that Kha was still on her side. Even after their fight, he was willing to listen to her and help her. She thought guiltily again of the Monkey King's hair in her pocket. She needed to tell Kha and Concao about it.

Then she remembered how they'd looked at each other, the silent conversation they'd had about her that echoed the many ones they probably had out loud, and she turned away. She wasn't the only one keeping secrets.

To hide the hurt that wrenched through her, she pulled out the map of the park they'd gotten from the tour guide yesterday, even though she wasn't interested in any of its features. Kha walked away to sit down on a nearby tree stump, looking exhausted, his cheeks pink, his hair shiny with sweat, and his clothes more rumpled than she had ever seen them. Concao followed him at first but then moved upward into the copse of trees behind him, slipping easily out of view.

Thom didn't know what to do while they waited. Should she sit with Kha? He probably just wanted to be left alone. He had folded his map into a fan and looked like he might hyperventilate.

"Hey, there's a café near here," she said. "I'm going to go get us something to drink." She paused. When he didn't say anything, she added, "You can wait here if you want."

Kha nodded and leaned back, trying to fit his body under the shade of the trees.

Thom breathed a sigh of relief and walked away, thankful to be alone for the first time all day. The café was a bit farther away than it seemed on the map, but the sun was starting to set, so the shadows of the trees were larger and cooler, and it wasn't an unpleasant walk.

As she neared the small coffee cart, she got that tingling sensation in the back of her neck that told her she wasn't alone.

"Where are we going?" the Monkey King asked, and even though guilt made her want to push him away, she was grateful for his presence. She could already feel the weight lifting from her shoulders. He had that effect sometimes, a reminder that nothing was as bad as it seemed and that, even if it was, he could always fix any problem he came up against.

"To get some boba, hopefully," she said, holding out the map, where a small menu had been printed next to the coffee shop. The Monkey King was invisible now, so she had no idea if he was even looking. Her mouth watered as she read the list of food options—marinated beef skewers, dried squid, fried shrimp, Cajun french fries.

The Monkey King's face appeared briefly in front of her, licking his lips. "Yum."

"Do you even eat?" she asked. She had never seen him do it.

"Of course I do. I'm not dead. I just don't need to, so I

don't waste my time, unless it's something utterly delicious, of course. Like demon spirit."

Thom almost stopped walking. "What?"

He giggled. "Kidding! Kidding. I haven't had demon spirit for centuries."

"Why would you eat demon spirit?" she asked, horrified.

"Like I said, it's delicious. And because some spirits give you more power and longer life. Before I ate the peaches of immortality and drank the heavenly wine and took the pills of immortality, I sometimes revived myself on demon spirit. I made a lot of enemies that way, though. I wouldn't recommend it." He gave a long-suffering sigh. "The things I resorted to before I became truly immortal."

Thom wasn't sure if he was being serious or not, but she was saved from having to reply because they'd reached the café. It was a simple window set inside a brick building and a large patio with half its chairs already put away. Still, the barista let her order—four iced boba drinks, barbecue skewers, Cajun-style potato discs on a stick—before closing the window to any other customers. Thom paid for everything with the last bit of cash she'd thought to bring with her.

"Your friends don't deserve all this food, do they?" the Monkey King asked, appearing briefly in front of her, walking backward with his hands behind his head. No one else seemed to see him. Tourists walked by and ignored Thom completely. She thought she might have looked pretty conspicuous, with a sword sticking out of her backpack, but no one cared. The park workers were too busy cleaning up trash or putting away chairs or hanging up closing signs to be worried about a girl walking by herself.

"We're all hungry," Thom said, clutching the paper bags of food, grease already soaking through the thin lining. She held out the container of four drinks. "One's for you."

"Oh." He looked surprised, but he took one of the cups and held it up to blink at the black blobs at the bottom. "What is it?" He licked at the straw experimentally, then chewed on it and made a face. "I don't think this stuff is good for you."

"You're not supposed to eat the straw," she said, laughing. "That's just a . . . like a utensil." She took a sip of her own drink to show him how it was done.

The Monkey King tried it and almost choked on a boba. He coughed it up and spat it into his hand. "Is this a magical pearl that gives you incredible strength?"

"No, weirdo, it's boba. It's a food."

"You . . . eat . . . this?" he asked, holding the black, jellylike ball up to his eye. "Are you sure you've never had demon spirit? It looks almost exactly like it, except demon spirit smokes a little."

"No, of course not. I mean, I don't think so? I've never had demon spirit." She grinned.

He smiled back at her. Then he popped the boba in his mouth, chewed, stuck out his tongue, flipped backward, and disappeared.

Thom was sad to see him go, but she had almost reached Kha by then, so she knew the Monkey King couldn't stick with her. Besides, she scolded herself, she shouldn't be talking to him in the first place. They didn't trust each other. They weren't friends, no matter how often he said so.

But still, she couldn't help feeling very lonely now that he was gone again. She clutched the bag of food and tried not to spill the drinks.

Concao was sitting with Kha when she got back, her fox face covered by her scarf so that she looked like a very regal grandmother resting with her grandson.

"Oh my God," Kha said, for the first time all day looking excited to see Thom, his eyes practically popping out of his head as he reached for the food. "What is it? Where'd you get it?"

"The café was about to close," she said. "I got there just in time." Thom held out the skewers and drinks, and no one talked as they spent the next few minutes burning their tongues on the meat and cooling them down with the iced boba.

"Why'd you get four?"

Kha asked, looking at the straw in the fourth cup the Monkey King had chewed on.

"Um, I'm really thirsty," she said, snatching it away. "I wanted two for myself."

"That's a lie," Concao said casually, as if commenting on how clear the sky was and not making an accusation. "It was for Wukong, wasn't it?"

Kha looked at the fox demon, then at Thom. "What?" There was a bubble of laughter in his voice, as if he wasn't sure if she was joking.

"She's been talking to the Monkey King," Concao said, finishing her food quickly. "She still has a hair of his."

Thom held both cups in each hand, frozen. *Lie, think of something.* But her mouth opened and closed like a fish's, and she couldn't think of anything to say.

"Oh my God, Concao's telling the truth, isn't she?" Kha said. He looked down at the remaining skewer as if debating tossing it dramatically, but instead he tore off the last bite, and *then* threw it in the trash. "What are you thinking?"

"It's not how—" Thom tried to explain.

"Where's the hair?"

"It's gone," Thom said. Too fast.

"Check her pocket," Concao said.

Kha moved toward her, the fox demon behind him as if backing him up.

Thom held up both boba drinks. "Stop, stop. Here." She

placed the cups on the floor, then flipped the pockets of her hoodie inside out. If the Monkey King had snuck his hair back in there, he would have hidden in the seam but she really had no idea where he'd gone when he'd disappeared. Kha inspected the pockets, turning the fabric over several times but didn't find anything aside from Jae's ring.

"I'm not, like, working with him," Thom tried to explain.

"But you're not exactly beating him, are you?" Concao pointed out. Her face was half hidden beneath her scarf.

"What would that do?" Thom said. "He's just a clone."

"Thom," Kha groaned. "We can't trust him."

"I *don't*! I know we can't."

"Then why didn't you tell us about him?" Kha asked.

"Because! I . . ." She felt awkward and dorky, standing there with her pockets sticking out, so she shoved them back in. "Look, he saved me. I didn't know about him—I mean, I forgot about the hair. It's the one the Monkey King gave me to take into the heavens and I just forgot." She shrugged. "But then, when I was drowning in the river, he saved me. I would have died. And, okay, I should have told you both, I know, but then he left. I thought he was gone. There was no point after that."

"You still should have told us," Kha said.

"He's trying to get in your head again," Concao said. "Tricking you."

Thom nodded. "I know."

"Don't listen to him," Kha said, his voice high, a sparkly sheen appearing on his face. "Don't fall for it again."

Thom crossed her arms. "I know," she repeated. When neither of them said anything, she added, "I'm sorry."

They didn't respond.

"How did you know anyway?" Thom asked Concao.

"I heard the two of you talking last night."

Thom closed her eyes briefly. "You have really good hearing."

Her scarf twitched where her ears were. "Yes," she said in a tone that suggested it wasn't something Thom should forget.

"What were you talking about?" Kha asked. "What does he want?"

Thom looked down. "He says he's here to protect me—"

"He's just tricking you again!" Kha practically shouted.

"I know!" The park was almost empty now, the daylight fading. "Can you just trust me? I didn't give in to him, and I didn't tell him anything."

"She's telling the truth," Concao said.

But still, Kha made a funny face.

"Look, it's getting dark," Thom said, gesturing at the sky. "We should go."

Kha glanced up as if realizing she was right. "Fine," he said, but the conversation wasn't over, judging from his voice.

Thom walked away and tossed the unfinished drinks in the trash.

12

THE ENTRANCE TO THE PARK was closed, the lights of the ticket windows turned off. Even in the darkness, Thom could make out the statue of the Sage. Was it her imagination, or had it changed again? The hat was no longer above his head but was lower, almost covering his face.

She stopped squinting as Kha transformed into a dragon. They were about to find out.

There wasn't enough room on the ledge above the gateway for Kha to land, so he hovered there while Thom slipped off. The ledge was only just deep enough that she could walk, but any wrong step meant a thirty-foot fall, unless Kha was quick enough to catch her. Concao remained on Kha's back, clearly not on board enough with Thom's plan to join her.

"We'll wait for you up there," Kha said, gesturing to the bridge above the gateway. "There's more room."

Thom nodded.

"If something happens, just shout for us," Kha added. There was a coldness in his voice, though.

"Okay." She patted the sword jutting out from her backpack. "I'll be fine." Though she had the sense that he wouldn't care now anyway, not after how she'd betrayed him.

He flew away, and Thom felt empty, wishing there was something she could do to instantly patch the damage she'd done.

The statue was hidden where it rested underneath the roof of the ledge. But there was no mistaking it now. The hat had moved to cover the figure's face. Even when Thom tried to peer behind the hat, she couldn't make out the features.

She wasn't sure what she had hoped to find up here, but the statue remained a statue. Disappointment made her exhausted. What had she thought would happen? That the statue would wake up and turn out to be the Sage after all?

She poked at its arm, but it didn't budge. "Hello," she whispered. Nothing. "Sage?" So silly, talking to a statue.

Instead of calling out for Kha and admitting that this was a bad idea after all, she stood to the side, looking out across the entrance to the park—the view the statue must see every day. She let out a long breath, took in a deeper one. It felt good, like a gulp of cold water after a grueling afternoon of soccer practice.

"Where's my drink?" the Monkey King asked, popping up next to her. He sat on the edge of the ledge, legs swinging, rocking dangerously like he might fall off.

"I threw it away," Thom whispered, afraid that Kha and Concao—especially Concao—might hear them.

"Why? I thought you were saving it for me. I wanted another taste of the fake demon spirit."

Thom turned her back on him. She didn't want to do it, but she had promised herself she would earlier, and she had told Kha she didn't trust the Monkey King. Kha and Concao were the ones on her side, not this demon-god who had betrayed her.

"Go away, Wukong," she said.

"Ooh-ooh?" He moved closer, studying her face. "What's happened? What's wrong?"

"You shouldn't be here. I can't be talking to you. You betrayed me, and I don't trust you."

"But I'm here to protect you—"

She reached above her head and touched the hilt of the sword. "I can protect myself."

"Oh yes, I forgot." His eyes flashed with anger. "Your magical sword, which you're going to beat me with. But tell me, do you even know how to use it?"

"Of course I do," she snapped. "Kha taught me."

"That snake noodle should stick to greasing his hair."

"Don't call him that. He's my friend, a better friend than you'll ever be."

The Monkey King stepped back, hand to his chest, jaw slack. "Him?" He gasped. "No!"

Thom couldn't tell if he was being sarcastic or not. "What are you really doing here? You're spying on me for the real you, aren't you? You're not here to protect me. You just want to find out how I'm going to defeat you. Well, I'll tell you how. I'm going to go up to the heavens. I'm going to find you, and I'm going to fight you, and beat you, and save everyone from your ridiculous rule."

His mouth opened and closed. "Why are you being so *mean*?" he asked, eyes watering.

She wasn't going to fall for it. She was *not*. She was done feeling sorry for him, being tricked by him, lying to her friends about him.

"Because we're not friends," she said. "Because you're my enemy. Because you're the bad guy."

A tear fell from his eye, soaking into the fur on his cheek. Thom wanted to take back her words. She'd gone too far. She had never seen him cry before, and it wrenched a hole in her chest.

But then he popped and disappeared. His hair fell. She had started to reach for him, an apology already forming, and it landed on her outstretched hand.

Thom studied the golden pinlike thing, wishing she could wake him up somehow. Had she been too mean? Was he really telling the truth, that he was the old Monkey King, the one who hadn't betrayed her?

But even if he was the old version of himself, he had

already been planning to betray her, hadn't he? He had always known he couldn't follow through with his promise to take her abnormal strength away. He had planned to trick her all along.

She closed her fist over his hair. What was right? Who was wrong?

"I'm sorry," she whispered. "I have no idea what I'm doing." A sob escaped her. Her legs wobbled like overcooked udon noodles. She lowered herself to the ground, pulled her knees to her chest, and stuffed her hands in her pockets.

"Well, of course you don't."

The voice startled her back to her feet.

She stepped back, slamming against the wall. She couldn't see very far in front of her—it was so dark—but there, unmistakably, the statue of the Sage was moving.

"You're just a little girl," he said. He lowered his hat, and his features looked like clay as they moved. "How old are you?"

"Al-almost twelve." Thom thought about the sword, but if she reached for it now, it might seem like a threat.

"Eleven. A baby. Really, why would they send a child?" He twirled the conical hat in one hand and swung his cane in the other, like he was a character in a musical, about to break into song.

"They didn't send me," Thom said. "I'm here on my own. I mean—not on my own. My two friends are helping me." Although *friends* sounded wrong as she said it. She wasn't sure about that, not now. Maybe *fellow soldiers*, or *teammates* even. "But we're here because we want to be. Or need to be. No one sent us."

If the statue had a reaction, she couldn't see it in the dark. He was so still that she wondered if he had moved at all.

"No one wants to help us," she continued because she couldn't stand the silence any longer. "We need to get to the heavens, but the Mountain God doesn't want to get involved. You're the only one left who can take us there. At least, I think you are. You are the Sage, right?"

The cane clicked. The hat twirled and landed on top of his head. "At your service."

"We found you because the Dragon Kings of the North and East helped us."

"Ah well, it's no secret. I like watching mortals."

Thom followed his gaze. She itched to ask him again to help her—but after her encounter with Sơn Tinh and Princess Mỵ Nương, she was aware of how entitled that seemed. Concao was right. They didn't know her. The Sage didn't know her. Why should they help? She had come all this way to ask for his help, but now she realized that she did not deserve it.

"You need to get to the heavens, I know," the Sage said, as if reading her mind. He crossed his hands behind his back. "But why?"

"To stop the Monkey King," Thom said.

"One does not stop the Monkey King. He will do as he pleases."

"Okay, then. To . . . make him . . . please . . . stop," she said lamely.

To her surprise, the Sage chuckled. "Yes, but why?"

"Because . . ." She groped for an answer. "He's a bad guy."

"Is he?"

"Yes! And he's going to destroy the heavens."

"Hmm."

That was not the response she'd expected. It was like talking to the Mountain God all over again. Shouldn't they be horrified that the heavens were in danger? It was the home of the gods after all, their home. *Her* home if she had had a choice, and maybe it could still be her home if she managed to fix everything—gain her father's forgiveness, convince the heavens that she deserved a second chance.

"Don't you think the heavens deserve saving?" she asked.

The Sage turned to her with a slow smile. "That's a very good question."

"I mean," Thom sputtered. "It was kind of rhetorical. Obviously, we need to help everyone up there."

"Why? You've been in the heavens. You've seen what it's like."

"Well, yeah, it's beautiful, the clouds and the temples and the flying."

The Sage studied her, his face frozen in a serene yet unreadable expression. "But it's not perfect, is it?"

No. Which was weird because it was the *heavens*. Wasn't it supposed to be perfect by its very definition?

And yet when she was there, it hadn't taken her long to notice the things that were wrong with it. How the fairies didn't respect Princess Jae because she was powerless, even though it wasn't her fault she was born that way. How the immortals all shuddered at the mention of the demons, even though not all demons were as bad as the heavens claimed them to be. And then there was Sơn Tinh. There was a reason he didn't want to live in the heavens even though he belonged there. And Concao—she'd made one mistake, and they'd stripped her of her name, turned her into a demon, and banished her to an island.

"So what should I do?" Thom asked. "I can't just abandon them."

"Why not?" The Sage twirled his cane. "You're perfectly fine down here, it seems. You can continue living your life, never having to worry about punishment for breaking in and stealing the cudgel."

He was right. Kind of. And yet a part of her longed for the heavens. A part of her belonged there. It wasn't perfect, but that didn't mean it wasn't worth saving. Worth fixing.

"But my mom," Thom said. "She's a cricket."

"So?"

"So! I need the Monkey King to turn her back."

"Then make another deal with him. Once he's done doing what he's doing in the heavens, he'll come back to the mortal world. What's stopping you from joining his side and getting what you want without the danger of retribution from the gods?"

Thom shook her head. "It's not right. I made that mistake before. He's a trickster. If I make a deal with him, it's never what I think it is—there's always a higher price or a . . . like a hidden fee."

The Sage's lips twitched. "You're quite clever."

"You have to help me," she said, encouraged by his compliment. Maybe he was on their side after all. "The heavens are in serious trouble. The Monkey King brought a whole demon army with him."

"And do you not think that the heavens have their own army?"

"They do, but they don't stand a chance against the Monkey King. He's undefeatable, and he'll just clone himself until he beats them. I can't just sit back and . . . go home when I know that he's up there."

"So why do you think you can succeed where the Jade Army cannot?"

"Because . . . because . . ." The Sage was right, wasn't he? What made Thom think she could defeat the most invincible demon-god to ever exist? "I have the sword."

"The sword?"

"The Sword of Heaven's Will. The Mountain God gave it to me. It will multiply my strength by ten thousand, and I'm already really strong."

She took the sword from her backpack and showed it to him. The Sage took it in his stone hands, studying the hilt and examining the blade.

"So it is," he said. "And with this sword you think you can defeat the Monkey King?"

Thom nodded.

"Hmm." He turned away, sword in one hand, cane in the other. Thom waited for his answer, heart pounding. "Okay." He thumped the cane. "I'll take you to the heavens."

"Really?" She nearly hopped with excitement, except she had never been a hop-with-excitement sort of person.

"But I want payment."

She deflated. "I don't have any money." She'd spent all she had left on food just that evening.

"I don't want money. I want this sword." He brandished it, or tried to, but it was quite heavy, so all he managed was to dangle it in his wrist.

"What?" Thom shook her head. "No, I just told you, I need that sword to defeat the Monkey King."

"Do you, though?"

"Yes. He's strong, and he has the cudgel. I'm strong, and I have the sword. We'll be a fair match."

"The Monkey King is strong, yes, but that isn't what makes him undefeatable. I should know. They don't call me the Sage for nothing. Ask me."

"Ask you what?"

"How to defeat the Monkey King."

Thom shook her head, not in defiance, but in disbelief. How could the Sage know something no other immortal or demon had ever found out? She humored him anyway. "How do you defeat the Monkey King?"

"You discover his weakness."

"Okay. How?"

"What is weakness, really, when you think about it?"

"Uhhhh." Thom wished he would just tell her the answer. He was one of those teachers who thought they could guide their students into figuring out a problem, stretching the silence into awkwardness.

He smiled knowingly. "Why do you really want to go after him?"

She sighed. "To stop him."

"Wrong answer."

"To save the heavens."

"Nope again." The Sage twirled his cane.

Thom took a deep breath. "To have him change my mom back from a cricket."

The Sage suppressed what sounded suspiciously like a chuckle. "We're getting closer, I think."

Thom thought hard of all the reasons she could give. "To bring him back to his brothers?"

The Sage laughed. "As if you ever intended to do that."

She turned away. He was right. She had promised Shing-Rhe she would try to save the Monkey King, to show him mercy. But she had also lied because she knew the truth. He couldn't be saved. He wouldn't want to be. And he wouldn't have deserved it.

Then she knew. When she looked at the Sage, she could tell he did, too, but she spoke out loud anyway. "To make him pay."

"For what?"

"For tricking me."

One side of the Sage's mouth quirked. "He tricks everyone. You've already met the Dragon King of the East—he stole the cudgel from him first. And your friend whom you travel with, the fox demon. He stole her fairyhood from her. Then there's the Lotus Master in the heavens, the countless gods and goddesses who wish him dead—"

"For betraying me," Thom cut him off. "That's why I want to go after him. To get him back."

The Sage waited, silence drawing out her answer.

"For," Thom said, her voice on the verge of cracking, "hurting me."

The Sage sighed, a contented sound like he had finally gotten to taste the meal he'd been craving. "There it is."

"I want to hurt him back," Thom said. Now that the truth

was out, she couldn't keep it in, not even a small bit. "I want him to feel what it was like to be promised the one thing you wanted more than anything, only to have it taken away."

The Sage chuckled quietly. "Who did you say was the bad guy, again?"

Thom clenched and unclenched her fists. "That's why I need the sword."

The Sage contemplated the weapon. For a second, she was afraid he wouldn't give it back, but then he handed it over, hilt first.

"No, you don't," he said. "But I know you won't believe me."

Thom took it anyway. He might be the Sage, the most intelligent being ever to exist, but she knew he was wrong. She could feel it in her gut, which was what had led her to him after all.

"There is still the matter of payment, however," the Sage added. "Have you anything else?"

Not money. Something valuable to an immortal. Not just any immortal, but one of the Four Immortals.

"I have this bracelet." She held up the golden string wrapped around her wrist. "From my father. But it might be useful. Um." She dug in her pocket and came up with two objects. "This is the Jade Princess's ring." The one she'd stolen from her only friend in the heavens. Another person who probably hated her guts. "And this is the hair of the Monkey King. Well, a hair of a hair."

The Sage's stony eyes lit up. "A clone of a clone?" He held out his palm.

Thom hesitated, but she wasn't sure why. The Monkey King had betrayed her, what did she need his hair for? And she had also promised her friends she wouldn't trust him again.

And yet she wanted to keep it. Why? The Monkey King couldn't help her—how could she trust anything he did or said? It was all fake. A trick. What he was known for.

Their last encounter still shadowed her. The hurt look in his eye. The one teardrop that had soaked into his fur.

"What are you going to do with it?" she asked.

"Study it. Observe it. Learn from it." The Sage shrugged.

"Are you going to hurt him?"

The Sage smiled. "Of course not. He's a powerful demon. I am a peaceful, scholarly god. I merely want to . . . talk. We have much to discuss, this monkey who calls himself the Great Sage of Heaven. Maybe we have things to teach each other."

Still, Thom hesitated. But it was either the hair or the ring, and she would need the ring in the heavens. She had to give it back to Jae. It wasn't hers to give to the Sage.

She dropped the hair into the Sage's hand. As he closed his fingers around it, she imagined them wrapping around her lungs instead.

"Accepted," the Sage said. He held it up to his face, pinched between thumb and forefinger. Then he turned to her with a smile. "Are you ready?"

WHEN THOM HAD BEEN WORKING with Kha on the Culture Day art project, she had made a joke about the Sage being like Mary Poppins. As he took off his hat, twirled it a couple of times, and then balanced it on top of the cane like an umbrella, she realized how wrong she'd been.

Of course, she hadn't expected him to be made of stone. Except that had just been a disguise, one he shed as Kha and Concao joined them. The gray surface of his statuelike skin grew red at first, as if being burned away, and retreated to reveal golden skin, a bald head, and knowing deep black eyes.

"I knew it," Kha said, having changed into his human form. "My uncles were right. We've been looking for you everywhere in the mountains."

The Sage inclined his head. "I prefer a good view."

Kha nudged Thom with his elbow. "Good job."

She smiled back, but her mind was still on the fact that she had just given away a hair of the Monkey King. It felt like the greatest betrayal. Even though he had betrayed her first, that didn't make it right. What if he appeared and found himself with the Sage instead of her? What would he think?

It didn't matter. She was about to do a lot worse to the real Monkey King in the heavens.

"Everyone ready?" the Sage asked, holding his hat-cane umbrella up to the sky.

"Do we—should we hold hands?" Thom asked, looking at the others.

The Sage chuckled. "Only if you want to."

Thom clasped her fingers together in embarrassment. But to her surprise, Kha reached for her hand, though he didn't meet her eyes. Concao's white paw joined their fists, like a team huddle. Something that reminded her of home.

"How sweet," the Sage said.

He twirled his cane. The ground dropped. The air rushed around them, only it was not just wind or sky, but little bubbles of something colorful, like a rainbow encased in teardrops. The same substance that had made up the Judgment Veil. A melodic tinkling tickled Thom's ears, and she couldn't hear or see anything else except the rainbow droplets, which had changed from multicolor to a pure essence, like mist or fog.

A cloud.

They burst through the surface and landed on a solid,

fog-covered floor. The familiar mist that permeated the heavens greeted them, but that was all she recognized.

Everywhere Thom turned, there was only more fog and empty clouds. Light infused the water droplets so it seemed as if everything glowed with golden magic, but there were no temples. No Forbidden Garden, Lotus Academy, or Jade Palace. None of the other buildings she remembered from her last trip to the heavens was here, either.

"Where are we?" Thom asked.

Kha and Concao looked equally confused.

The Sage tipped his hat back on his head. "We're in the most secluded area of the heavens," he said. "My home, if you can call it that. Although, after Father decided to be reincarnated, I never really saw it as such."

Kha tapped Thom's shoulder. "If we go up there, we could get to Guanyin's temple."

"That's right," the Sage said, looking up. "The Goddess of Mercy is the only one who likes her privacy in the heavens more than I do."

"But where's the Jade Palace?" Thom asked. Where were the Monkey King and the demon army? Where was the battle?

The Sage pointed down. "Just follow these clouds until you reach it."

Thom, Concao, and Kha leaned down to watch the swirl of mist beneath them.

"Remember, Thom," the Sage said. "The key to defeating the Monkey King is discovering his weakness."

When the Sage had first said that to her, Thom had had no clue what he meant. But now she remembered what the Dragon King of the East had told them.

"He doesn't have a weakness," she said, but the Sage was already gone.

The three of them were alone in the foggy landscape. Clouds curled around them like wet cotton candy, but instead of being damp and cold, it felt like a warm, soft hug.

They had done it. They'd made it to the heavens. After all the days of searching, almost dying, always feeling like they were alone, someone had finally helped them, and Thom realized with guilt that she hadn't even said thank you.

She secured her backpack straps, then took out the sword, just because she found the weight of it comforting. "Let's go," she said.

"Wait," Kha said. "You don't want to go see Guanyin first?"

"What? Why?"

"Because of what Shing-Rhe said, about asking her to give the Monkey King mercy."

"The Monkey King doesn't deserve mercy," Thom said.

Kha frowned at her.

Thom met Concao's eyes. "Does he?"

The fox demon squared her shoulders. "No. And we've wasted enough time getting here."

Concao didn't even wait for them to be ready. She jumped off the cloud.

Thom smiled apologetically at Kha. "She's right. We need to go find him."

Kha glanced up, uncertain.

"Why don't you go see Guanyin," Thom suggested. "And catch up to us?"

"What, split up?" He shook his head. "No, we're in this together."

It wasn't the first time Thom had felt both warmed and yet unsure of his friendship. "Kha, I'm so sorry for not telling you about the Monkey King's clone."

He shook his head. "It's okay. It's over. We're here and we're going to get him."

Her chest swelled. She didn't deserve his forgiveness or his friendship. "Why? Why are you sticking with me?"

He had trouble meeting her eyes. "I promised my father and yours I would look out for you."

Of course. Kha had always been there because of his father. The general had sent him down to watch out for her in the mortal world, and now he was only still here to prove to his father that he could be a great dragon.

She gripped her sword. It was never because of her that he wanted to be friends; it was an agreement he'd made with someone else. It seemed lately that the world only ran on bargains. Payments in exchange for a favor. The Monkey King had only befriended her because he needed her to steal his cudgel. The Sage had only taken her to the heavens because she'd given him the Monkey King's hair.

But then Kha's next words surprised her. "And we're friends," he said. "Remember?"

She smiled at him and nodded. Together, they stepped off the cloud, and followed the fox demon into the battle.

◆ ◆ ◆

Demons were everywhere. On every cloud, in every temple. Thom heard their shrieks before they reached the Jade Palace. She, Concao, and Kha hid on a cloud above the green building to observe what they were up against and to figure out their next move.

The Jade Palace was the most crowded, with demons patrolling the entrances and windows, their hooves and paws stepping carefully on the clouds like those who weren't used to something so luxurious and soft, unsure it would hold them. The other temples were also guarded, but not as heavily.

And in the air between the floating buildings, hundreds of Monkey King clones flew, giggling as they kicked and twirled and somersaulted as if they were not at a siege but instead at the most anticipated party of the year.

"I think they're holding almost everyone captive in the Jade Palace," Thom said. "You can kind of see through the windows." She recognized the black-plated hats that the officials wore, as immortals and fairies were crowded inside the buildings. Demons towered above them, shoving them to move along faster.

"Yeah," Kha agreed. "There's the emperor." He pointed at a wide balcony on the top floor of the palace.

Through the open doors, Thom spotted the heavily robed figure of the heavenly king. The Jade Emperor looked almost exactly as she remembered him, skin glowing with a golden light, black hair exposed and tied back in a style that would have allowed for a crown. A crown that was missing. He sat on the bed, the large sleeves of his gold-and-red robes draping on the floor.

Pacing in front of the Jade Emperor was the real Monkey King. She could tell it was the real Monkey King and not a clone because he was the only one carrying the cudgel, swinging it over his shoulder and out in front of him, holding it behind his head with both hands, looking relaxed and carefree, grinning as if this were all a big joke and he would reveal the punch line soon.

Then he flew out the window and rose above the other temples. His clones turned and danced, and demons cheered as they saw him.

"Brothers!" the Monkey King shouted, his voice booming across the heavens so that everyone stopped to listen to him. "Today, we will make history!" Applause came in feral growls from the crowd of demons. "We have escaped our island, yes.

And it's true, I have freed you all. But not in the real sense of the word. Because the truth is, are any of us really free?"

"No!" the crowd responded, although it came out in angry screams and dismayed crows.

"No!" the Monkey King agreed. "Not when the gods and fairies and dragon kings rule the heavens! Not when they ban us from what should equally be shared. Is that fair?"

"No!" Shrieks and screams roared across the clouds.

"Brothers!" he called again to catch their attention. "We have stricken our names from the Book of the Hells, and now, on this day, we will add them to the Book of the Heavens. We will eat the peaches of immortality."

"Peaches!" someone called from the demon audience. "Peaches, peaches, peaches!"

"We will drink the heavenly wine!"

"Wine!" a chant started. "Wine, wine, wine!"

"And I will never ban any of you from taking the pills of immortality!"

"Immortalityyyyy!" a demon roared.

The Monkey King's laugh echoed across the sky. "They thought we weren't worthy of notice. They thought we were scum. But we have breached the Bridge of Souls and overtaken the heavens. We have bested the immortals and contained their soldiers. The Jade Army was no match for us!"

The demons roared, stomped their feet, and pounded their chests.

The Monkey King raised the cudgel. "And soon, their precious emperor will bow to me, and I shall become Ruler of the Heavens and create a place for you all!"

At the resulting applause, the Monkey King flew back into the palace and dragged the Jade Emperor out onto the balcony. Despite being roughly handled, the emperor held his head high, his face turned away from the Monkey King as if the demon-god did not deserve even the slightest glance.

"The emperor can't bow," Kha said. "That would mean he's relinquishing his authority over the heavens to the Monkey King."

"He's refusing," Concao said.

She was right. The Jade Emperor stood tall, even as the Monkey King raised his staff.

"You will bow to me," the Monkey King said.

The Jade Emperor turned his face away.

"Will you risk the safety of the heavens?" the Monkey King demanded. "Of everyone in the Jade Palace? I will keep them there forever. I will starve them. I will hurt them, one by one, until you bow."

Still, the Jade Emperor kept his chin high.

"No?" The Monkey King rested his cudgel over his shoulder. "How about we start with your daughter?"

"Jae?" Thom clutched the sword.

The Jade Emperor looked hesitant, as if he might actually give in. Only he didn't. He held his arms stiffly at his sides.

"But he can't hurt Jae," Thom said. "She's just a kid. I mean, she's innocent in this. She hasn't done anything wrong."

"She's the Jade Emperor's daughter," Kha said. "The Monkey King knows that's the one way to get the emperor to do what he wants."

The Monkey King grabbed the Jade Emperor and dragged him back into his room. He said something, but the emperor just ignored him. The Monkey King laughed, pacing, unguarded, the balcony doors wide open. He was so arrogant. He thought no one could reach him or defeat him, and he had been right.

Until now. Because Thom was here, and she was as strong as he was—well, almost as strong—especially now that she had the sword. She could beat him.

She took off her backpack, checked inside to make sure the cricket was okay, and then placed it gently on the cloud at her feet.

"What are you doing?" Kha asked slowly.

"Keep my mom safe," Thom said. "I'm going after him."

Before Kha or Concao could stop her, Thom launched off the cloud, sword thrust in front of her, and shot straight for the Monkey King.

She thought she'd forgotten what it was like to fly in the heavens on her own, but it came back to her almost immediately, the weightlessness and freedom of it. Her determination to reach the Monkey King sped up her flight. Even the sword

grew heavier in her grip, warmer, as if it was ready, finally, to fulfill its purpose. Because she really meant it this time. She planned to use it and make the Monkey King pay for all he'd done.

She landed on the balcony much harder than she'd intended, her feet slamming onto the green jade flooring and cracking the stone into several branching webs.

The noise caught the attention of everyone in the room—the Monkey King, the Jade Emperor, and Princess Jae, held down on her knees by a pig demon. All of them turned and stared at Thom. Jae gasped. The Jade Emperor held an arm out in front of his daughter as if Thom were the one they should be afraid of.

"What an entrance," the Monkey King said, giggling and

clapping. He sounded almost like his old self, like *her* Monkey King, not the serious one that had been freed from under the Mountain. But when their eyes met, she knew it wasn't him. This older, wiser, angrier Monkey King had a hardened gaze, its mirth lost and replaced with cruelty.

Thom knew that now was her moment to say something clever, but she froze with all the attention on her. All she could do was raise her sword and point it at the Monkey King, hoping he would understand it as the challenge it was.

His eyes widened. "Ooh-ooh," he giggled, his body going very still as he observed her stance.

She became aware of how awkward she looked, legs shaking and feet too close, shoulders squared, right arm outstretched. This was the exact opposite of how Kha had taught her to stand.

"What is that?" the Monkey King asked.

She didn't move, remaining on the balcony, hoping he would join her instead. She didn't want to fight the Monkey King in the enclosed room, where Jae and the Jade Emperor could get hurt.

"Where did you get that sword, Thom-Thom?" he asked again, his tone calm and steady, an animal moving with careful grace before attacking.

"Don't call me that," she snapped, his nickname for her bringing back happy memories that warred with the anger and hatred she kept fueled against him.

He eased closer, his feet moving even though he floated several inches above the floor. "That's a big sword for such a small girl," he sang.

She didn't respond. He was wittier than her, smarter. The only advantage she had was her strength, especially since he didn't know the sword would make her even stronger.

He was out of the room now, meeting her on the balcony, careful not to add his weight to the cracked floor. "What are you doing here, Thom-Thom?" His voice lost its singsong quality now that no one else could hear them.

"What does it look like? I'm here to defeat you."

He eyed the sword wearily. "Go home. You'll get hurt."

Anger flared inside her, as if he'd thrown a log carelessly onto burning firewood, sparks flying, flames thrashing. She swung the sword, not even aiming, just hoping to hit him.

The blade met the solid metal of the cudgel. He'd barely moved, flicking his wrist to block her attack, while she'd put her whole weight behind the hit. Their eyes met—his in surprise, hers in fury.

She swung again, and he moved to defend himself. She kept going, hoping to catch him by surprise, each blow meeting his cudgel with a clang that echoed across the sky.

When she'd backed him against the edge of the balcony, Thom knew it was working. The sword made her much stronger. She could do it. She was beating the Monkey King.

She pressed down on the sword, the blade sliding across

the cudgel until it caught on an engraved indentation. The Monkey King bent under the weight, dropped to one knee, back pressed against the balcony ledge. His face was tense, jaw tight, the muscles around his eyes clenched.

Thom smiled. She was doing it. It had been so easy. Well, not getting here, but now that she faced the Monkey King, all her fears had been for nothing. She'd hyped him up so much in her mind, made him invincible. When what she'd needed all along was to believe in her own power—

He opened his mouth, threw his head back, and laughed. The familiar bouncy giggles made her lose her grip just slightly.

But it didn't matter.

He lowered his cudgel. Her sword glanced off it. The Monkey King pressed his hands to the floor, slapped a palm on the jade as he laughed until he couldn't breathe. His wheezes echoed across to the other temples and slowly, as if his laughter were a plague, it spread among the demons. They shrieked and jumped and threw their heads back, mouths wide, and roared with mirth.

This time, the heat that filled her was not anger, but embarrassment. Her ears burned. Her sword swung limply by her side. The hilt was cold in her hand, like a prop, a child's toy, not an ancient weapon that imbued her with power.

The Monkey King leaned back on his heels, wiping at his eyes. "You really . . . think," he choked between laughs, "that you can defeat me? You?" He pointed at her. Then at himself. "Me?"

He grinned, sharp incisors flashing. He wiped the corner of his eyes with one hairy finger.

And then, just as easily, the smile faded—ripped off was more like it. His face tensed again, the cudgel back in his grip and swinging at her.

Thom blocked it, but barely, and even so, she skidded across the floor. She moved the sword only just in time to catch his next blow, nearly flying off the balcony. He was strong— he was so strong. Each hit of his cudgel sent a tingling shock down her arms, reverberating through her body and straight into her toes. Her knees buckled. Her legs threatened to give out. How could she forget? How had she even thought they could compare?

He came at her, again and again. She could barely hold up the sword. Her shoulders ached in an unfamiliar way she hadn't felt in years.

When he hit her once more, she almost didn't block in time, and as the cudgel pressed down on the sword, pain shot up her wrists and elbows. She cried out.

His face softened. His eyes took on that rounded, concerned gaze. But it was just a flash. He drew the cudgel up, and in his face, she understood that this would be the killing blow. For a second, she wondered if anyone would come save her. That's what usually happened to heroes in movies—someone conveniently coming to their rescue at the most dramatic moment.

But she was not a hero. Not in this story anyway. She had caused this. The Monkey King wouldn't be here if it weren't for her. No one had wanted to help her. Maybe the Sage was right when he'd posed that question.

Who was really the bad guy?

14

AS IF WONDERING THE SAME thing, the Monkey King hesitated a bit too long, and Thom acted out of instinct.

She delivered the best goal-scoring kick she'd ever made, only this time she didn't hold back. Her foot connected with his shin, and the Monkey King's legs swung back.

He fell flat on his face.

Thom scampered back, clutching the sword. It was cold in her hands, the stone digging into her palm.

The demons went quiet. A hush fell over the heavens.

Then someone snickered. Another demon laughed. Soon they were all guffawing, but now *at* the Monkey King, not *with* him.

His head lifted. He pinned Thom with a murderous look that would have been a match for Ma's Asian stare of death. The whites of his eyes bulged, the pupils narrowed to pinpoints.

Before he could get up and attack her again, Thom turned and jumped off the balcony. She launched up into the air, jumping from cloud to cloud.

He was close behind, and she turned in time to dodge a blow. The cudgel swung so fast above her head that her pony-tail whipped up.

She swung the sword hard, and it met the cudgel this time with a heavy clang. They twisted in the air from the momentum of their hits, like two dancers spinning, climbing higher up in the heavens.

Soon they lost sight of the Jade Palace and the demons, and were surrounded by white mist and swirling clouds.

She kicked away from him and slammed onto a solid fog so hard that the cloud threatened to break apart, mist particles scattering beneath her feet before gathering together again. Her sneakers sank into it like it was wet mud. The Monkey King landed behind her, and mist swirled around them.

"I told you to go home, Thom-Thom," he said. He pounded his cudgel down, making the cloud shake, and she stumbled to all fours, barely managing to hang on to the sword. The cloud was no longer solid ground, but sand slipping away, as if pulled back by a receding wave. Each time she tried to get up, the Monkey King slammed the cudgel, and she slipped again. "I told you, you could get hurt."

A shadow fell over her, and she swung the sword without looking. He stepped back, and she managed to get to her feet and jump up to another cloud before that one disintegrated into fog.

"Why did you come here?" the Monkey King asked, following her easily. He was unhurt and unfazed, while Thom might as well have been walking underwater, her limbs heavy and exhausted, her arms shaking with fatigue and pain. Her right wrist ached, and she couldn't grip the sword without trembling. Her fingers were so weak, she couldn't make a fist.

Why wasn't it working? Why didn't the sword give her the strength she needed?

"Please," she whispered down at the blade, feeling as silly and crazy as the last time she had asked the Ruyi Jingu Bang for help. The sword remained cold and dormant. "Please . . ." But she couldn't remember its name. The Sword of Heaven's Will—the Mountain God had told her its real name, something that started with a *th*—thien thuan? But it slipped from her thoughts no matter how hard she tried to form the words. She let out a sob.

"Did you really think you could come here to defeat me?" the Monkey King asked, looming behind her.

She turned to face him. Beads of sweat dripped off her forehead. She was breathing hard, heart pounding. She wasn't used to this level of exertion, wasn't used to being so . . . weak. Since she'd developed her superstrength, physical activities had come easy to her. She could run faster and longer than her teammates, she could kick harder, she could lift anything without breaking a sweat. She was supposed to be strong, and the sword was supposed to make her stronger, but even with the weapon, even fueled by her anger and determination, she was no match against the Monkey King.

She had thought, naively, that the sword was the answer. That she was enough. But she wasn't. She wasn't strong enough after all.

"Why did you come here?" the Monkey King asked again. He looked like a warrior, feet apart, knees bent, ready to attack at any second.

Thom couldn't even stand up straight. "To hurt you," she said.

His face registered surprise. And then a grin stretched his lips slowly over sharp teeth, spreading so wide it became more of a grimace. "My little apprentice," he said, giggling. "There's hope for you yet."

And then he attacked. Thom dropped to her knees. His cudgel swung above her. She struck at his legs, but he somersaulted before the blade hit him. Then they both spun to face each other. She raised her sword in time as his cudgel came down and met her blade with a reverberating clang. She grunted as pain shot down her arms.

Then something gave way, and she fell back, dropping the sword. The hilt landed next to her. The blade sank into the cloud in several pieces.

Thom stared at the broken shards in disbelief. Her fingers

dug into the ground beneath her, trying to find something to hold on to as the cloud seemed to shift. The world tilted and spun. Was she sliding off the cloud? Was she falling?

How could this happen? The sword was magical, just like the Monkey King's cudgel. Yet it lay in pieces all around her.

She looked up. The Monkey King towered over her as if he'd grown taller or she had shrunk. She swallowed. A part of her knew she should get up. She could still try to fight—she was still superstrong without the sword, and she'd been able to hold him down before. Kind of.

But what was the point? She was defeated. He had won. Just like everyone knew he would.

She waited for him to raise his cudgel and . . . knock her out? Kill her? She wasn't sure. But instead, he held it at his side like a walking stick.

Then he giggled, his head tilting back and forth.

"I haven't had that much fun in centuries," he said. "You're just as delightful as I remembered. But you're untrained."

"What?" The world was still whirling, clouds swirling around her like she was on a spinning carnival ride. She closed her eyes, but when she opened them, he was still in front of her, and the mist twisted and looped around them.

"I can teach you, you know," the Monkey King said. "How to fight, to really fight, the way I taught you to control your strength. You wanted to be a warrior, remember? We could still work together. Be a team." He held out a hand.

Thom breathed hard. "You're not going to kill me?"

"Kill you? Why would I do that?" He smiled, his face widening, the apples of his cheeks lifting to crinkle his eyes. "You're my friend."

She looked at his hand, at the pink pads of his palm and fingers, and imagined what it would be like if that were really true. She would come back to the Jade Palace with him, stand next to him in front of his demon army. It would be so easy to be on the winning side. To have the Monkey King as an ally again. Why did she fight so hard to do the right thing anyway? Her only option had been to defeat him, to show the heavens that she could single-handedly save them so that they had no choice but to forgive her for putting them in danger. But that wasn't happening. Nothing was happening the way she'd hoped.

But no one else seemed to care, and most of the heavens probably thought she was just as bad as the Monkey King anyway. Why not join him? Why not make a new deal, like the Sage had suggested?

She raised her hand toward his, and light reflected off the golden bracelet wrapped around her wrist. The magical string that her father had given her. To keep her safe, he'd said. Other memories flashed in her mind. The Boy Giant bringing her cookies, offering her condensed milk, his fingers holding a tiny teacup with the gentle touch of someone incredibly strong. His hopeful face when he offered to teach her how to be a fighter, a hero for those who couldn't fight for themselves. She would never be the person he wanted her to be if she joined the Monkey King now.

She reached for the Monkey King's hand. His eyes crinkled, and his smile deepened. He leaned down and grasped her fingers in his warm, rough hand.

"It's good to have you here, Thom-Thom," he said, his words like little needles in her heart.

She fell back, pulled him with her until he hovered above her, eyes as wide as saucers, and then kicked at his ribs as hard as she could. He fell off the cloud, flipped through the air, and tumbled out of sight.

Then she scrambled to her feet, collected all the pieces of the sword she could find, and launched into the sky. She didn't know where to go, really; she just knew that she needed to get as far away from the Monkey King as possible, at least for now. She needed to find a place to rest. Her arms were shaky. She was going to collapse. She had never been so tired before.

Kha and Concao must be here somewhere, but a look around the misty white landscape told her it would be impossible to find them. The higher she went, the thicker the air became.

Thom paused to breathe and bit back the tears that burned her eyes and stung her nose. How could it have all gone so terribly? They'd worked so hard to get here. She had been so sure that she could defeat him once she confronted him.

She had to keep moving. Exhausted, she launched herself up and up to the next cloud, not knowing where she was going, not knowing what her next plan was, just knowing that she couldn't sit still.

Then she saw it. A castle, glittering as if made of glass. On a closer look, she realized it was ice, the air around it filled with hand-carved snowflakes, sitting on a solid block that was more like a glacier than a cloud. Nothing else above it, no more clouds to escape to, just pure, empty sky.

This, she realized, must be the temple of Guanyin, the Goddess of Mercy.

Thom didn't know what else to do. She pulled herself up to the steps of the palace and raised her hand to knock. She barely managed to make a sound. Her muscles were so weak, she couldn't bring herself to try again. She was cold, exhausted, and so sleepy.

She slumped against the door and closed her eyes.

15

"WE TOLD YOU TO COME here first," Kha said as soon as she woke up. She sat up straight but regretted it as a wave of dizziness hit her. "But you're so hardheaded, you know that?"

He sat on a chair next to her bed. Concao was on the other side of the room, reading through one scroll, with more piled on the desk in front of her.

"What happened?" Thom asked, touching her forehead.

"After you charged off to go get yourself beat up," Kha said angrily, "Concao and I went up to Guanyin's temple to ask for help. Then you showed up like an hour later, passed out on the step."

"The sword," Thom said.

"Oh yeah, your precious sword. It's broken. You broke it."

She groaned and laid back. Her body ached everywhere, and she just wanted to go back to sleep for days.

Kha's angry expression softened. "Are you okay?"

"I feel like someone tried to put me in the washing machine," she said. "And then the dryer."

"Well, the fairies who took care of you said nothing is broken. You just need to rest for a few days."

Thom closed her eyes. "We don't have a few days. How long do you think the Monkey King is going to wait before he starts hurting people?" She couldn't imagine him as a torturer, but then she remembered how the monkey brothers had been hurt. He hadn't done it himself, Concao had said, but he had let the demons do it. If he allowed that to happen to his own brothers, then anything could happen to the people in the heavens. To the Jade Emperor. To Jae.

"I don't know what to tell you," Kha said. His face was a mask of indifference, but beneath the exterior, the muscles around his mouth and brows twitched, as if he was trying to control his anger. "We don't have a choice."

Why couldn't she get better instantly? Like that one time, when she'd gotten a cold, and the Monkey King had taken her to the Mountain, to the cave behind the waterfall, and she'd been healed by the rainbow water.

"We have the water that the monkey brothers packed for us," she remembered. She tried to get up too fast and grimaced. Her backpack was on the ground next to her bed, and she dug through it for the gourd.

"Where's the cricket?" she asked when she realized the mason jar was missing.

"I left her with Guanyin, to see if she could do anything to lift the spell," Kha said.

Thom uncorked the gourd and, out of habit, sniffed it to make sure the contents hadn't gone bad. Then she gulped it down, sitting back as the familiar coolness spread into her belly. A refreshing tingling sensation traveled down her arms and legs. Her muscles relaxed, the aches receding like a stove fire being turned from high to low until it went out altogether.

She set the empty gourd aside and got up from the bed but realized she didn't have anywhere to go.

"Where's Guanyin?" she asked.

"Busy, probably," Kha said. "She said she'll come to us when you're awake."

"Oh." Thom tried to sit. Then got up and paced the room. She was antsy and energized, with the nervous excitement that usually came before a soccer match or after she'd eaten way too much sugar. She knew it was partly the magical rainbow water giving her back her energy, but she was also impatient to do something. Head back into battle, challenge the Monkey King again. She knew what his fighting style was like now. She just needed more practice before she could beat him.

"I forgot the sword's name," Thom said.

"What?" Kha looked rightfully confused.

"The Sword of Heaven's Will. That's how you command magical weapons. You call their name and treat them with respect."

"How do you know that?"

"The . . . Monkey King . . . told me," Thom said hesitantly.

Kha's eyes flashed with anger. "And you trust him?"

"It worked with the cudgel. When I stole it." She paced. "If we could fix the sword, I could try again. I remember what it was now. Um . . . Uh . . . Thuan Thien?"

"Thuận Thiên," Kha corrected her, the tonal changes over the vowels such a simple difference that Thom slapped a hand over her forehead.

"I can't believe I forgot," she said. "If I had remembered, if only I'd—"

"Sit still," Concao said. She'd remained at the desk reading through scrolls. "You're making me dizzy."

"But—"

"The Monkey King still would have found a way to beat you," Concao said. "Even if you knew how to use the sword correctly, it's not strong enough to take on his cudgel."

Thom wanted to argue some more. The sword hadn't worked correctly because she hadn't known how to use it, hadn't been able to wake it up the way she'd called on the cudgel last time. But Concao, still bent over her scrolls, wasn't interested. And maybe the fox demon was right. The Monkey King had been so powerful, even stronger than she remembered. What if he was still going easy on her? If the sword had worked correctly, there was a chance he would still beat her.

"What are you doing?" Thom asked, taking the seat next to Concao.

"Studying ancient weapons," the fox demon said distractedly.

"Anything useful?" Thom asked, picking up a random scroll.

"Nothing that would be a match against the Monkey King's cudgel," Concao said, not bothering to look up from what she was reading. "It is a singular weapon of ancient magic."

Kha remained standing, looking at Thom with an angry, expectant expression. She tried to ignore him, mostly because she was tired of arguing. It wasn't that she didn't care about how he felt, but that they had bigger issues to worry about. When he didn't stop glaring, though, she put down her scroll and turned toward him.

"What is it?" she asked, trying to sound concerned, but it came out wrong. Flippant and cold.

"*What is it?*" His face reddened a few shades. "You're not even going to say sorry?"

"For what?"

Kha opened and closed his mouth. "For not listening to us! For just charging off and attacking the Monkey King without a plan."

"I had a plan."

"Oh, what was that? Get yourself beat up and then run away? Great plan."

"I had the sword."

"And what good did the sword do you?"

She swiveled in her seat. "How was I supposed to know that the cudgel would break it?"

"Exactly! You didn't know. You should have consulted with us first."

"We've been consulting for days, trying to get here. I couldn't waste any more time—he was about to hurt Jae!"

"But he hadn't hurt anyone yet. You were rash, and you paid for it."

"He's right, you know," Concao said, still not looking up.

"Of course you're on his side," Thom said. Heat boiled in her veins, making her face and ears grow warm. "I know you two have been talking about me behind my back."

"Because you won't talk to us about any of your plans," Kha said.

"You didn't even ask us what to do," Concao agreed before Thom could defend herself.

"You just ditched us to be the hero," Kha said. "You want all the glory for yourself. You want to take the Monkey King on because you want to prove that you're good enough or whatever so the heavens will forgive you. It's always about you and what you want and need, not about us at all. You don't care about what we want. You're not even here to do the right thing—you're just here to look out for yourself!"

"That's not why I did it!" Thom couldn't believe he thought she was so selfish. "I don't want to be the hero."

"Don't you? With your giant sword and your 'I can beat the Monkey King on my own!'"

"It's my fault he's here, so it's my *responsibility* to beat him!"

"Yeah, you're right!" Kha shouted back. He had never looked so angry, face red, steam literally flowing out of his nostrils, skin shimmering into scales. "And it's also your fault that *I'm* here. I've been helping you, too, and you just ignored me! You don't even ask me for any ideas! I'm not your little sidekick!" His hair burst into blue feathers.

Thom held up a hand, remembering how he'd shot that ball of fire at the Lord of the Waters. "I never asked you to come with me," she said calmly.

He growled, the guttural dragon sound deep in his throat. "What choice did I have?"

"You could have stayed with your uncles," Thom pointed out. "Or your grandparents, if they were even your grandparents. You could have gone to so many other immortals who would have taken you in. I don't have anyone but my mother. I'm the one who doesn't have a choice."

"Who's fault is that?" Kha was nearly screaming now.

Thom got to her feet. "It's my fault! I know it is. I'm taking the full blame for everything, so stop reminding me that I'm the one who messed up. I already know that!"

"And because you messed up, I have to go with you and help you!"

Thom hadn't realized that she and Kha had been moving closer to each other, arms out and ready to fight, until they were just a foot apart. Heat wafted from Kha's body, his skin glittery, the outlines of scales appearing on his exposed neck. His very fragile human neck, which she could easily wring if she moved fast enough. She gritted her teeth.

"Why?" she asked. "Because your father asked you to look after me?"

He grimaced at her, his teeth sharper than usual in mid-transformation. "Because I was assigned to help you."

"Stop using your father as an excuse," Thom snapped.

The steam stopped. The heat dissipated a bit. "What are you talking about?"

Thom wasn't even sure what she was saying anymore, she was so angry. "You want to show your father that you can be a strong dragon, but you're afraid to do anything real. You're just using me as a way to—" There, her words stopped. She stumbled over them, annoyed at herself for never being able to get anything out right. "I don't know."

"No, say it," Kha insisted.

"You're afraid," Thom said. "You want to do something tough to make your father proud, but you can't, and the only thing that you can hide behind is me. If you help me, then you succeed, too. But you're right, Kha. You're not a sidekick. You can't be my sidekick because I'm not a hero. I don't even know if I'm the good guy in all of this! I'm just trying to fix what I messed up in the first place."

Kha didn't say anything. Thom stepped back from him and plopped onto a chair, looking down, feeling drained. Was what she said even true? Or was she just making things up to win this argument? She had gone too far. Kha was sensitive about his father. She shouldn't have brought the general into the discussion.

"Kha, I-I'm sorry," Thom stammered. "I shouldn't have said that. This *is* all my fault. I fell for the Monkey King's lies, I broke into the Forbidden Armory and stole the cudgel. I broke the Judgment Veil—"

"No," Kha cut her off. "I mean, you did, but you wouldn't have done it if I hadn't told you to."

Thom looked up, surprised to hear him admit that.

"I did." He twisted his fingers together, not meeting her gaze. "I freaked out, too. I didn't want the Jade Soldiers to catch up to us and see that I hadn't been able to stop you and then report to my father that I failed. I wanted to buy more time for us . . . for myself, really."

"But it's not your fault," Thom said. "I'm the one who broke it."

"Only because I told you to."

"But I'm the one who did it."

Kha let out an exasperated huff.

"Does it really matter which one of us did it?" Thom asked. "Let's just fix this. It's not too late. We'll figure it out together."

He didn't respond, looking away. He had grown so hot that the temperature in the room rose by several degrees. Thom was starting to sweat. Even Concao's fur looked a bit wilted, but neither of them said anything about it.

A lady's voice came from the door. "My, my, should I come back another time?"

Thom's chair scraped back as she got to her feet. Concao rose much more gracefully. A goddess had entered the room. Thom knew she was a goddess and not just a fairy because she glowed with the same pure aura that had surrounded the Boy Giant and the Jade Emperor. She was incredibly tall, dressed in creamy chiffon robes that seemed to float over her slender frame. A diadem twinkled from her dark hair, and between the draping sleeves of her robe, her hands held the mason jar where Ma the cricket was still a cricket.

After the initial relief of seeing her mom safe, Thom couldn't help getting a sinking feeling. Despite the Mountain God telling her that the transformation could only be lifted by the Monkey King himself, she'd hoped someone in the heavens would be able to change her mom back.

She looked up at the goddess. Thom had been in the

presence of other immortals before, and even though she had been awestruck and awkward then, she was even more insecure now. Should she bow? Curtsy, kneel on the floor? On the hierarchy of gods and goddesses, Guanyin was pretty high up there, maybe even equal to or above the Jade Emperor. But Thom couldn't move, frozen by the goddess's beauty and otherworldly presence.

"You must be Thom," Guanyin said, gliding into the room.

The aura around her was not as golden as that around the Boy Giant or the Jade Emperor—but it was purer somehow. It reminded Thom of the magical droplets in the Judgment Veil, the ones that had surrounded them when the Sage had taken them into the heavens.

"Your friends told me about you, and how you went after Sun Wukong. You must be very brave."

Glancing at the broken shards of the Sword of Heaven's Will, Thom didn't feel brave.

"Here you go, child," Guanyin said, handing Thom the mason jar. The cricket hopped around in excitement, as if happy to be reunited with Thom.

A small bit of tension eased from her shoulders. At least someone was happy to see her.

"Were you able to find anything?" Thom asked. "About the enchantment?"

"I'm afraid it's nothing you don't already know." When Guanyin spoke, a calm settled over the room. Thom let out an involuntary sigh. Even Concao gazed at the goddess with adoration. "The transformation spell is strong and can only be lifted safely by the one who placed it there. Of course, I can try to remove it, but it may cause unforeseen damages. Your mother might not remember who she is, or we might end up hurting her in another way. One can never tell with enchantments this . . ."

"Evil," Concao said. "The monkey did it after all."

"I was going to say 'strong,'" Guanyin said with a kind smile.

"So the only way to change her back is for the Monkey King to do it," Thom said. "He'll never agree to, not after the way I tried to beat him."

"Tell us what happened," Guanyin said, taking a seat on a lounge chair. She looked so understanding, her expression calm and neutral, that Thom found it easy to describe the fight with the Monkey King. She told them about how he had tried to convince her, again, to join his side, but left out the part about how tempting it had been, how she had really thought about taking his offer.

Even now, the idea beckoned to her like cold water on a

hot, dry day. If she joined the Monkey King, she wouldn't be in trouble anymore. She would be in charge. What even awaited her if she did somehow defeat him and saved the heavens? The Jade Emperor and the other immortals would still blame her for releasing the Monkey King and for causing the upheaval in their lives. She would be sent to the hells, or worse, though she couldn't think of anything worse than that.

And what the Monkey King wanted—for the demons to be able to live in the heavens—was it really that bad? Why didn't they deserve a place up here? Why couldn't the fairies and immortals share?

Except Thom knew better than to believe him, not completely. He'd said he wanted equality for his brothers, but he was also a trickster who never did anything for anyone without gaining something in return.

"So I have to defeat him," Thom said. "He can't just take what doesn't belong to him. He can't just, like, conquer the heavens, even if it's to create a place for his demon brothers."

"Yes, there are certainly more peaceful and effective ways to achieve equality," Guanyin said. "If he wants to convince the heavens that the demons belong up here, he's not making a very good point by attacking the immortals, is he?"

Thom looked up at the goddess. "Do you think he's right?"

"No!" Kha jumped in. "You're doing it again. You're letting him get in your head."

"She has the right to question herself," Guanyin said.

Kha looked like he wanted to argue some more, but he stopped himself.

Guanyin smiled at Thom. "I don't believe Sun Wukong's motivations are wrong."

"He just thinks his brothers deserve a chance," Thom said.

Guanyin nodded, but Thom couldn't tell if the goddess was just letting Thom talk or if she agreed with the Monkey King.

"It's just . . . his methods that are wrong," Thom continued.

"Right," Guanyin said.

"He can't just barge in and steal what isn't his and hurt everyone who doesn't give him what he wants," Thom said. "The fairies didn't ask for this, either, just as much as the demons didn't ask to be banished to the island. That's why we need to stop him." She told them how she had been thoroughly beat up by the Monkey King in front of the entire heavens. "I have to try, even if it means I'll only be punished for helping him in the first place. I know what I did was wrong, and I want to make it right. But the sword is broken. I'm no match against him unless I have a weapon."

Guanyin clicked her tongue. "Do you really think a weapon will make a difference when thousands of others have tried to challenge Sun Wukong—beings much more powerful than you?"

"But I'm strong," Thom said. Funny. She had never been

proud of her superstrength before she met the Monkey King, yet now she knew it was her greatest asset against him. "With the sword, I was stronger. I just need more practice. Another chance. If we can fix the sword, maybe . . ." Her voice trailed off as she realized no one agreed with her. They all looked at her with sympathetic expressions, as if they all knew she was sick but didn't know how to tell her.

"Actually, Thom is right about something," Concao said, surprising them. The fox demon picked up a scroll. "There is an ancient weapon—a headband—that will render the wearer completely under the control of the person who wields it."

Guanyin took the scroll and skimmed the section before handing it to Thom. Kha stepped up beside her. Thom held still, not quite certain how things were between the two of them. They read the passage together, studying the illustration of the golden band. It was quite pretty, a simple gold piece of jewelry that curled into twin swirls where the metal joined in a circle.

"This looks like the bracelet your father gave you," Kha pointed out.

He was right. The golden string, which Thom wore as a bracelet, and the headband were both made from thin strands of gold, almost flimsy to look at, but stronger than any other material.

"They were made by the same forger," Concao said, taking the scroll back. "The Lotus Master. The one who taught the

Monkey King the Seventy-Two Transformations. It's almost as if he foresaw a need for weapons that could contain someone as powerful as Wukong." She flipped to another section of the scroll. "Like the bracelet, the headband, once placed on the head of the prisoner, can only be removed by the wielder, who will have complete control over the prisoner, with the power to inflict incredible pain on the prisoner at will."

No one said anything. Thom swallowed. Could they really do that to the Monkey King, to any other living being? That would essentially turn the "prisoner," as the scroll put it, into a slave.

"Can we do that?" Thom asked out loud. "I mean, should we?"

Concao rolled up the parchment. "Do we have another choice?"

"No," Kha said, too decisively. "There's no other way to beat him."

Thom didn't want to argue, not again. And they were right anyway. She needed to stop defending the Monkey King, to stop believing he could still be her friend.

"Where can we find it?" Thom asked.

16

THEY ALL SPOKE AT ONCE, talking over one another, shouting out plans and ideas, but there was one thing they all agreed on.

"The Monkey King will know what we're trying to do," Thom said. "We can't just drop a headband on his head. He might not know what it's for, but he won't sit quietly and let us."

"We have to trick him into wearing it," Concao said.

"How?" Kha asked. "If we try and fail, he'll know for sure, and there goes that idea. We only have one chance."

Guanyin watched all this with calm amusement, like a teacher observing her students figure out the answer to the same problem she taught year after year.

Thom readjusted her ponytail, which she'd tied so tight it was giving her a headache. "The Sage said we have to find out his weakness."

"He doesn't have a weakness," Kha said.

Up until that moment, Thom would have agreed. But she remembered the Monkey King's face. There had been rare moments when he'd lost his smile, when his eyes were stripped of mischief, when there was only raw want and pure longing for something he could never have.

"He wants . . ." Thom said, searching for the right word. Was it love? No. He had his monkey brothers, and Shing-Rhe would do anything to save the Monkey King, even betray him.

Was it power? But the Monkey King was the most powerful being in the universe.

And then, it came to her.

"He wants respect," Thom said.

Concao's ears twitched. "But he has it. His army of demons are proof—they worship him."

"It's not enough," Thom said. "He wants the heavens to respect him, too: the Jade Emperor to bow to him, the immortals to take him seriously. It's not just power, or he would have made everyone do what he wants—he could have bullied them into it. But it wouldn't be real to him. He wants their genuine acceptance. He wants to be one of them."

She looked at everyone's faces to see if she was right, even though she knew in her gut she had found the answer. Everything the Monkey King had done in the past led to this. He'd wanted to be more than a monkey demon, so he left his cave, found a master, and studied the ways of humans. Then he wanted to be like the immortals, so he learned magic and developed abilities and ate a bunch of peaches and crossed his name out of the Book of the Hells.

Then when that wasn't enough, he wanted to be part of the heavens, so he begged for a title, a real place among the immortals. But they had given him a fake role, a made-up title as Master of the Horses so they could all laugh at him behind his back.

None of them were laughing now.

"I know how to defeat him," Thom said as a piece of the puzzle clicked into place. All this time, she'd thought she needed to beat him with pure strength. She'd thought she was a match for the Monkey King—because he had always told her they could be a team, because he had convinced her to accept her strength. But maybe that was another trick he had played. Because while they were both strong, that was not the Monkey King's greatest ability. He was a trickster god.

Thom looked up at Kha and Concao. All this time, she'd thought she was the one who had to defeat the Monkey King, that she was the only one strong and powerful enough. She had been wrong.

"I can't do this alone," she said. "I'll need your help."

Concao rolled her eyes. "We know," she said. "Come on, let's go."

◆ ◆ ◆

First, they had to sneak back into the Jade Palace.

Thom felt a mixture of guilt and embarrassment as she stood next to Kha. It had taken her much too long to realize that she couldn't do any of this without them. But now that she'd accepted that she wouldn't be able to prove herself to the heavens, she still knew she had to do the right thing and recapture the Monkey King. And she also understood that she, Kha, and Concao couldn't do it alone, either. They needed even more help. She only hoped that she would be convincing enough this time.

"Kha," Thom said softly into Kha's ear from where she sat on his back. He was a dragon again, slipping from one cloud to another. He had made himself invisible, but they still had to be careful in case any demon or one of the Monkey King clones happened to spot them. "Kha, I'm really, really sorry," she said. "About everything. About ignoring you and not trusting you more."

He didn't say anything, but his feather-tipped ears lay flat against his head to catch her voice. Concao was silent behind Thom, probably focused on their plan. She had the toughest job out of all of them.

"After the way the Mountain God and Princess My Nương rejected us, I don't know," Thom tried to explain, her words jumbled and awkward again. "I just felt like no one wanted to help me, that I might as well be on my own. Even though you were both helping me, it seemed like I had to figure it out by myself. But I know I can't. I know I need you."

They were close to the Jade Palace now, only a few clouds away.

"I'm sorry I said that about your father," she continued. "You don't need to prove anything to him. You're already a tough dragon. You're the toughest dragon I know—you used to be the only dragon I know," she added with a soft laugh, "but I've met a few of them by now, and you're my favorite."

He still didn't say anything.

"Anyway, I get it if you want to be mad at me forever. But I want you to know that I know I've been a terrible friend."

Kha landed at the back entrance of the Jade Palace. A Monkey King clone zipped in the air above them, supposedly keeping guard on the palace but too lost in his own antics to notice them.

Thom and Concao slipped off Kha's back. He changed into his human form to fit through the doors, looking down at his hands as he turned to face her.

"I'm sorry, too," he said. "For blaming you for the Judgment Veil."

She shook her head. "It wasn't your fault—"

"Yes it was." He finally met her eyes. "I was using you. I needed you to succeed so that I can prove to my father that I'm worthy of his praise."

"I shouldn't have brought your father into this."

Kha smiled gently. "You were right, though."

"Guys," Concao said. "Do we have to do this here?"

Kha and Thom bit back their laughs, like trying not to giggle when they got caught talking in class.

"Let's do this, then," Thom said, before all three of them slipped inside the Jade Palace.

They ran together at first, slowing down and being especially careful around corners. When the hallway split into three different directions, they stopped, and Thom took out the ring the Monkey King had stolen from Jae the last time she'd been in the heavens.

"Keep it safe," she said, handing it to Concao. They all looked at one another one last time with too many words to speak out loud, and then headed in different directions.

The last time Thom had roamed these hallways, they had been crowded with servants, officials, and fairies. Now the palace was eerily quiet. Her steps sounded like thunder on the jade flooring, and she stopped before every corner to make sure she wouldn't run into any demons. But the halls were empty.

As she came to the end of one hallway, she saw why. Demons were posted outside huge double doors, and even though everything was hushed and controlled, she could hear whispers and mutterings coming from the room, punctuated by shouts of "Quiet!" in a rough voice. This must be where the Monkey King's army had cordoned off most of the people in the heavens.

Thom backed away before the demon guards noticed her. She ran down a different hallway, but loud footsteps echoed from the other end.

Panicked, she slipped into the closest room and closed the door, breathing heavily.

"Thom?"

She whirled around at the familiar voice. She was in some sort of makeshift infirmary. There were small beds separated by curtains, though no one else was there except for one person.

"Ba?"

Her father, the Boy Giant, sat on the bed near the window, dressed in a simple white shirt and loose pants, which made his golden skin glow even brighter. A white bandage was wrapped around his head, looking almost eerily like the sashes you wore at funerals. His face was frozen in a hard expression, one that made her grow weak.

He was still angry. Of course he was—the last time he'd seen her, she'd bludgeoned him with a magical, seventeen-thousand-pound staff.

Thom walked slowly to her father. "Ba, I'm so sorry," she said. "I didn't mean to. I didn't know—I thought I was doing the right thing. I mean—" Her words stumbled out, and there was no way to right the balance. "Obviously, not hitting you. I panicked but I'm so, so sorry."

Her father didn't say anything for a long moment, just stared at her.

She clasped her fingers together, tried to shrink into her shoulders. What if he hated her? After all these years, she'd finally met her father just to mess it up.

"You," he said.

Thom flinched. His footsteps were light on the floor as he approached her.

"You . . . called me 'Ba.'"

She looked up. "Well, you are. You're my dad, right?"

He smiled. And then he hugged her.

Thom sank against him, relief making her limbs turn to jelly. She blinked back tears. "Are you okay?" she asked, her voice muffled against his shoulder. "Are you hurt? I mean, obviously you're hurt, but is it bad?"

He chuckled, patting her back. "I'll be fine. I just need to rest." He pulled back so he could meet her eyes. "One good thing out of it is that the demons left me here instead of making me go with the others. They figured I'm too injured to do much harm to their plans."

"I'm so sorry," she said again, sniffling.

"It's okay." He patted Thom's shoulder a bit awkwardly. "It was a mistake. We all make those from time to time. It's my fault, really. I should have taught you. You were right—I've had a lot of time to think on it. I could have showed you how to control your power. I could have guided you and taught you what you needed to know. None of this would have happened if I had been a real father."

She had already forgiven him. If he could forgive her for whacking him in the head with an iron cudgel, she could forgive him for doing what he thought was the right thing.

"I think we were all just trying our best," she said.

"You're probably right." He smiled. And then he really looked at her. "What happened, Thom? What are you doing here?"

"I don't have much time," she said, and gave him the short version of what she'd done since she'd left the heavens. "But I have to go, Ba. I need to find Jae and the Monkey King."

"Go? You can't go." He tightened his grip on the sleeves of her hoodie. "You'll get hurt. You can't defeat him, Thom. I know you're strong, but you're still too little. You need training, you need more time—"

"I don't have time. The Monkey King is running out of patience, and he'll start hurting people. I have to go."

He shook his head. "You can't do it alone. Wait for me. Let me get better and I can fix this for you."

Finally, a grown-up stepping in and helping her, which was what she'd been searching for on the quest for the Four Immortals. But she knew she couldn't let him. She had to take care of her own mistakes.

"Don't worry, Ba. I'm not doing this alone."

"But . . ."

"I have to go."

"Thom, wait—"

"I'll find you. When this is all over. I promise."

She gave him one last hug, ignoring the pleading look in his eyes, and then left the room before she could change her mind. It was too tempting to stay safe and hidden with her father, hoping he really could get rid of all her problems for her. But it wasn't the right thing to do.

The stairs were empty as she found her way up to the highest room in the Jade Palace. That was where the Jade Emperor and his daughter were being held prisoner.

But first, she made a stop at the only other room she'd been in the last time she was in the heavens: Jae's suite.

Pushing aside the repulsion she felt at looking through someone else's things, she dug through Jae's closet. She couldn't show up in front of the demons in her hoodie and jeans—she would stand out immediately, since everyone else in the heavens dressed in elegant robes, armor, or flowy chiffon dresses.

Like any princess, Jae owned an assortment of clothes ranging from garden-banquet fancy to shabby uniforms she must wear to disguise herself. At least, Thom could picture Jae dressing down so she wouldn't have to act like a princess all the time. Luckily, Thom found a plain gray áo dài—something a servant would wear—that would be perfect. The buttons weren't too difficult to do by herself. Then she shook out her ponytail. The Monkey King would recognize her immediately, but hopefully the demons wouldn't look twice at her, not at first anyway.

Before she left the suite, she grabbed a tray still set with a teapot and cups and carried it from the room.

Her fingers shook as she found the floor leading to the Jade Emperor's suite. She knew she was close because familiar voices echoed down the hall—the Monkey King shouting the same threats, the Jade Emperor's loud silence as he ignored him.

Two huge demons stood on either side of the entrance to the suite, both oxen in nature, one part lion, the other a mixture of eagle and tiger. Their muscles bulged as they turned to survey her. Thom breathed. She could take them if she had to. She was stronger than them. But she needed to get past them, or else the plan wouldn't work.

Their beady eyes sharpened as their lips pulled back to reveal knifelike teeth.

"What do you want?" the eagle-headed one growled. He held a three-pronged spear in one hand, tipping it at Thom now, but only in a casual way. He didn't see her as a real threat, which she didn't blame him for, since she only came up to his waist.

She bowed her head. She didn't have to fake being afraid. The teacups rattled on the tray. "The princess needs her medicine," she said, her voice shaking and high-pitched. "She must take it now, or she'll get really sick."

The lion-headed demon growled. "Who sent you?"

Uh-oh. "I-I'm the princess's personal maid. I must administer her treatment, or she'll . . . die."

She glanced up to see the two guards looking at each other questioningly.

"Please," she said, dropping her eyes when they turned sharply to her. "If she dies, the emperor will be too distraught to do as the Monkey King wishes, and all his plans will be ruined."

"What do you know about his plans?" Lion Head growled, stomping toward her.

Wrong thing to say. Thom bowed deeper, holding out the tea tray, porcelain clinking. He was going to bite her head off for sure. She waited for the sharp sink of his teeth in her flesh. But instead, he made a funny, sniffling sound. Was he crying?

No. He had smelled something on the tea tray. His black, wet nose twitched. It would have been almost cute except that he had been ready to kill her just a moment before and could alert the others at any second.

"What—what is that?" Lion Head asked, his nose nudging against a jar. "It smells delicious."

Eagle Head joined him. "Cookies. Smells like cookies."

"I'm starving," Lion Head growled. "He hasn't fed us since this morning."

"He doesn't need to eat," Eagle said. "He forgot."

"He's too focused on the Jade Emperor. Too greedy for power."

"Well, that's why we're here, eh? He promised us he'd look out for us demons once he's in control." Eagle Head nudged the tray. "Give us the cookies then, girl-flesh."

"Okay," Thom said. She would have brought a hundred jars of cookies if she had known that would have distracted them so easily. "You can have the cookies. As long as I can bring in the princess's medicine."

The guards looked at each other.

"It's just medicine," Lion Head said. He eyed Thom up and down. "And if she tries anything else, I'll eat her, too."

"Go on, then," Eagle Head said, already snatching up the cookie jar, his furry hand swallowing the dainty porcelain.

"Save some for me," Lion Head growled.

Eagle Head nodded, but Thom doubted there'd be any cookies left from the way he licked his lips.

Lion Head grabbed Thom's arm in what might have been a painful grip for any normal mortal, but Thom barely felt it. Still, she whimpered and made herself go limp so he could drag her into the room.

17

THOM STUDIED EVERYTHING QUICKLY–THE SUITE was split into two rooms, the adjoining door opening to reveal the Jade Emperor sitting at the end of the bed while the Monkey King paced in front of him, the demons guarding the Jade Emperor on either side.

Lion Head took Thom to the corner table in the first room, where Jae was seated. One very large boarlike creature towered behind her.

Jae looked so small and prim, her hands in her lap, back straight, frightened eyes fixed on her father through the open door.

Then she looked up at Thom, and her face stretched into shock before tensing with fury.

"I brought your medicine, princess," Thom said before Jae could lash out and give her away.

Lion Head pushed Thom into the seat next to Jae before

leaving the room quickly, probably scared to leave Eagle Head alone with the cookies for long.

"What are you doing here?" Jae hissed.

The boar demon behind them snorted a few times as if in warning but didn't say anything.

Thom picked up the teapot with shaking hands and poured the brown liquid into one of the small cups. "I've brought you your medicine," she repeated, and as she placed the cup into the princess's hands, she also slipped a piece of paper up the long sleeve of Jae's áo dài.

Jae's eyes widened, but she took the cup and pretended to sip at it. The tea must have been old because she made a face.

"Jae," Thom said, leaning close so the boar demon wouldn't hear. "I'm really sorry. I'm here to make things right."

But the princess's face hardened. "Don't bother."

Thom knew she deserved it, but the words stung. "I betrayed you, but I didn't know exactly what I was doing. The Monkey King tricked me—"

"Oh please. As if I haven't heard that before."

The boar demon snorted again, so they quieted, looking down at their hands.

"We have a plan," Thom whispered, so quietly she was afraid Jae might not hear her, but she didn't dare speak louder. "But we need your help for it to work. And the Jade Emperor's."

Jae didn't respond, lifting the teacup to hide her face.

"Jae, I'm sorry," Thom blurted out. "I really am."

Jae froze. Her shoulders tensed and started shaking. "Did you only become my friend so you could steal the ring from me?"

"What? No!"

They spoke in hushed whispers. Jae thought Thom had used her this whole time, but that wasn't the truth at all. Thom knew how much it hurt to feel like people were only friends with you because they needed something from you.

"I had no idea who you even were," Thom said. "I didn't know you were the princess until we got to the garden banquet and I met your father, I swear. I didn't know about your ring. It was the Monkey King who stole it, and then . . ." Thom wanted to blame the Monkey King for everything. It would be so easy. But she couldn't. He wasn't the only one who had made mistakes. "He stole it so I could get into the armory."

A muscle in Jae's jaw twitched. "Did you know how much trouble I got in after you left? After they found out how you managed to get into the armory?"

Thom shook her head, even though she had a good guess at the answer.

"You knew. I confided in you, how much they . . . looked down upon me. Because I'm weak." Jac looked up at her, tears in her eyes. "And yet you still had no hesitations about using me to get what you wanted, knowing that it would only put me down further in their eyes."

"No, that's not it—" Thom started to say.

"They already didn't trust me—Father and his advisers. They didn't think I should have been given something so important. They always thought I was too weak. Me, a princess. My own father didn't trust me."

"But I'll tell them what happened. I'll explain—"

"As if they'll listen to you, Thom."

Thom's shoulders fell. "I'm so sorry, Jae."

"Stop saying that. Of course you're sorry. Look what you caused." Jae glanced toward the adjoining room, where the Monkey King paced in front of her father.

"Please, Jae," Thom said, desperate, not just because she wanted Jae to forgive her, but because she needed her help. Not for the first time, she was painfully aware of how little she deserved it. "I know you probably won't ever forgive me. But I need you to trust me, just for a little bit, if we have any hope of defeating the Monkey King. I'm about to do something really dumb and dangerous. And I hope it's worth it. It will be, if you help us."

Then she looked up, glancing to study Jae's reaction. The princess showed no response, and Thom wished more than anything that she knew how to convince the princess that she was sorry for all she'd done. She wished she knew what to say to make Jae forgive her. But right now, it didn't matter if Jae forgave her as long as she followed along with the plan.

The boar grunted and came closer to the table as if it sensed something was going wrong. Instead of cowering this time, Thom met its gaze with her own challenging one. The boar snorted louder, a high-pitched squeal.

Thom stood up, right foot back and fists raised, a challenging pose.

"Thom?" Jae asked.

She reached out as if to pull Thom back down, and Thom was grateful that, as angry as the princess was, she still cared about Thom a little. Enough not to want to see her hurt.

"Read the note," Thom whispered.

The boar grabbed her arm—to throw her out maybe. She snatched his wrist and swung him across the room.

The boar crashed against the door between the two rooms of the suite, his hurt and angry squeals drawing everyone's attention. Lion Head and Eagle Head rushed in. Thom braced herself, bending her knees the way Kha had taught her, as Lion Head came for her first. But just as they were about to meet, a teacup smashed against his forehead.

Jae breathed heavily, more surprised at what she'd done than they were. Thom used the moment of surprise to thrust shoulder-first into Lion Head's stomach, sending him crashing back against Eagle Head. They slammed against the wall, their heads bashing with a loud knock, and slumped unconscious on the floor.

"I knew you'd be back," a giggly voice said from the adjoining door.

Fueled by adrenaline and determination, Thom didn't hesitate. She rushed at the Monkey King, satisfied when his eyes rounded right before she slammed into him. They crashed through the other side of the room.

The Jade Emperor got up from the bed. The two demons guarding him grabbed his arms.

Thom took hold of the Monkey King's cudgel. His mouth grimaced in anger and disbelief. No one else had dared to take the staff straight out of his fingers. But she wasn't trying to steal it—she could barely hold it on her own.

Instead, she swung it across the room. He didn't loosen his grip. Thom didn't let go, either, swinging him against the demons holding the Jade Emperor. They moved out of the way just in time.

But the Monkey King slammed into his brothers and knocked one down. Thom swung him again and got the other one, before the Monkey King finally dug his feet against the floor and skidded to a stop. He gaped at the demons' slumped bodies.

"Run!" Thom shouted at the Jade Emperor, who stood to the side, his golden robes slightly crooked. His mouth dropped at the sight of her—at first glance, she must have looked like a servant barking orders at the king of the heavens. But then he recognized her, and she had no idea what he could be thinking. "Get Jae and go!" she shouted.

The Monkey King wrenched the cudgel out of her grip. His foot embedded itself on her chest for a split second, and then she was falling backward, the world spinning. She landed on her back, wheezing. She tried to roll up to all fours, but her body wouldn't obey.

The Monkey King advanced on the Jade Emperor and pinned him to a corner.

Thom coughed and got to her feet slowly. She jumped onto the Monkey King's back, arms wrapped around his neck the way she used to ride piggyback on him on their way to the Mountain of a Hundred Giants. Only this time she aimed to hurt, to drag him down. Her hands tightened on his fur. She wrapped her arms around his neck and squeezed as hard as she could.

He grappled with her hands, his grip loosening on the cudgel. She snatched it, but her angle was all wrong. It slipped from her fingers, dropped, and rolled across the floor.

Thom launched herself off his back to go after the cudgel, but the Monkey King grabbed her ankle. He leapfrogged over her.

Just as he reached the staff, she slammed onto his back again. They slapped like stacked pancakes onto the balcony floor, the cudgel rolling away. It smacked against the railing and spun, slipping through two of the railing poles. For a second, it looked like it might drop and fall through the heavens, balanced on the edge of the balcony like a seesaw.

The Monkey King tried to throw Thom off, but she clung to him. She loosened the golden string, wrapped like a bracelet on her wrist, and started to lengthen it. He saw what she planned to do and thrashed, almost throwing her off. She managed to loop the string around his chest, one end still connected to her wrist, but he moved too much for her to tie it securely.

When he went after the cudgel, he dragged her along with him. She dug her feet in, her heel catching on a crack in the jade flooring. No matter how he tried to get rid of the golden string connecting them, it wouldn't obey, sticking to him like duct tape.

"Agh!" he shouted, finally facing her. They stood just a few feet from the cudgel, her hanging on to the string as if he were some circus animal. "You are the stubbornest person I've ever met!"

Thom wasn't used to being called that, so she wasn't sure

how to respond. She yanked on the golden string instead, tugging him away from the staff.

"I am not your pet," the Monkey King said, grabbing the loose string between them and pulling. Thom jerked to her feet. The Monkey King couldn't untie the string, but there was nothing stopping him from pulling it tighter so that they were suddenly inches from each other. "Why does everyone think they can control me, like I'm some sort of animal?"

"I don't want to control you," Thom said. "I just want to stop you from hurting people."

There was a commotion in the distance. The Monkey King whirled around, leaning over the balcony railing. On the next cloud over was a huge stone building—Thom had learned earlier that it was the Jade Army headquarters. The doors burst open, and horses galloped into the air. Giant horses, the size of elephants, dressed in red-and-gold armor.

A group of demons guarding the door tried to stop them, but the horses kicked them down and bounded into the air. Some of them bore soldiers on their backs, but most of them were riderless as they neighed and charged after the demons clambering to get away.

"Get back to your stables!" the Monkey King shouted at the horses as if he thought he was still their master. They ignored him, so he turned to the demons instead. "Hold your stations! Pax! Stop them!"

Thom recognized the pig demon she had arm-wrestled

with once. He tried to stand in front of a giant horse, but the heavenly animal almost flattened him. Several demons from other clouds jumped over to fight the horses and the Jade Soldiers escaping the building, meeting them in a brutal battle of teeth and claws against swords and armor.

The Monkey King turned on Thom. "You did this, didn't you?"

"No." Thom clutched the golden string between them. "Not me."

The real person in charge of the Jade Army's release flew out of the building now, his white scales shining as he whipped his blue-feathered tail against a demon about to attack a horse. Seeing Kha fight, Thom understood that he was destined to become a dragon king. He moved with swift grace—taking out several demons at once, helping the soldiers who had fallen—and seemed never afraid to put himself in danger.

As they watched, a man dressed in heavy armor that indicated he was someone more important than just a soldier—a general, maybe even *the* general—fell down the steps of the building, his helmet flying off. A demon ran after him, about to slam his unprotected head with a bat. Kha whipped toward the demon so fast, the demon didn't see him coming until the dragon shoved the demon right off the cloud, sending the creature spinning down and out of sight.

Thom almost smiled. Except the Monkey King turned to her, his face scrunched in fury.

"Is this what you wanted?" he asked as shrieks and shouts of fighting filled the air. "Real war?"

The battle was spreading as more horses and soldiers escaped from the building, demons and armored warriors meeting on different clouds and temples. Thom didn't know who was losing or winning, but at least the heavens were no longer held prisoner. Thanks to Kha.

"I want you to stop," Thom said to the Monkey King.

"Stop what? Defending my brothers and trying to gain them freedom and equality?"

"That didn't look like equality to me," Thom said, pointing inside the room. "You have the people of the heavens locked up. You're destroying their home. Hurting the immortals."

"No one will get hurt if they do what I say."

"So it's okay to control people as long as you're the one doing the controlling?"

The muscles on his forehead puckered, making his eyes round, puppylike. "Let them see what it's like for a change. Let them take the place of the demons and see how long they last."

"You're planning to send the immortals to the hells?" Thom asked. "But how is that any different from how they treat you and the demons?"

"I want them to have a taste of what it's like."

"Don't do it, Wukong," she begged. "Please, if you stop now, your punishment won't be so bad."

He threw his head back and guffawed. "You really think that they'll forgive either of us for what we've done?"

Thom knew she was going to have to pay for her mistakes, but being reminded that she was on the side of neither the heavens nor the demons made her uneasy.

"They'll be more forgiving if you stop and give up now," Thom said.

"Why should I stop? I have come so far. And I am still winning."

"You're losing." She nodded at the battle below. With the heavenly horses now released, the Jade Army had a fighting chance against the demons, even with the Monkey King clones added to their numbers. The horses were so large and powerful, soldiers in their own right, that at least ten Monkey Kings were needed to bring one down. "Just give up now, and . . . we can figure something out. I'll tell them that you didn't mean it. I know you don't. You just want good things for your friends and brothers—you're not really that bad." Once the words left her mouth, she knew there was some truth to them. "Come on, Wukong. It's not too late. We can both make this right."

He chuckled. "Oh, Thom-Thom. These people don't care about us. They don't care about you. They don't even know you, except as the girl who brought carnage down upon their heads."

Before she could respond, he slammed his foot on the

teetering cudgel. It flipped into the air, and he caught it in one hand before swinging it onto the string between them. Thinking back to when the cudgel had snapped the Sword of Heaven's Will into several pieces, Thom had a moment of déjà vu.

But the string didn't break. It remained intact as the cudgel hit the floor and dragged the Monkey King with it. The section wrapped around Thom's wrist lengthened, however, so that she remained standing and unharmed.

The Monkey King grabbed at the string and thrashed, kicking his legs and flailing his arms like a toddler throwing a tantrum. "Take this thing off me!" he wailed. Thom stood over him in disbelief. Had she done it? Had she finally captured the Monkey King? With a piece of string? A magical string, sure, but was that really all it had taken?

A giggle came from above her. Then another one. And another, until the air filled with hundreds of staccato laughs, a symphony of mischief.

Monkey Kings everywhere. His clones made a whole army of their own. They somersaulted and skipped, swam backward, jogged in place. Some waved at her, but soon all the smiling faces disappeared, replaced by an angry grimace.

"Take this off me, Thom," the Monkey King said, the real one on the balcony with her. "Or I will attack."

Thom froze. Could she take on all the clones at once? No,

definitely not. She had never even been able to take on just one of them.

They eased in, surrounding her. Some grinned. Others bared their teeth in a more menacing way.

Thom stood up straight, breathing fast. What were her choices? She could jump off the balcony again, but one of them would catch up to her. She could untie the Monkey King, but . . . well, that seemed like an even worse idea. She had only managed to secure him, and there was no guarantee he wouldn't attack anyway even if she did what he wanted.

One of the clones landed a kick to her head that made her ears ring. She was prepared for the next hit, blocking the punch, grabbing another clone's ankle, ducking a swing aimed at her face. But there were so many, and they came from everywhere, and soon her world became nothing but golden fur and maniacal giggles and punches and kicks that felt like they would never end.

18

THOM COVERED HER HEAD AND curled into a ball, as if doing so would help absorb all the attacks.

"Enough!" someone shouted.

The clones didn't move off her at once, but the beating stopped. Thom shoved her way out of the pile of the Monkey King clones, still hanging on to the golden string, which secured the real Monkey King to her. She followed everyone's gaze to inside the emperor's suite, frozen along with the rest of them.

The Jade Emperor was there, even though Thom had told him to run, and Jae was next to him.

And so was the fox demon. Concao stood tall and magnificent, void of any disguises so that her white fur glistened and waved beautifully in the breeze. Except for one thing.

"What in heavens name is on your head?" the real Monkey King asked, getting to his feet, encumbered by the string that attached him to Thom's wrist. He tried to tug himself free, groaning with frustration when nothing worked. Several clones pulled on the string, but their fingers slipped off as if it were made of slippery silk.

"Stop it, Wukong," Concao said, and to everyone's surprise, he did, though he gave her a funny look, seeming more shocked that she dared to command him than anything else. The fox demon turned to Thom. "Untie him."

Thom didn't pause, immediately untying the string from the Monkey King's chest. His eyes widened, but he stayed still until he was released. Then he bounded away from her, skipping through the air in his relief to have his freedom back. The clones copied him, the suite filling with a dozen Monkey Kings twirling and dancing on the ceiling and walls, holding hands and spinning, and turning to stick their tongues out at Thom.

"I said stop!" Concao commanded. She had the perfect authoritative voice and, standing tall with her shoulders thrown back and her fluffy tail curled around her legs, she looked regal and elegant. Like a queen. Even the Jade Emperor stared at her in awe.

The real Monkey King tossed his cudgel from his left hand to his right. He landed on the ground in front of her. "My dearest friend. It is good to see you here. I'm glad you've changed your mind and joined me after all. But tell me: Why should I listen to you?"

"Because," Concao said, "I am in charge now."

The Monkey King laughed. "In charge?"

The fox demon tossed her head, and the hat above it rocked back and forth like it had a mind of its own. It was a very weird hat, made of several layers of fabric, as if many headdresses and headpieces and scarves had been sacrificed in its making. The multiple colors shone in the sunlight, and the glittery pieces caught everyone's attention—most of all the two antennalike feathers that rose three feet in the air and curled dramatically at the tips. They waved each time Concao so much as breathed.

"Yes, I am in charge now," Concao said. "Because of this hat. Don't you recognize it?"

The Monkey King prowled around her, ignoring everyone else in the room, even the people who were starting to come in through the adjoining room—fairies and immortals, the citizens of the heavens. Concao must have freed them from the main hall. They all stopped, straining to see over one another, but not daring to come any closer to the Monkey King. Thom wondered if that was because they were afraid of him or disgusted by him.

"I have never heard of such a thing," the Monkey King said, but he sniffed the hat curiously. "How can such a magical weapon exist without my knowledge of it?"

"Perhaps you were so lost in your greed for power, you forgot that real power lies within wisdom. You neglected the ancient scrolls that reveal such knowledge. This one I found today. Imagine how much advantage you would have had over me, if only you had stopped to conduct some research."

Despite his skepticism, the Monkey King peered closer at the hat. "What does it do?"

"It gives me command over all beings. I simply have to speak the words, and they will do my bidding."

The Monkey King, already forming plans of what he would do and whom he would command if he owned the hat, flicked his gaze to the Jade Emperor and then back to the fox demon.

"Give it to me," he said.

"Why should I?" Concao said. "It's mine."

The Monkey King reached for the hat, and Concao darted away faster than Thom had ever seen her move. The Monkey King's clones came after her, but she was too agile, zipping around the room and escaping their grasp.

The real Monkey King crossed his arms, turned his face away, pretended to look indifferent. But Thom knew him better. Curiosity sparked in his eyes, even while his mind whirred with possibilities of being tricked, and he studied the hat for any hidden deceptions.

"She's lying," Thom said.

Concao scowled at her. "How dare you?"

"A hat that gives you control in the heavens?" Thom made an amused sound. "How come the Jade Emperor doesn't wear it?"

The Monkey King raised his brows at Concao.

"He's already the emperor," the fox demon said. "He doesn't need it. He probably forgot it even existed, locked it up in the Forbidden Armory."

"I don't believe you," Thom said. "You're a demon, just another one of Wukong's lackeys. The hat won't work for you."

Concao bared her teeth.

The Monkey King narrowed his gaze at Thom. "How dare you say such things to my friend?"

"It's just a hat," Thom said. "What if the fox is lying?"

The Monkey King studied her, and for a second Thom wondered if she had gone too far. But then he turned on Concao.

"Thom-Thom is right," he said. "You didn't want to join us before. Why should I believe you now?"

"We've never lied to each other, Wukong," Concao said. "I had a lot of time to think about what you said, and you were right. Why should demons be banished to the hells? Why can't we have what the immortals have? I want to gorge myself on peaches. I want to drink heavenly wine. I want to be a fairy, too. You know I do, more than anything in the world."

"Yes, but I still want proof," the Monkey King said. "It won't be hard. Tell me to do something."

Concao came closer. "I'll make it even better." She turned to the Jade Emperor.

The emperor stepped back from her, holding a sleeve up to his face as if she smelled. "How dare you, you filthy demon."

The Monkey King clones hissed and shrieked at him.

Concao, almost tall enough to meet the Jade Emperor's eyes, straightened her shoulders. The feathers of her hat tickled the top of his head, and he jerked away in disgust, grabbing Jae's hand to pull her back.

"Bow to me," Concao demanded.

At first, nothing happened. The Jade Emperor remained standing, clutching his daughter's hand. The Monkey King started to snicker, an amused clicking reverberating in his throat.

But then the Jade Emperor moved. His knees bent.

"Father," Jae protested, but he released her hand and dropped to the floor.

"Lower," Concao said in her deep, throaty voice.

The Jade Emperor dropped to all fours and touched his forehead to the ground.

The adjoining rooms erupted into chaos. Monkey King clones shouted with laughter. The fairies and immortals in the other room gasped in shock. Some fainted, others ran from the suite. The king of the heavens had bowed down to a lowly demon. The world was ending, the heavens collapsing.

The Monkey King clapped his hands in glee and bounded over to Concao. "Now give it to me," he said.

She turned away. "No."

"Please, my friend." He started to reach for her, then remembered how fast she was and stood calm. Patient. "Power is a great responsibility. You have never wanted to be in charge. Imagine all the decisions you have to make. What will you do with the fairies? The officials, the gods? Will you banish them to the hells now? And the demons? They will want answers. I can help you. Let me be in charge, and I will take care of all of that."

Concao paused. "You are right. I have never wanted that responsibility."

The Monkey King clapped and hopped in excitement. "Here, here." He held out both hands to the hat as if about to pick up a baby.

"Under one condition," Concao said.

The Monkey King nodded. "Yes, anything."

"Once you are ruler of the heavens—"

At this, the Monkey King could barely contain himself, flipping into the air, the real Monkey King as well as his clones. They looked like the ensemble cast of a musical, their movements synchronized, their dance steps choreographed to complement one another.

"Once you are the ruler," Concao repeated over their shouts of excitement, "you must make me a fairy."

"Yes, yes!" The Monkey King flipped into the air. "You'll have what you've wished for all these years. I promise, my friend. Now hand me the hat, please."

Concao tipped her head forward, reaching up with both hands, but the Monkey King paused.

"No, no," he said. "This isn't right."

He pinned Thom with his gaze. The fox demon froze. Thom's heart skipped.

"A ruler must be crowned. Come, Thom-Thom."

Thom hesitated, then moved forward, trying to remain calm.

"Yes, yes," he said, more to himself than anyone there. "I will be crowned, by one of their own. By the daughter of one of the Four Immortals. Yes, this is right. You will do the honors," he said to Thom, gesturing at the hat.

"You . . . want me to . . . crown you?" Thom asked.

"Yes, you. It must be you. We would not be here had you not helped me. Released me. Stolen the cudgel from the Forbidden Armory for me."

She cringed with each incriminating item and hoped the Jade Emperor wasn't listening too hard. But it was all true, of course.

"Do it, Thom-Thom," the Monkey King said, his face so full of happiness and . . . trust. How did he trust her, even after all this time? After all they'd been through. Or was it just another trick?

He nodded, and she didn't see any other way out of the situation.

"Kneel down," she said.

He did, looking up at her in wide-eyed innocence. She took the hat off Concao's head, and as she held it high above the Monkey King's, a glint of light reflected off the golden lining inside the hat. The Monkey King bowed.

With everyone watching, with the Jade Emperor still kneeling on the floor, Jae by his side, the fairies and immortals in the crowd, Thom officially crowned the Monkey King.

19

THE MONKEY KING LIFTED HIS head and blinked.

"Well?" Thom asked, stepping back. "How does it feel?"

"A bit anticlimactic." He adjusted the hat and grinned. "How do I look? Like a king?"

Thom didn't have the heart to tell him that he looked ridiculous, not when he reminded her so much now of the Monkey King she knew once, the one who wasn't so serious, so hell-bent on gaining power in the heavens. She knew he was the enemy, the bad guy, knew he had to be defeated. But looking at him now with the silly-looking hat, she was reminded of all the times they'd shared, how he'd helped her on the soccer field, how he'd taught her to stand up for herself and accept her strength when she'd tried so hard to get rid of it.

She nodded.

He smiled. He held one hand out to her. "Let's put our fight behind us, huh, my friend?"

Her chest twisted. She didn't take his hand.

He wiggled his fingers. "Come, then. I told you we would make a great team. Together, we will make the heavens a liberated kingdom. Demons and immortals living peacefully together, with equal rights and liberties and benefits. And as many peaches as we want to eat!" He giggled and took her hand without waiting for her to give it to him. He pulled her into the air, and they spun in circles as if they were dancing. The Jade Emperor, Jae, Concao, and the fairies watched them with expressions of disgust.

Thom was tempted to believe the Monkey King, to enjoy the dance with him, to hope that he was telling the truth. Because the words he spoke, the world he wanted to make . . . it didn't sound bad at all. Why couldn't the demons have what the fairies had? Why were they banished to an island or condemned to the hells?

Okay, so the ones who had attacked the heavens might deserve to be punished. But what about the others? Shing-Rhe and the monkey brothers, and the rest who lived peaceful lives and didn't bother anyone? They weren't bad at all. Some were good.

What defined whether you were good or bad anyway?

Then the Monkey King placed her back on the floor. He stepped up to the Jade Emperor, who held out an arm to protect Jae, even though the Monkey King didn't even glance at her.

"Bow to me," the Monkey King commanded.

This time, the Jade Emperor looked like it really did pain him. He lowered to his knees slowly.

"Lower," the Monkey King said.

The Jade Emperor touched his forehead to the floor. Some fairies ran from the other room, but Monkey King clones darted after them. Those who remained were barred from leaving, forced to watch as their emperor surrendered to the demon-god who held them hostage.

"Lower," the Monkey King said again.

"Wukong," Thom whispered.

The immortals in the other room gave cries of despair. Some sobbed into their sleeves. Others clutched one another.

"Lower!" the Monkey King shouted.

The Jade Emperor obeyed, his stomach, chest, everything flat against the floor.

The Monkey King shrieked and laughed and danced. He twirled his cudgel and looked up at his clones, who formed lines like soldiers in a formation.

He pointed his staff at the Jade Emperor, who still lay flat on the floor. "Lock him up," he commanded. "Lock them all up." He swept his staff to indicate Jae and the rest of the crowd.

"What? No!" Thom said. She rushed to stand in front of Jae, but a clone picked her up as if she were a doll and held her back. Thom kicked at the clone. "No, you can't do that! He bowed to you. He peacefully obeyed—you said you want the fairies and demons to live in harmony."

"Yes," the Monkey King said. "Eventually. That kind of thing doesn't happen overnight, Thom-Thom. First, we must change their minds. Show each side what the other has been dealing with. All the demons will get to see what living in the heavens has been like. And all the immortals will be sent to the hells."

Cries came from the crowd. Jae clutched her father's arm.

"You can't do that," Thom said.

"Of course I can." The Monkey King gestured to the silly hat on his head. "I am the ruler of the heavens now. You crowned me yourself." Then he nodded at his clones, and dozens of Monkey Kings dove for the immortals.

"No!" Thom cried. "You can't."

But the Monkey King only giggled.

"Please, Wukong," she begged, desperately using his name.

But he ignored her, dancing in the air as his clones grabbed at fairies and officials. As two of them reached for the Jade Emperor and Jae, Thom realized she had no other choice. A part of her had still been hoping the Monkey King wasn't as bad as everyone thought he was, that he might change, that she could still convince him to be good. But the proof was right in front of her, had been again and again.

"Stop!" she cried.

She had no idea how the magic of the golden headband worked, the one that the Monkey King had commanded her to crown him with, the one that Concao had gone to take from the Forbidden Armory with Jae's ring and sewn inside the lining of the silly hat. So she wasn't really sure what she was supposed to do at this point.

She only knew that because she had been the one to place it on his head, she now had power over him through the headband. She held out a hand as if that might help to wield it. A deep pull yanked somewhere inside her. The longing that pulsed and tugged at her when she wanted something so bad—and this time, she wanted the Monkey King to *stop*.

The tugging grew harder and twisted painfully. At the same time, the Monkey King dropped to his knees and clutched his head. All the clones did the same, falling from the air like dead flies, releasing the immortals, Jae, and the Jade Emperor. The clones groaned and rolled around on the floor in almost overexaggerated agony—only Thom knew it wasn't another trick, because she still felt that painful tug inside her. It was more than just a discomfort, but a twist in her chest. She tried to stop it, to release the Monkey King from the pain she was causing. But she didn't know how. His agony was tethered to a desire in her she couldn't fathom how to sever.

"What's . . . happening . . . to me?" He looked up at her, still curled over his knees, hand clutching his head. His eyes bulged and watered. He ripped the hat from his head, only to reveal the golden headband, which remained strapped to his forehead. It looked too tight, creating a deep indent in his fur. And it was getting smaller, squeezing the Monkey King's head until he writhed in pain. "Make it stop. Please, Thom-Thom, stop it, stop, please."

She had never heard him sound so hurt, so desperate. "I can't," she gasped. She couldn't breathe, all her focus on the connection between them. Her chest throbbed. In the distance she could hear the demons still shrieking, the Jade Army swords clanging, the heavenly horses crying out as they fought, though the sounds were dying away.

"They're leaving!" someone shouted.

A soldier landed on the balcony and ran into the room. It was the general from earlier, the one Kha had saved. He took in the scene with surprise on his face and turned to the Jade Emperor. "Sire, the demons are retreating. Their army has escaped through the Bridge of Souls."

Thom clutched at her chest.

"Do not let them escape," the Jade Emperor said. "They will be punished and banished for eternity in the hells."

"No!" the Monkey King cried. "Don't. They were only following my orders."

Pop. Pop. Pop. Each of the Monkey King clones disappeared, transforming back into his hair. The strands floated down, scattering around the room.

The Jade Emperor ignored him. "Send the soldiers after them. We will capture each and every one of them and make them pay for what they've attempted here today."

The general nodded and left the room.

"Thom," the Monkey King begged. He clutched at the headband, but it wouldn't budge. "Please, stop this. Let me go. I will take the demons. I will leave the heavens forever. You will never see us again."

Thom bit back a sob. "I . . . don't know how."

The fox demon bounded over to her. "Thom," she said. "Are you okay?"

"It hurts." She clutched her chest.

"Yes it hurts!" the Monkey King wailed.

"Try this," Concao said, her hands out in front of her as if she were holding a book, trying to remember what she'd read. "*Tayata om—*"

"Stop," the Jade Emperor said, pushing the fox demon aside.

The Monkey King groaned and crawled toward Thom, grimacing with each inch closer. She was both afraid of what he might do and relieved that he would be able to help her, to fix everything, the way she always thought he could. His fingers reached out and grazed her neck, whether out of affection or a desire to strangle her, she had no idea.

Because then the Jade Emperor loomed behind the Monkey King, grabbed him by the back of his neck, and pulled him out of Thom's sight. Then the emperor drew his arm back and slammed a palm into Thom's chest. Hot, white pain lanced through her, followed by a release, like the snap of a metal chain, and she was free.

20

ONCE AGAIN, THOM WOKE UP in a room she didn't recognize.

Well, *room* was maybe too pleasant a word for the place she was in. It was an empty concrete box with one small window no bigger than her arm and too high to reach. No one bigger than a toddler would be able to escape through it.

She wasn't completely alone. Slumped in a corner at the other end of the room was the Monkey King.

She was surprised that neither of them were shackled or tied up in any way, but then again, they were both strong enough to break any bonds the heavens might attempt to place on them.

His head lifted when he realized she was awake. Gleaming in the small amount of light through the window was the golden headband. It fit a bit too snugly, sinking into his fur as if welded to his forehead. If she had just met him, she might have thought it was a diadem or a crown, something dignifying. But she knew it was a symbol of imprisonment. One she had placed on him.

"Wukong," she started to say, an apology bubbling to burst out of her throat.

He giggled, surprising her. He should have been angry, but instead, a grin brightened his face. "It's funny, isn't it?"

She studied him carefully. Why wasn't he attacking her? Why wasn't he angrier?

"What is?" she asked slowly.

"You did all that to capture me, save the heavens, but they locked you up here with me anyway." He giggled again.

She looked down. She had known this would happen, that she would be punished and blamed for everything, but a part of her had still hoped that the Jade Emperor and the others would see how hard she'd tried to fix everything. "They think we planned this together."

"We did."

He grinned at the incredulous look she gave him.

"Don't you remember, Thom-Thom? You stole the cudgel for me. You helped me escape the Mountain."

"I stole the cudgel so you could take my superstrength away. I didn't know what you were really planning to do with it."

"Oh, come on." He tucked his chin into his chest and smiled. "You must stop using that excuse."

"It's not an excuse."

"Did you really think you could make a deal with a trickster god, and not . . . I don't know." He held out his palms.
"Get tricked?"

She met his grin with a serious expression. "I thought you
were my friend."

"So did I."

"Then why did you turn my mom into a cricket?"

"She called me dirty and smacked me on the nose. Don't
you remember?"

Thom blinked. "Oh yeah, she did do that. But still, that
doesn't mean you can turn her into an insect."

He placed a hand over his heart. "I promise to turn her
back. If they ever let us out of this room." He grinned at her.
"Okay? Can we be friends again?"

When she didn't return his smile, he waved a hand, letting
it fall limp on his crossed legs.

"I was hoping you'd be on my side."

Thom scoffed. "You gathered a demon army and attacked
the heavens!"

"What about when we talked about how the demon
brothers deserve to be in the heavens, too, huh?" he asked,
like they were reminiscing over soccer practice and not a
celestial war.

"I didn't think you meant it literally."

"Why not? Why don't they deserve to be here? Why
should they be called dirty and evil when they did nothing to

earn it?" He leaned forward. "Do you know how demons are made?"

"Shing-Rhe said that when you try to heal something that wasn't meant to be healed—"

"Oh, sure, that. The very first demons, yes, centuries and eons ago, but the demons you meet now. My monkey brothers."

Thom shook her head.

"They were born. Just like the fairies are born, just like you were born. Did you get to choose what you were? Part mortal, part immortal? Did you get to choose whether or not to have superstrength?"

Again, she shook her head.

"Neither did they. Neither did we all." He let his words hang in the air, let them gather weight and sink. "You and me—what we want is not so different. To be accepted. To belong somewhere. Tell me, am I wrong?"

"No," Thom had to admit.

"It's what everyone wants. It's what the demons want, too. Why is that so bad?"

It wasn't. It wasn't bad at all.

"But you shouldn't have attacked the heavens," she said. "You can't just take what isn't yours."

"Why not?" he demanded.

"Because it doesn't work like that. Because it's not right."

"The heavens selfishly keeping everything to themselves

is not right. Banishing demons to the hells when they've done nothing wrong is what's not right."

"It's the heavens—you have to be good to make it up here."

"Says who? The people who were already here? How do you know they're not lying?"

Maybe Kha had been right—maybe she was letting the Monkey King get in her head again. But what Wukong said made sense. And the more she pictured the demons being hunted and dragged to the hells by Jade Army soldiers while the fairies enjoyed the beauty of the heavens without doing a thing to deserve it other than being born on the right side of the world, the more she agreed with the Monkey King. His *motivations* weren't wrong—it was just his *methods* that were wrong.

"Just because you're more powerful than everyone else doesn't mean you can take everything by force," she said. "They'll never accept you like that. And the fact that you brought a whole demon army with you to attack the heavens just proved to everyone here that the demons deserve to be banished to the island after all. Now everyone will think the demons *should* be sent to the hells. Maybe before this, we might have been able to convince everyone that the demons haven't done anything wrong, especially Shing-Rhe and the monkey brothers. But now . . ."

"What do you suggest I should have done?" the Monkey King asked.

"I don't know. But there are more peaceful ways. You could have spoken to the Jade Emperor."

"The last time I spoke to the Jade Emperor, he and Buddha imprisoned me for five hundred years under a mountain."

"Okay, but you deserved it. You stole the peaches and pills and wine, and you destroyed a bunch of temples."

He giggled. "You've been talking to the others about me."

"You could have spoken to someone else, someone in charge, someone who might have understood," Thom continued. "And explained what you really wanted. A place for your brothers. Fairness and equality—those aren't bad things. They're actually great things. If you could have found someone to listen. Guanyin maybe, or even the other immortals and fairies—"

"Oh yes," the Monkey King said with a giggle. "And how did that go for you, the last time you asked anyone in the heavens to change their mind?"

Badly. At the garden banquet, when Thom had tried to argue for the demons' sake, the fairies and immortals had all been repulsed. Just the mention of the Monkey King had made one of the goddesses faint.

"We were so close," the Monkey King said, speaking more to himself now. "We'd never come so close before." He looked distant.

"Why aren't you mad at me?" she asked. She thought he would be bitter, angry.

He shrugged. "Winning the heavens was a long shot anyway. But I'm glad you're the one who defeated me." He giggled again. "I was right about you. We are a match, both in strength and in wits. You outsmarted me. No one has done that in a long time."

Heat spread into her face. She wasn't exactly proud of what she'd done. She couldn't look directly at the golden headband. "Concao came up with the idea," she said.

"Ah. Betrayed by my closest friends." He laughed. "A great honor."

Thom gave him a funny look. What a weird thing to be proud of.

"Kha helped," she added. "And we wouldn't have been able to do it without Jae and the Jade Emperor."

If Jae hadn't read the note and convinced her father to go along with their plan—to obey the fox demon when she asked so that the Monkey King would believe the hat really did confer power—they wouldn't have succeeded. While Thom had slipped Jae the note and distracted the Monkey King in a fight she knew she would lose—again—Concao had gone to the Forbidden Armory with Jae's ring, found the golden headband, and hidden it inside the silly hat so that they could trick the Monkey King into wearing it.

Meanwhile, Kha had gone to his father, the general, to help free him and the rest of the Jade Army so they would have a winning chance against the demons and the clones. Thom had played only a small part—her friends had done most of the dangerous work.

"Take the credit, Thom-Thom," the Monkey King said. "You outwitted the Great Sage of Heaven, the Handsome Monkey King, the trickster god." He looked ready to bounce into the air but scratched at his head around the headband instead. "You could take this off, you know. Now that you've defeated me, you don't need it anymore."

"Right," she said dryly.

"No, I mean it. You've bested me. I owe you my deepest respect."

"I'm not taking off the headband."

He giggled. "Worth a try." He looked around the dark room. "This is almost as bad as the Mountain. Enclosed. Not enough space, no light, incredibly dusty, no one to talk to, nothing to do. Not even a book to read. For four hundred and ninety-eight years." He sighed.

"That sounds miserable," Thom said.

He met her eyes with a genuine smile. "When you released one of my hairs from the temple, it was like I could breathe again. I could see the world. I could talk to other people."

"How did that hair get there in the first place?" Thom asked, thinking back to the evening she'd gone with Ma to the Thien Than Temple when she'd accidentally released the Monkey King from the gourd where he'd been held prisoner.

"A battle with a monk." He shrugged. "He placed an enchantment on the little gourd and locked it up, but that was so long ago, everyone forgot, thought I was just a story, and the gourd was just an ornament. Until you came along and freed me." He looked around the room again. "I'm glad I'm not in here alone."

Thom didn't want him to know how much she felt the same. "You also helped, you know."

"What? How?"

"Your clone. One of your hairs, the one you gave me to take into the heavens when I broke in to steal the cudgel. You saved me from drowning and rescued me from the Water Lord. I gave you away, though. I'm sorry."

"Oh, that. Yes, he and I are having a great time with the Sage right now. Wise fellow. Asks a lot of questions, and actually listens to the answers. Not a lot of people I know are that smart."

"What? But I thought . . ." Thom frowned. "He—your clone, I mean—said you won't know what he's been through, and like, the other way around, until he rejoins with you."

"Oh, Thom-Thom. Did you really believe that?"

"Well, yeah. He—I mean, you—were really convincing. He said he didn't remember anything after we were together in the heavens."

The Monkey King shrugged. "I was lying. I wanted you to trust me."

How could she have been such a fool? She had believed him when she had known at that point how little he could be trusted.

"Not because I wanted to outsmart you or anything," the Monkey King added when he saw her face. "Because I really did want to protect you. And the only way I could ensure that you would be kept safe is if you kept my clone on you. If you didn't trust me, you would have just tossed me away."

"Why did you want to keep me safe when you knew I was coming after you?" She didn't understand him at all. He was supposed to be her enemy, but things were so confusing. Enemies didn't protect each other. But he couldn't be her friend, either, because he had tricked her and turned her mom into a cricket.

"We're not enemies," he said, as if he knew what she was thinking. "We just happened to be on different sides for a while. Now we are not. Someday we may be again." He shrugged. "We're alike, you and me. We have never truly belonged anywhere—the mortal world, the demon island, the heavens. Except with each other."

The door opened, and two tall soldiers of the Jade Army stepped into the room, holding out swords as if afraid Thom and the Monkey King would attack. But the Monkey King remained cross-legged on the floor, scratching at his headband, and Thom held up both hands to show she meant no harm.

"Come with us," one of them said, brandishing his sword.

He stepped out of the way as Thom moved through the door. The other soldier grabbed the Monkey King, who giggled and hugged him around his neck, lifting his legs up so that it looked as if the soldier was carrying the Monkey King romantically in his arms, like a groom carrying his bride over the threshold.

The room where they were being kept was in the dungeons of the Jade Palace, and as they moved up and through the halls, they passed by several servants and fairies. The Monkey King blew kisses at them, delighted the more they stared. The soldier he clung to tried to extract the Monkey King, but Wukong didn't budge a finger, just giggled and kissed the soldier on the cheek.

They finally came to the throne room, where Thom's steps faltered. The Jade Emperor sat on his throne on the dais, Jae on a smaller throne next to him. On the Jade Emperor's other side, the general of the Jade Army stood tall, and next to him was Kha in a minimalistic guard uniform that looked too plain and wrong on him. Officials formed lines along the walls, looking identical in black hats with plating across the backs of their heads.

The soldiers marched Thom and carried the Monkey King to kneel before the throne, though the Monkey King refused to let go of the soldier, hugging his neck with a death grip. The soldier struggled to remove him while the crowd looked on, but the Monkey King clung to the soldier's neck, his eyes full of love.

Thom couldn't help biting back a laugh. Several officials held their billowy black sleeves up to their faces as if hiding smiles. A strange huffing sound came from the back of the room as if someone was trying not to laugh.

"Enough," the Jade Emperor said.

But the Monkey King only turned his face to the throne and blew a loud, smooching kiss. The soldier looked like he might use his sword to manually extract the Monkey King, when he finally let go and floated toward the throne.

"I said enough, monkey," the Jade Emperor declared, "or I will have the girl invoke the torture of the golden headband upon your head once more."

The Monkey King landed heavily next to Thom. "The girl," he said, "has a name: It is Thom. And Thom has no reason to hurt me, not when I've done nothing wrong." He laughed, tucking his chin and pulling his wrists up to his chest. "This time."

The Jade Emperor turned to Thom. "Well?"

She bowed her head. "I . . . I want to do what I can to make things right."

The Monkey King giggled as if she'd delivered the most hilarious joke.

"Silence!" the Jade Emperor commanded, slamming a palm on his wooden armrest.

"Ooh, ouch." The Monkey King winced. "That looked like it hurt."

The Jade Emperor breathed in deeply through his nostrils. "You stand here accused of attacking the heavens, invoking a war, disturbing the peace, and attempting to overthrow the current rule."

"Don't forget, allowing the dirty, nasty, bad, bad demons into your clean, precious temples," the Monkey King said.

The Jade Emperor closed his eyes and breathed in deep. "Do you deny it?"

The Monkey King held out his palms and turned to the rest of the court, as if he were a performer and not a prisoner on trial. "Well, we have so many witnesses, how can I?" He pulled his hands back to his chest and beamed.

"And you . . . Thom." The Jade Emperor said her name with the greatest difficulty.

Thom's knees shook.

"You stand accused of helping him."

"Only at first," she said. "I didn't know what his real plans were. I only stole the cudgel because he promised me he would take my superstrength away. I didn't know he planned to wage war on the heavens."

"Nevertheless," the Jade Emperor said, "you did break in. You lied to the gatekeeper. You lied to the Jade Princess. You lied to everyone you met. You stole from a member of the royal family, you broke into the Forbidden Armory, and you took a very valuable, incredibly dangerous, highly forbidden weapon."

Thom winced at each infraction. It sounded so much worse listed out like that.

"And," the Jade Emperor added, clearly not finished, "you used that weapon to fight and incapacitate several Jade Soldiers. *And* your own father, the Boy Giant, a respected immortal of the heavens. He—and the rest of the beings you attacked—remain hospitalized to this day. Do you deny it?"

"No," she said.

Murmurs moved over the crowd.

"For your crimes, Thom Ngho, mortal of the earth, befriender of demons, accomplice to the trickster monkey," the emperor said, "you will be sent to the hells."

21

NEXT TO HER FATHER, JAE looked startled, turning to him in protest. Kha opened his mouth as if to say something, but the general held out an arm to stop him. The general must be Kha's father, Thom realized. He even looked like the Dragon Kings of the North and East, but much younger, his hair still black, his jawline shaven and firm.

"Come now, Jadey," the Monkey King said.

"Jadey?" the Jade Emperor repeated in horror.

"Thom-Thom tried to stop me, you know," the Monkey King said. "I mean, none of your other 'loyal servants' were going to step up to the task. You should have seen how easily they surrendered, one by one. The fairies gave up their peaches without even a second's hesitation. You'll have them to thank for the immortal demons roaming the earth now. The Lotus Students all dropped their weapons before we even attacked. And the Jade Army, well, one can't blame them when one considers that my demon army and my clones posed an intimidating threat. But you can't possibly call them the great army of the heavens now, after the way they sniveled and begged. They didn't even *try*."

He snickered into his furry hand. The Jade Emperor looked like steam might start spouting from his nose.

"This girl, who is a quarter of your size, by the way," the Monkey King continued, "was the only one who dared to challenge me. Not once, but twice."

The Jade Emperor bristled.

"In the end, she did what you couldn't," the Monkey King added, gesturing to the golden headband, tracing the swirls at his forehead. He held his chin high as if he bore the most elegant crown in the world. "No one else could have managed this."

"That's right!" Kha blurted out, ignoring the look his father gave him. "Thom stopped the Monkey King! We would still be surrounded by demons if it hadn't been for her."

"If it hadn't been for her," the Jade Emperor said through clenched teeth, "those demons would still be locked up. Instead, most of them have escaped into the mortal world. Apparently, they are now imbued with the gift of the peaches of immortality! Who knows what havoc they will wreak on the humans? We will be spending centuries cleaning up her mistake."

"But I can help," Thom said. "I can help you capture them."

Others started speaking at once, Jae trying to catch her

father's attention, Kha trying to agree with Thom while his father shushed him. The officials around them shouted their opinions, a mixture of agreement and, mostly, doubt.

Next to her, the Monkey King giggled, delighting in the mayhem. "This is good," he whispered. "Soon, they'll be so enraptured by their own problems, you and I can slip away."

"Stop it," she said. "I'm not on your side."

"You're not?" The Monkey King flattened his palm over his chest. "Why, that's not fair. I'm certainly on *your* side."

"No you're not. You've never been on anyone's side but your own." She ignored his hurt expression. "You call me friend, but you've never been a friend to me. You've only done what you've wanted—it's always been about you."

He looked startled, his brows pulled together.

The Jade Emperor slapped his armrest again, and the room hushed. "Well, Thom? How do you plead your case?"

She turned to him, palms sweating. "I am guilty of what you said."

A murmur ran through the crowd. Some were surprised, but others sounded almost pleased.

"And like I said, Your Majesty," she continued, "I want to make everything right. I'll help fix the Judgment Veil. I'll help recapture the demons. But . . . but I'm not going to send them to the hells."

The courtroom grew silent, as if everyone was unsure of what she'd just said.

"In fact . . ." Thom said, taking a deep breath. She looked at Kha, who smiled reassuringly, then at Jae, who just looked confused and unsure. "I'm going to release the Monkey King . . ."

At this, the officials around them all gasped. Some stepped forward as if to stop her. The Monkey King shrieked with laughter and backflipped. The Jade Emperor moved forward on his throne, one hand already gesturing for a guard.

"Unless . . ." Thom said, cutting everyone off.

They froze and waited for her next words.

"Unless you create a place in the heavens for the demons also."

Silence. Even the Monkey King didn't know what to say, staring at her with round eyes.

Then the Jade Emperor rose slowly to his feet. "How dare you," he said.

Thom's knees shook, but she held her ground. "It's not fair," she blurted out, trying to get as many words in as possible before the soldiers came for her. "The demons didn't do anything wrong—I mean, before the attack on the heavens, obviously. But you banished them to an island and to the hells when they haven't done anything to deserve that, when they were just born demons, just like fairies are born fairies."

The two soldiers who had escorted Thom and the Monkey King to the room came toward her now. The Monkey King landed in front of her and bared his teeth at them.

"Stop it," she said, swatting him on the shoulder. "You're not helping."

"Seize her," the Jade Emperor said.

"I will release him!" Thom shouted, reaching for the Monkey King's headband.

"No!" The Jade Emperor held up a hand. The soldiers stopped.

"Do it, do it, do it, do it," the Monkey King whispered.

"The demons deserve a place here as much as the rest of you," Thom said. "A place of their own. Bring the ones who haven't done anything wrong. There are some who didn't join the attack."

The Jade Emperor's face had turned red, and his robes shifted as he breathed heavily.

"And punish me by sending me after the ones that escaped. I'm strong," she said, desperate to convince him. "I can do it. I can bring them back here, and you can teach them to be good, give them a chance. That's all they want."

Still nothing.

"And if you really want to punish Wukong," she added, fighting the hopelessness that was starting to weigh her down, "make him come with me. Nothing will be worse than forcing him to capture his own friends." Thom, glancing at the headband on the Monkey King's head, knew the truth of this from experience.

"The heavens are no place for demons," the Jade Emperor said.

"Why not?" Thom asked. "You don't know them. Not all of them. There are peaceful monkey demons on the Mountain of a Hundred Giants. They haven't done anything wrong."

"Because they are demons—"

"But what makes that so wrong? They didn't ask to be demons. Just like I didn't ask to be superstrong." She held up her hands. "Even though I've accepted it now, I wanted to change it, but I couldn't. Maybe they want to change their demon-ness, too, but they can't do a thing about it. So why don't they deserve a place up here?"

"They've done nothing to earn it."

"Neither have the fairies and immortals who were born up here," Thom pointed out.

The crowd murmured, but she didn't know if it was in agreement or dissent.

"Please," Thom said, "just give them a chance.

Let me help capture the demons and bring them up here so they can prove themselves."

"You are a thief and a liar, a traitor to the heavens. Why should we trust you?" the Jade Emperor asked.

The words crushed down on Thom's shoulders. She looked at Jae, whose blank expression told Thom she was still angry. Jae might not have wanted Thom sent to the hells, but she mostly agreed with her father that Thom was a traitor. Kha looked helpless, unable to do a thing for her. Even the Monkey King was silent, looking at Thom to see what her reaction would be.

Thom knew why they should trust her: Because she wanted to make things right. Because even when she was unsure if she was really the good guy, she still wanted to do the right thing. Because even though defeating the Monkey King and freeing the heavens meant that she would be punished, she had done it anyway. But she couldn't find the words to say it. She didn't trust herself to speak the truth without stuttering and stammering and making herself look even guiltier. No one would believe her. No one was on her side—no one who could do anything about it anyway.

"Because she's right," a voice declared from the back of the room. Guanyin glided across the floor, a fairy servant on either side of her.

As they moved closer, Thom did a double take. One of the fairies was Concao! She was still a fox, of course, but dressed in the soft chiffon robes, she could have passed for a goddess. She almost smiled at Thom's reaction, but simply nodded. Even the Monkey King ogled her with openmouthed fascination, but she ignored him completely.

"Guanyin," the Jade Emperor said with an exasperated sigh. "Now is not the time for one of your charity cases."

"It's not charity." Guanyin stood next to Thom and placed a hand under her elbow as if to steady her. "It's mercy."

The Jade Emperor cut short his groan of annoyance. "Did you hear what she suggested? A place in the heavens for demons? Preposterous."

"I don't think so at all," Guanyin said.

The Jade Emperor stared at her in disbelief. "You—" he sputtered. "You agree with her?"

"Well . . . yes."

"But—"

"She's right. The demons didn't ask to be what they are."

"They attacked the heavens!"

"Yes, but perhaps, as their leaders, we failed in teaching them right from wrong."

"So you're saying that the war was *our* fault?" The Jade Emperor was practically spitting, his face almost as red as the general's armor.

"I'm saying that we were responsible," Guanyin said, "at least in part. Perhaps if we had treated them better, gave them a chance, like Thom suggested, we could have prevented the attack. But it's not too late. We can provide a space for them up here and teach ourselves and everyone in the heavens to accept the demons. To understand them, to teach them, and to learn from them."

"That one wanted me to bow to him!" The emperor pointed a finger at the Monkey King.

"Sun Wukong will be punished. But the demons deserve our mercy. I will make it my own personal project to . . . rehabilitate them and to help the fairies and immortals welcome them into our community."

The emperor sat down hard on the throne. He glared at Thom, then away. "We're not letting the girl get away with everything she's done. Did you not hear her list of infractions?"

"Of course I did," Guanyin said. "She must be punished, I agree. But she's right—sending her and the demons to the hells would be of no use."

"I don't want her to be of use. I want her to be punished."

"And she has already offered the perfect solution."

The Jade Emperor looked away and flapped a hand, annoyed.

"Send her after the demons," Guanyin continued. "She's one of the few beings strong enough to take them on. As an added torture, she'll have to take the Monkey King with her."

The Jade Emperor made a sound of protest, but Guanyin kept talking.

"Locking him up has already failed," the Goddess of Mercy said. "He always finds a way to escape. If you do as I ask, you'll have a free . . . hmm . . . babysitter."

She glanced at the Monkey King with a mischievous expression of her own. He bowed deeper to her than Thom had ever seen him bow, his nose touching his knees.

"Even if she wasn't one of the few beings strong enough to subdue him," Guanyin continued, "Thom now has the power over him no one else will, with the golden shackle on his head."

The Jade Emperor eyed Thom and the Monkey King, probably trying to think of a way to object.

"It will be dangerous, hard, grueling work," Guanyin said. "And she will spend years thinking about all the wrong she has done. The perfect punishment."

"What about school?" Thom asked the goddess quietly, thinking about how Ma would react if she found out Thom had been assigned a full-time job on top of her studies. Ma was not going to be happy about the fact that the Monkey King would be following them home, but if that meant that Thom would get to go home, she would have to find a way to tell Ma later.

"You'll be allowed to live your mortal life," Guanyin said. "As long as you don't neglect your demon-hunting responsibilities."

Thom looked up at the Jade Emperor. Everyone awaited his decision.

He took a deep breath and glared at the Monkey King as if he wished more than anything he could incinerate the demon-god on the spot. The Monkey King blew a kiss at him and batted his eyelashes.

The Jade Emperor looked up, as if communing silently with another god. He muttered to himself. "Fine," he said to the court finally.

Thom sagged, but thankfully, the Goddess of Mercy still held her arm. She patted Thom gently.

"But only as a trial," the Jade Emperor added. "We will see how she fares for the first year. If no progress is made, if she has captured no demons, if she allows the monkey even an inch of freedom, if I suspect for one second that she is not holding up her end of the deal"—he leaned forward and glared at Thom—"they will both go to the hells."

"And the demons?" Thom asked.

"Guanyin will personally be responsible for providing

them a rehabilitation temple," the Jade Emperor said, though his jaw was stiff as if it pained him.

"And you'll teach everyone to be nice to them, right?" Thom asked. She knew there was a difference between being in a place and belonging there. Just because the demons would be allowed to live in the heavens didn't mean they would be accepted unless everyone committed to welcoming them.

"Yes, yes," the Jade Emperor said dismissively.

"Don't worry, Thom," Guanyin said, smiling down at her. "You're not the only one who wants to make things right. Everyone here will work hard at fixing our mistakes. I'll make sure of it."

◆ ◆ ◆

Guanyin led Thom and the Monkey King to the infirmary next, escorted by the two Jade Soldiers who had taken them to the throne room earlier. Thom held the Monkey King's cudgel, but only because the soldiers couldn't handle the weight, and the Monkey King couldn't be trusted despite the power she held over him now. He giggled and waved at everyone they passed as if he were a celebrity on tour surrounded by his entourage. No one knew how to react to him, so they mostly gawked. Thom ignored him, even though he kept whispering in her ear and trying to make her laugh.

"Oh, look at that guy," the Monkey King said, pointing to an official. Thom didn't turn her head, but it was hard not to at least glance that way. "Looks like he has a mushroom for a nose, doesn't he?"

"Stop it," she said. "Be nice."

"That one might fall in love with me—look at the way he stares."

"He's staring because you're a prisoner, not because he's going to fall in love with you."

"I'm hurt, Thom-Thom. Truly I'm hurt."

This time, the beds in the infirmary were filled with resting fairies, immortal officials, and soldiers. Thom stopped outside a privacy screen. She could see the golden glow from inside the sectioned area, and her palms started sweating so much, she almost dropped the cudgel.

"It's okay, Thom," Guanyin said with a nod.

Next to her, Concao the fox demon turned fairy smiled, a rare sight on her otherwise stoic face. They had learned that Concao had been rewarded for her valiant efforts to stop the Monkey King: Guanyin had offered her a place in the Temple of Mercy. After a few decades of serving there, she would be made a true fairy goddess, something she had worked so hard for all of her existence.

The Monkey King was the one who nudged Thom forward, bumping into her. She stumbled into the Boy Giant's screened-off room.

He was sitting with his back to her, looking out a window with a view of the Forbidden Garden. At the sound of her footsteps, he turned. His head was still covered in a white bandage. He looked relieved and . . . happy to see her.

"Thom!" he said.

She fought back tears, rushed forward, and buried her face in his robe, wrapping her arms around him. The cudgel clattered to the floor at her feet.

"I was so worried about you," he said. "But you did it—you stopped him all on your own, and you convinced the Jade Emperor to do the right thing."

She pulled back. "You heard about that?"

"The whole heavens have heard about it. Some are saying you were very brave for standing up for the demons. I'm so proud of you, Thom."

A knot lodged in her throat, and even though she wanted to say something just as heartfelt in return, she couldn't. She looked down instead.

In his hands, held in the careful way she knew too well, was the glass mason jar that housed her mother. The cricket.

"I've been trying, but I can't lift the enchantment," he said, holding the cricket up to meet their eyes.

"That's true, you can't," Thom said. "We asked every powerful being we ran into—the Mountain God, the Dragon Kings of the North and East, and the Sage. Even Guanyin can't lift the transformation. That's why I brought this." She bent down and fumbled a bit before she picked up the cudgel.

"And him." She nodded toward the screen. The Monkey King poked his head through the opening and waved.

To his credit, the Boy Giant didn't look shocked to see the demon-god. Just weary. "Wukong," he said.

"Thánh Gióng," the Monkey King said, just as solemnly, using the Boy Giant's name. "I've come to make things right."

"Really," the Boy Giant said skeptically.

"Well, I've come to make Thom happy."

Thom frowned at him.

"Okay, fine." The Monkey King pressed his palms together and bowed to her. "I shouldn't have turned your mother into a cricket in the first place. She had nothing to do with any of this, and we're going to have to learn to get along now." He leaned down and winked at the cricket.

The Boy Giant looked questioningly at Thom, who nodded.

"We're being punished together," she said. "We're stuck with each other now."

"Oh dear." Her father looked down at her mother. "Perhaps we should keep her a cricket."

Thom almost agreed. She had no idea how Ma was going to take the news that the Monkey King would be coming home with them and that Thom would be working with him until all the demons who had escaped were brought back to the heavens.

The Monkey King giggled and skipped into the room. "But how else will I show you that I've reformed? I have so much to prove, and for my first act of repentance, I shall turn your mother back into a human." He held out his hand for the cudgel.

Thom paused. "If you try to run away, I can hurt you."

"Oh yes. I haven't forgotten. Seeing as how you don't even know how to control the headband, we may both be stuck in a twisted torment for the rest of our very long lives."

"Exactly." She gulped. "And if you try to hurt anyone, they'll send us both to the hells."

"Yes, yes, I know." His eyes gleamed as he stared at his cudgel. Then, when he realized she was observing him, he shook his head and plastered on a more serious expression. "You're going to have to trust me eventually, Thom-Thom, if we're to work together."

Thom hesitated just another moment, and then placed the cudgel into the Monkey King's hand.

He stepped one foot back as if getting ready to fly away. She stood up and prepared to lunge for him if he tried to escape. The Jade Soldiers were on the other side of the screen, but she knew it would be down to her to keep him from causing any trouble.

But then he gestured at the mason jar. "Let her out," he said.

Gently, the Boy Giant unscrewed the lid and shook the cricket out onto the bed. Her round eyes blinked up at them.

The Monkey King moved, twirling the cudgel faster and faster until it became a blur. The wind gusted around them like a twister. Thom hung on to the bedpost. The privacy screens around them fell with a clatter. The Jade Soldiers shouted something, but the Boy Giant held up a hand, so they stayed in place.

And then, all was still. Thom searched the bed for a sign of the cricket, but it wasn't there.

Instead, sitting next to her father was her mother. Her mother as a human.

Ma squinted as she looked all around her, frowning and lost. She still wore the dress she'd had on the last time Thom had seen her, right after Culture Day at school. That felt like it had been years ago, but it had only been a couple of weeks.

"Ma," Thom said, and Ma finally looked up at her.

"Cưng?" Ma's voice was hoarse.

Thom walked over slowly as if Ma would break if she moved too fast. "How do you feel?"

Ma swallowed. "Thirsty."

They got her some water, everyone watching. Ma drank at least two cups before she finally gave Thom a good look.

"Do you remember anything?" Thom asked.

"Of course I remember," Ma said, and even though her

voice was harsh, Thom was so relieved that she sounded like herself that she didn't care.

Thom sat down on the bed, and Ma pulled her into a hug. She smelled exactly how Thom remembered, a hint of lavender lotion and something clean, like laundry detergent. It felt so good to hold her that Thom almost forgot about everyone else in the room.

"A cricket," Ma muttered.

Thom pulled away.

"A cricket! You." She pointed a finger at the Monkey King, who stepped back and held his cudgel up to his chest like a shield. "You." But she couldn't seem to think of what to say to him. She turned to Thom instead. "You think just because I was cricket, I don't know anything? I don't see you do some really dangerous thing? You grounded for life."

"Now, now," the Boy Giant said. "That's a bit harsh."

"And you!" Ma turned to him, a new lecture already forming, probably. But then she really looked at him and stopped.

Ma, speechless? Thom glanced back at the Monkey King, but he was gone.

Her heart skipped several beats. But then she spotted him, floating near the ceiling, hands behind his head. He smiled and winked at her. He had handed his cudgel to the Jade Soldiers, who even between them still couldn't hold it upright.

"It's really you," Ma was saying to the Boy Giant, to Ba. He smiled and took her hand. "Are we really here? Together?"

He nodded, and once again, Ma didn't seem to know what to say. She only leaned her head down on his shoulder, so he put an arm around hers.

Guanyin touched Thom's arm and nodded at the door. Thom got up and led everyone else out, leaving her parents alone with each other.

NEXT, GUANYIN TOOK THEM BACK to her temple. There were logistics to discuss, terms to negotiate, although Thom didn't have much say in her own punishment. She already understood it was nothing short of a miracle that she wouldn't be sent to the hells.

The Jade Soldiers who now escorted Thom and the Monkey King everywhere had to remain outside the temple since Guanyin didn't like their presence in her home.

"They just take away from the merciful ambience," Guanyin said with a sigh. "You'll be under my command since I vouched for you. The Jade Emperor has his soldiers searching for the demons who escaped during the battle. Once we have a lead, we will send you to convince them to come back to the heavens."

"What will happen to them once they're here?"

"I'm working on a place for them, somewhere they can learn to be good."

"Not a prison," Thom started to say.

"Of course not. But it won't be unlike their island. They'll finally get the chance they wanted. And I've convinced many goddesses to help welcome them. Not all of the heavens see our side of things. Centuries of believing the demons are inherently bad won't be easily fixed, but at least we're trying now. First, we'll need you to bring the demons back from the mortal world."

"How will I know where to go?" Thom asked.

"I will reach out to you with your assignments." Guanyin gave Thom a compact mirror. "With this."

Thom flipped it open as Guanyin did the same to an identical mirror. Instead of her own reflection, the Goddess of Mercy's ethereal face smiled back at her.

"And you're sure it won't interfere with school?" Thom asked. "Ma will kill me if it does."

"We'll try to work around your mortal schedule. But demon-hunting comes first, Thom. That was the deal. Now, even though we're bringing the demons back to the heavens, they'll be resistant to capture. I know you're incredibly strong for a mortal, but you'll need to learn how to fight properly." Guanyin led them to a room where groups of fairy goddesses were training and sparring with one another. "My ladies are not part of the Jade Army, but they are still taught to fight so that they can protect themselves on their missions. You'll stay at the castle and learn from them while we wait for the Judgment Veil to be repaired."

The Jade Soldiers had taken the cudgel and locked it back in the Forbidden Armory, and the Monkey King looked a bit lost, as if he didn't know what to do with his hands.

"They can't expect me to capture many demons if I don't have my cudgel on me," he grumbled now.

"You won't be fighting the demons so much as convincing them to come back with you to the heavens," Guanyin said.

"They'll think it's a trap, believe me. I'll need my cudgel."

"You've proven that you are a danger with that thing," Guanyin said.

"Yes, but Thom is in charge of me now." The Monkey King rested his head on Thom's shoulder and batted his eyelashes at Guanyin. "I won't do anything that will make her unhappy."

Guanyin, not easily fooled or seduced by his charms, gave him a steadying look.

"He's right, though," Thom said. "I could hang on to the cudgel, or at least another weapon. We'll need something to defend ourselves with."

Guanyin sighed. "I'll see what I can do, but I make no promises. The cudgel is a dangerous weapon, and if we knew how to destroy it, we would have done so by now."

The Monkey King gasped and pretended to faint.

"It was already enough of a fight to convince the Jade Emperor not to send you to the hells," Guanyin said. "Not to mention the demon cloud. So don't get your hopes up about the cudgel."

◆ ◆ ◆

Training with Guanyin was not what Thom had expected it to be. She learned more about how to fight, but she spent most of her time studying the best ways to negotiate with demons.

"You may want to attack them at first sight," Guanyin said, "but remember that you are one of my girls now. You will be an instrument of mercy. You must show them compassion first, something they have not encountered before. It will be a great weapon."

"I like her," the Monkey King whispered to Thom.

Later that evening, they met Concao in the training room.

"I'm going to teach you how to control the headband," the fox fairy said. She'd discarded the soft, flowy chiffon robes and wore something more suitable for fighting. "I've been studying the ancient scrolls, and I think we can channel the power through an incantation so that you can stop it at any time and it doesn't torture the both of you."

"Hello, dearest friend!" The Monkey King floated all around Thom, trying to pull her into a dance, but she evaded his touch with her sharp, agile movements, and otherwise pretended he didn't exist. "How is it, being a fairy? Was it everything you ever wanted?"

"Focus on the headband, Thom," Concao said. "Do you feel a tugging in your chest?"

Thom stared at the collarlike diadem on the Monkey King's head. He floated in front of Concao and batted his eyelashes at her, but she pretended to see right through him.

"Yeah, like a string is tied to my heart," Thom said.

"Okay, focus on that feeling, and repeat this incantation." Concao slapped the Monkey King's finger away, and he flipped in the air, laughing at the fact that he'd finally gotten a reaction out of her. "*Na mô a di dà phật.*"

"What does it mean?" Thom asked.

"It means you rely on the light of Buddha to guide you."

"But . . . I don't."

"It doesn't matter. It's just a saying to invoke the power of the headband. Now focus on that tug in your heart and repeat the incantation."

"Okay." Thom looked at the Monkey King, but he was busy skipping in the air, and she couldn't get a good look at the golden headband.

"Wukong, get back down here," Concao ordered.

"Why? So you can teach Thom-Thom how to torture me?"

Concao narrowed her eyes.

Thom took a deep breath. She didn't want to torture the

Monkey King, but she knew she would have to learn how to control him eventually. If they were both going to succeed as demon-hunters, or at least stay out of the hells, she needed a way to subdue him.

Plus, there was Ma to think about. If the Monkey King wouldn't listen to Thom, how was he going to obey all of Ma's house rules?

"Okay, I think I have it," Thom said to Concao, keeping her eyes glued to the golden reflection on the Monkey King's head. He turned upside down, met her gaze, and disappeared.

She closed her eyes. "*Na mô a di đà phật*," she chanted. That terrible pull in her chest made her stop almost immediately.

Nothing else happened. The Monkey King was still gone. Invisible, probably sticking his tongue out at them now.

"Keep chanting it," Concao encouraged her. "Only stop when you want the pain to stop."

"Okay." Thom took a deep breath. "*Na mô a di đà phật. Na mô a di đà phật. Na mô a di đà phật—*"

"Aaaah—stop, stop, please!" the Monkey King groaned. He reappeared curled up on the floor in the corner of the room, clutching his forehead. "It works. It works. Don't do it anymore. I beg you."

"Oh my God," Thom gasped, clutching her chest. "Um, uh—"

"Try this," Concao said. "It's a Sanskrit incantation known

as the Medicine Buddha mantra, used to heal pain. It might work on the headband: *Tayata om, bekandze bekandze, maha bekandze, radza samudgate soha.*"

Thom repeated the fox fairy's chant, and the Monkey King uncurled his limbs, body limp like a puppet with its strings cut. She dropped to her knees and touched his arms. Her own chest felt like she had tried to stretch it tight and wring it like it was a wet towel. He uncovered his head, his eyes shining with tears.

"Don't let them do this, Thom-Thom," he said, whimpering. "Take the headband off. Please. I'll do what you say. I'll be your partner. Your teammate. We can capture those bad, bad demons together. I promise. Just . . . don't control me like this. I'm not . . . I'm not an animal—and even if I was, animals don't deserve this. Not even the worst, cruelest monsters deserve this, Thom-Thom. Not even our most hated enemies."

Thom's own eyes filled with tears. "I can't take it off," she whispered. "This is the only way they'll let us be free." It wasn't just the Monkey King she had to think about, or herself. What about Ma? If Thom didn't hold up her end of the bargain and they sent her to the hells, Ma would be devastated. And the demons might not get their temple in the heavens after all.

"Are you truly hurt?" Concao asked, her mask of coldness gone, her eyes concerned as she studied him.

"It's not so bad now," he said with a whimper.

"If you take it too far, keep chanting the healing

incantation," the fox fairy told Thom. "It should make him feel better."

His mouth stretched back in a grimace and he sobbed, tears soaking into the fur around his eyes. "Oh! That I were not immortal!" he wailed. "And invincible! And forced to live this life of cruelty! And—"

"Oh for mercy's sake," Concao said, yanking him to his feet. "Is it worse than being under the Mountain?"

He paused and wiped at his face. "No, I suppose not."

"Do you want to be locked up in the hells instead?"

He looked sheepish, clasping his hands together. "At least I would have a lot of fun—"

"No, you wouldn't. They would lock you away in the deepest corner in the most isolated realm, and you would be alone and lonely and made to feel even worse torture. At least Thom feels sorry for you, don't you, Thom?"

Thom wanted to be cool and collected like Concao, but one look at the Monkey King's wilted expression made her wish she hadn't been the one to put the headband on him. Why couldn't it have been someone else? Even the Monkey King's fur looked dull. His shoulders sagged. His feet dragged on the floor. He wasn't even floating. What had she done to him?

"How does it feel when I do that?" she asked. "Use the headband on you?"

"As if my very existence were being squeezed," he said. "As

if my soul were being crushed. As if my head were a grape you are trying to chomp. As if my heart were a tomato you—"

"Give me the power of the headband," Concao said, "and I will show him true pain."

"No—no!" The Monkey King held Thom in front of him like a shield against the fox fairy.

"Can I do that?" Thom asked. "Just hand over the power to you?"

"You would have to remove the headband first and then I would put it back on him. We can get the army in here to hold him down."

The Monkey King hugged Thom harder, attaching himself to her back like a turtle shell. "I'm happy with our current arrangement. We both are. Thom and I will make it work, won't we, Thom-Thom?" He patted her hair.

Thom didn't want to be the one with so much responsibility over the Monkey King, but she understood now that others would not hesitate to hurt him. Concao looked like she might enjoy it. Anyone else would be happy to do it just to watch the Monkey King suffer. At least she could keep his torture to a minimum. She would try to control him only when she needed to, only when he was about to hurt someone or do something incredibly stupid. She wouldn't abuse the power.

She nodded. "Yeah."

Concao eyed the Monkey King suspiciously, but she didn't make them practice the torture anymore.

♦ ♦ ♦

Thom visited her parents often in the infirmary, where they shared lunches and had tea together. They were both recovering quickly, but Ma was eager to go home, especially after she'd learned how much school Thom had missed.

"I have to get you tutor," Ma said. "Do extra work to catch up."

Thom rolled her eyes. Her father winked at her. Her heart sank as her parents started discussing how much tutoring she would need, how often she would have to return to the heavens for training, and what they could do to keep her workload manageable on top of the assignments she would receive from the heavens. The closer they came to returning home, the sooner she wouldn't get to see her father anymore.

They were still awkward around each other, but Thom enjoyed being with the Boy Giant. He was nice—and he had a way of convincing her mother to be nicer, too. He had lots of tips on how to live as a mortal even when you were abnormally strong, and even though he was still recovering from his injury, he tried to teach her how to fight and how to defend herself against demon attacks.

The best part about Ba was that Ma was different around

him. She laughed more, scolded less. Lectures were often cut short just because Ba patted her hand or murmured disagreement in his gentle voice. They were total opposites, but they belonged together. Anyone could see it.

Thom also hung out with Kha often during the remaining days in the heavens. He lived in the building with the Jade Soldiers, but in a wing with his father, who was technically the Dragon King of the West, but preferred to be called the general. Kha didn't like to spend much time there, though, so they usually took walks in the Forbidden Garden, where his mother, a fairy goddess in charge of a huge orchard, often invited them to tea.

"Have you talked to Jae?" Kha asked as they sat outside under the swaying leaves of a peach tree, eating lemon cookies and sipping tea. The Monkey King had been summoned by the Lotus Master, and Kha's mother had made the other Jade Soldier wait outside the orchard, so Thom and Kha had a rare moment to themselves.

"No," Thom said, stomach clenching. "Is she still mad at me?" She hadn't been back to the Jade Palace, mostly because she didn't want to face the Jade Emperor, whose disappointment frightened her. But also because she was afraid to run into Jae.

"You should talk to her," Kha said. "And find out for yourself."

"Aren't you going to tell me about how you took down an

entire demon army?" Thom asked, taking a bite of a lemon cookie. "You saved the day! You were a hero!"

"Stop it," Kha said, face turning pink. "I know what you're trying to do."

"What? You did. We wouldn't have won if it hadn't been for you."

"Nah. Once the Monkey King was defeated, everyone knew the demons didn't stand a chance. It was all you."

"It wasn't, though," Thom said. "It was you and Concao and Jae and the Jade Emperor. But mostly you." She nudged him.

Kha tried to hide his smile. "It was pretty awesome. I snuck into the building and freed the horses. They were very indignant and uncooperative at first. They don't like dragons—think they're better than us. Very arrogant. But once they realized that I had let them out, they rampaged the place. They like demons even less, so it wasn't hard to convince them to fight them off."

"Wow."

"Yeah, after that, the demons scattered like cockroaches. Then I freed the Jade Soldiers. You should have seen the look on my father's face." There was a bounce in Kha's step.

"I saw you save him from a demon," Thom said. "That was pretty cool. What did he think?"

He shrugged. "The usual."

"He wasn't impressed?"

"I mean, maybe a little. But that's the thing. Even when he is impressed, he always turns it around and says that I should be expected to be that great." Kha picked at an imaginary fleck of dust on his sleeve. He'd changed into a bright turquoise áo dài that looked more suitable on him than the army uniform had. "But I did talk to him about something. About what you said. You know, how I should be a fairy if I want to. But I don't, not all the time. So we came to an agreement. I'm going to spend half of my time with the dragons, training to be a dragon king, but the other half with my mom, tending to the orchards."

"That's . . . that's great, Kha," Thom said. "That's what you want, right?"

Kha nodded. "It's a start anyway."

"So . . . does that mean you're not going back to the mortal world?"

"I don't know. I was only sent there to help you, and now you won't need it. You'll have the Monkey King."

"I'll always need your help," Thom said, wishing more than anything that Kha was coming with her.

Kha grinned. "I'll think about it."

"What about school?" Thom asked. "They'll wonder what happened to you." And Thom wouldn't have anyone to sit with at lunch anymore, although the idea of that didn't worry her as much as it used to. After almost being sent to the hells, sitting alone at lunch wasn't such a bad thing. She shook off the thought and changed the subject. "Kha, about what I said, about you being afraid—"

"Hey, it's okay. We were both very stressed."

"I know, but I wasn't right. You were the hero—you *are* the hero. You don't have to prove anything. You're already amazing just by being you."

He grinned. "Yeah, I know."

"I really hope you come back," she said. "School won't be the same without you."

Kha didn't give an answer, just smiled and ate a cookie, and Thom wished more than ever that she could stay in the heavens, even if things weren't perfect. At least she would have her best friend and her father.

✦ ✦ ✦

When she got back to the Temple of Mercy, Guanyin was waiting for her. "They've approved my request for the cudgel," the goddess said. "Though they tried to petition me for a different weapon, none of the others would help you in your quest."

"What about the Sword of Heaven's Will?" Thom asked. "Will they be able to repair it?"

"Yes, but that sword has already served its purpose for you. Its destiny is to find the next ruler to aid them in their guidance of Vietnam. You have enough on your plate already, I think." Guanyin led Thom back to the entrance of the temple, where the Jade Soldiers stood waiting. "You'll have to retrieve the cudgel from the Forbidden Armory."

"But I don't have access to it."

"I've asked the Jade Princess to meet you there."

"What?" Thom reached for Guanyin's sleeve, as if the goddess could protect her. "But I—"

"You'll have to talk to her eventually, Thom."

"But she doesn't want to talk to me."

"She is a kind and gentle soul. She'll forgive you. Someday. But not if you don't make your heart known to her. Not if you don't apologize."

"But I have apologized. She hasn't forgiven me."

"Then keep trying."

Thom looked at the Jade Soldiers as if they might be able to help, but they stared straight ahead, expressions blank.

Luckily, she didn't have to make the trip on her own, because the Monkey King returned just as she was about to take off. The soldier escorting him looked like he was seconds away from hacking the Monkey King to pieces with his sword. He darted off as soon as he saw the Monkey King was back with Thom and her own guards.

"Trying to escape without me?" the Monkey King asked, dancing through the air around her head.

"We're going to pick up your cudgel," she said.

His eyes widened. He settled into step next to her. She could already tell that his mind was whirring with possibilities.

"It's to protect us so we can bring the demons back," she said. "Not to plot your revenge."

"Revenge? Me?" He cartwheeled off a cloud. "I am an agent of mercy now. I belong to Guanyin, the most beautiful goddess, the most wonderful immortal, the most lovely celestial ever to grace the heavens with her presence. With her guidance, I only seek peace and compassion, you know that."

"What did the Lotus Master want?" Thom asked.

"Oh, the usual threats and promises," the Monkey King said, but he didn't clarify.

Thom didn't pry further. The Monkey King and the Lotus Master had a rich history she would never truly understand.

They neared the Jade Palace, and her stomach clenched. Soon she would have to face Jae.

The princess was waiting for them in front of the armory. She heard them coming down the hall but didn't acknowledge Thom at all, just turned to face the door when Thom and the Monkey King reached her. Thom's heart beat faster, her face heated. The Monkey King raised his brows at Thom but, thankfully, didn't say anything to make fun of the princess.

"Jae," Thom started to say, but the princess averted her eyes. Jae unlocked the door to the armory and stepped inside, and Thom had no choice but to follow her. Thom paused as she passed the princess, but Jae turned away, so she went farther into the armory with a heavy heart, a soldier escorting her.

The Monkey King stayed outside with the other soldier.

The cudgel was where it had been the last time, perched on the pedestal without any other protection. Thom took it. It was still heavier than anything she'd ever carried, but it was getting easier, as if her muscles were getting even stronger, her power growing.

When she came out of the armory, Jae had a strange look on her face. The Monkey King looked as mischievous as ever. Had he said something to her?

"Thank you," Thom said as Jae closed the door.

Jae didn't say anything, instead turning to walk away. Thom realized she would have to leave the heavens with the princess still mad at her. She tried to tell herself there would be other opportunities to talk. Thom worked for the heavens now. She would have to come back to report to Guanyin.

But what if something happened to her? She would be doing dangerous work after all. What if this was the last chance she had alone—almost alone, anyway, with the Monkey King and the two soldiers watching them—with the princess? Guanyin was right. She needed to apologize and make sure Jae knew how much she regretted her choices.

"Jae, I'm really sorry," Thom said, rushing after her. The Monkey King remained behind, giving them space. "For lying to you and . . . using you."

Jae stopped and sighed, shoulders tense. "It's fine."

"No, it's not, I'm—"

"Look, Thom," Jae cut her off. "It doesn't matter anymore. I thought we were friends and I was wrong and that's that."

Thom wanted to say more, but it was obvious that Jae wasn't going to forgive her, and even if she did, it wasn't like they were going to see each other much. "Thank you, then," she said instead. "For helping us earlier, with the Monkey King, I mean. For convincing your dad to bow to Concao. It must have been really hard for him."

Jae shrugged. "It was in our best interest to go along with your plan."

Thom nodded. She started to leave, but then Jae said something.

"Why did you come back?"

"What do you mean?" Thom asked.

"You could have just abandoned us and stayed in the mortal world, but you came back even though you knew you would be punished once the Monkey King was defeated. Why?"

"Because it was the right thing to do. And, you know, it was kind of personal. The Monkey King had turned my mom into a cricket, my dad was still up here, and . . . the heavens are kind of my home, too. I wanted to make things right."

"Wasn't it hard?" Jae asked.

"Yeah. Yeah, it was really hard," Thom said. "Especially when we went looking for the Four Immortals to help us."

Jae looked startled for some reason. "Why did you need the Four Immortals?"

"The Judgment Veil was broken, and the Bridge of Souls was blocked off. The only other way into the heavens was through the paths the Four Immortals created when they ascended. The Boy Giant was already up here, so he was out. We found the Mountain God and he didn't really want to help, but he did give me the Sword of Heaven's Will. The Sage was the one who got us up here, but only after I gave him a hair of the Monkey King. We never found Princess Liễu Hạnh."

"That's because she was in the heavens, too."

"Really? Do you know her?"

"Thom," Jae said, sounding exasperated, "*I'm* Princess Liễu Hạnh. I'm the Jade Emperor's fourteenth daughter, the thirteenth reincarnation of the same soul."

"Are you serious?" Thom stared at her. "You're one of the Four Immortals? The Mother Goddess?"

Princess Liễu Hạnh was the infamous troublemaking daughter of the Jade Emperor, the one who had been punished after she broke his favorite teacup. Sent down to live with the mortals, she fell in love with them and continued to live her lives on earth with each reincarnation. Because she helped them survive several famines, people considered her the mother of all things good. At least that was what Thom remembered reading about when they were researching her for Culture Day.

Thom and Kha and Concao would have tried to find her if the Sage hadn't been willing to help them, but they would have had no idea where to start looking. Even the Dragon Kings of the North and East had said that no one had been able to find the princess for over twenty years, and this was why: Jae had chosen to stay up in the heavens this time instead of being sent down to the mortal world.

"You were here all along," Thom said. "We wanted to look for you. We would have asked you for help."

"What could I have done? I don't have any powers."

"You could have gotten us into the heavens," Thom said, "even without any powers." It occurred to her then that all of the Four Immortals had aided Thom and her friends in some way. "And you *did* help us, in the end."

"I thought you knew who I was," Jae said. "With each reincarnation, I'm different—different powers and gifts. This time, I was weak, so my father suggested that I stay in the heavens. I didn't have enough strength to survive in the mortal world, and I wouldn't have been able to protect myself or help anyone. He didn't think I would be able to handle the responsibility of the ring, either. The others all thought you overpowered me."

"But that's not what happened."

"Either way," Jae said, bitter lines bracketing her mouth, "you proved them right."

"I'm sorry," Thom said for what felt like the hundredth time. "If there's anything I can do to make you understand that, I'll do it. Maybe . . ." She looked away. "Well, like, I know you really love the mortal world, or at least you did in your previous lives. So if you ever want to go back down there, you can always stay with us. I'll show you around . . ." She trailed off lamely.

Jae left Thom standing in the hallway, alone with her sinking heart.

23

FINALLY, IT WAS TIME FOR Thom to leave. The Judgment Veil was fixed, her mom was better, and Guanyin's instructions were clear. There was no more reason to stay.

Thom said goodbye to Kha in his mother's orchard, trying not to cry as she inhaled the scent of peaches. He had decided to stay in the heavens. Their farewell was quiet, full of hugs and tears, but there was nothing left to say.

At Guanyin's temple, she was glad to see that she was leaving Concao where she had always belonged. The fox fairy had never looked so happy as she did as part of the Goddess of Mercy's team, and even happier now that she knew Thom had a way to torture the Monkey King at will.

"Want to give it another go?" Concao asked. "Make sure the headband really works?"

The Monkey King cowered behind Thom. "I'm pretty sure it works wonderfully."

"I think we're good," Thom said.

The Monkey King patted her shoulder in thanks.

"Goodbye, Concao," Thom said, pulling the fox fairy into a gentle hug before she could dart away.

Concao resisted for only a few seconds before hugging her back.

◆ ◆ ◆

The Goddess of Mercy was waiting for her at the door of her temple.

"Guanyin, thank you so much for everything," Thom said, bowing to her. "For helping us when we needed it most, for standing up for me and for the demons."

Guanyin held out an arm to Thom. "Before you leave, I want to show you something." She looked at the Monkey King. "Both of you."

She led them to a cloud not far from the Temple of Mercy.

Thom's mouth fell open when she saw it. It was an oasis, a garden secluded from the rest of the heavens with a waterfall flowing into a shining lake, surrounded by trees and flowers. The Monkey King paused next to her, then sped ahead, zipping around the cloud so fast, mist swirled behind him.

Thom stayed next to Guanyin. "Wow. Is this . . ."

"The demons' new home," the Goddess of Mercy said.

The Monkey King came back. "This is ours?" he asked. "You made this for us?"

Guanyin nodded. Thom studied the Monkey King's face for his reaction, expecting him to do backflips and somersaults, to skip through the air or shriek with laughter. But he just looked out across the cloud. And then he floated up without a word.

Thom and Guanyin walked on the path circling the water, the falls roaring in the distance, creating ripples in the lake over the pink lotus blossoms dotting its surface. Thom couldn't stop looking right and left, taking in the beauty of the sanctuary. The demons would finally have a home, and it would be beautiful, not some dark corner to keep them out of the way. She couldn't wait to bring the monkey brothers here.

"I wanted to create something the demons would want to come back to," Guanyin said. "Not a punishment, but a real home."

"They're going to love it," Thom said. "It's even better than their island. It's much better than the hells, not that I've ever been there, and won't be, thanks to you."

Guanyin laughed softly. "I'm glad you like it."

Thom looked up. The goddess was so tall that she really had to lean her head back. "Why did you help us? I mean, I'm grateful, but . . . no one else did. Why did you stand up for the demons?"

Guanyin gazed out at the lake. "You opened my eyes to a problem I didn't know we had. Despite its name, the heavens are not perfect. You were right about the demons. How unfairly we've treated them. Yes, I know some of them do deserve to be punished, but for the most part, they've done nothing wrong. And even if they have, it is because we never taught them anything else. We never allowed them the chance or even the knowledge that they could be good." She placed a hand on Thom's shoulder. "So it is I who should thank you, Thom."

"It was really the Monkey King," Thom said. "He was the one who showed me that first."

They both looked up at where the Monkey King perched on a boulder at the top of the waterfall. His elbows rested on his knees, his chin in his hands as he gazed out at the island. His face was unreadable, blank for the first time since she'd met him. Gone was the usual mischief in his gaze.

"He's really not a bad guy, you know," Thom said.

Guanyin smiled. "No, he isn't."

◆ ◆ ◆

Last, Thom went to the Lotus Academy to say goodbye to her father, but he wasn't there. His classroom and bed-chambers were empty. She lingered, sitting at the table where she'd had tea with him and Jae, when he'd asked so many questions about Ma, she should have seen through him. When he'd served way too many cookies and dumplings, when he had wanted to know so much about her.

She wiped her eyes, got up, and went to meet her mom at the Judgment Veil.

The Monkey King was already there with the usual escort of Jade Soldiers. Her mom stood with him and, next to her . . . was Thom's father.

Thom jumped onto the cloud, so happy she hadn't missed her chance to say goodbye that she almost knocked him over.

"I looked for you at the Lotus Academy," she said. "But you weren't there."

"What's wrong?" the Boy Giant asked. "Did you need something?"

"I wanted to say goodbye."

"Goodbye? But why would you need to say goodbye?" He frowned. "I'm coming with you."

"What? You are?" Thom looked at Ma, who smiled. "He is? When—how? I thought gods aren't supposed to live with mortals."

"The Jade Emperor want you to go after dangerous demon," Ma said, "without any training? No way, I said. You're only eleven."

"Almost twelve," Thom pointed out.

"Still, you're just a baby. I say he can go catch demon himself if he think it so easy."

"But I was getting trained," Thom pointed out.

"By Guanyin? She no warrior. Your ba." Ma patted the Boy

Giant on the back. "He a true warrior. I say he will teach you or no one else, and the Jade Emperor finally say okay."

Thom was horrified at the image of her mother going up against the Jade Emperor. She didn't know who she felt sorrier for. What if the Jade Emperor took it the wrong way and took away the demons' cloud or sent her to the hells after all? What if he punished Ma, too, for defying his judgment?

"Don't worry, Thom," Ba said, wrapping a comforting arm around Ma. "The Jade Emperor, your mother, and I struck a deal. I will come to the mortal world with you to train you. Help you. That way, he gets what he wants—the demons out of the mortal world. And you receive guidance. You'll need it, even with the Monkey King's help."

"And that another thing," Ma said, eyeing the Monkey King, who was still guarded on either side by soldiers. "He have to come with you? More like punishment for me, not you."

"Which is why," Ba said, squeezing her shoulders, "you'll have my help. And I'm tired of being away from my family." He smiled.

Thom couldn't believe it. Ba was coming to live with them. She would have a father. She didn't have to say goodbye.

"I . . ." the Boy Giant said, looking shy. "I hope that's okay with you, Thom. We should have asked, of course . . . But I thought . . ." He glanced at Ma hesitantly.

"Ask?" Ma said. "She our daughter, why ask? She just need to obey."

"Yes, but it's also her choice," he said in a low voice. "Her life."

Before Ma could argue, Thom grabbed both of their hands. "Of course it's okay," she said. "It's more than okay." Then, because her voice was starting to crack, she nodded and added, "Let's go home."

Ba smiled. Ma tried not to.

Thom looked back at the Monkey King, who was watching all of them with guarded amusement.

"Wish I had a family," he said with a sad chuckle.

"But you do." Thom stepped back to walk next to him.

"You have Shing-Rhe and your monkey brothers. And me, now. We're stuck with each other."

He made a satisfied monkeyish noise in the back of his throat. Then he hopped onto her back, weightless as he wrapped his arms around her. "And there's no one else I'd rather be tortured with, Thom-Thom."

With the Jade Soldiers escorting them, they stepped together through the Judgment Veil.

◆ ◆ ◆

"First thing first," Ma said to the Monkey King as soon as they got home. "If you live here, you have to pick up your hair."

"My hair?" The Monkey King looked at the floor behind him. "But what's wrong with my hair?"

"I can't have your hair falling everywhere. The dog is already enough. Where is the dog?" Ma looked around the kitchen. "Mochi?"

"Oh," Thom said, stopping halfway up the stairs to her room. "I took him to my friend Kathy's house to watch him."

"Your . . . friend?" Ma asked, looking confused. "Kathy?"

"Yeah, she's on the soccer team." Thom came back down. "I can go pick him up. Wukong will take me."

The Monkey King bowed. "At your service."

"You can't go by yourself," Ma said.

Ba came to her side. "Why not? She just explored the whole world by herself, searching for dragon kings and immortals. And she saved the heavens. I think she can handle a trip to her friend's house." He gave Thom a wink when Ma wasn't looking.

"But . . ." Ma started to say.

Ba dug through the pantry and pulled out a bag of flour. "I'm making cookies. Want to help?"

Ma looked from Thom to Ba, probably unsure how to respond to the new situation.

"We won't take long," Thom said. "Kathy doesn't live far. We won't go anywhere else. You want Mochi back, don't you?"

"Maybe we go as family," Ma said.

"But what about the cookies?" Ba asked, opening the fridge.

Ma sighed. "Do you have your phone?" she asked Thom.

Thom pulled it out of her backpack. It hadn't worked in the heavens, so she had turned it off to save the battery.

"Okay, then," Ma said. "You call if anything happens?"

"Yes."

"And you tell Kathy thank you for watching your dog?"

"Of course, Ma."

"And ask her parents to call me."

"Ma," Thom said, exasperated.

"Okay, okay." Ma still looked unsure. She put her hands on Thom's shoulder and leaned down to meet her eyes. "You all big now, hah? Not my baby anymore."

Thom gave her a hug, surprising them both. "No, not a baby," Thom said. "But still yours."

Ma's lower lip wavered. "Okay, go." She pushed Thom gently away. "And, monkey."

The Monkey King hovered above the door. "Yes, Mother?"

He had meant to goad her, but Ma was unfazed. "You take care of her."

The Monkey King saluted. Thom grabbed his hand and dragged him out the door before he could do something else to change her mom's mind.

As they flew past Kha's empty house, a heavy nostalgia dragged her down over the thought of not seeing him again. Or at least, not as often. Not at school. Not living next to her. It seemed wrong somehow, that they had spent almost every day together for the last few weeks, and now he was just gone. She had no idea when she would see him again. And even if she did, they might never be as close as they once were.

"Wait here," Thom told the Monkey King when he dropped her off in the nearby park.

He swung onto a tree branch and leaned back against his arms.

Thom walked the remaining block to Kathy's house. The neighborhood looked different from the last time she saw it, when she had been so fearful of what was to come, when she had been so determined to stop the Monkey King, so angry at what he'd done. Now the sidewalks seemed cleaner, the air lighter and clearer. Things were going to be okay. A lot of hard work lay in front of her, but at least she had everything she needed. Her mom and dad, a good friend, and the help of a powerful goddess.

She knocked on Kathy's door. When it opened, she didn't know who was more surprised—her or Bethany Anderson. Instead of the soccer uniform or practice clothes that Thom was used to seeing her in, Bethany wore jeans and a T-shirt, and didn't have any shoes on. Her bare feet made her look so vulnerable that Thom wondered why she'd ever been so afraid of her.

"Um, hey," Thom said when Bethany just stared at her. Thom looked at the number on the house. "This is still Kathy's place, right?"

"Right." Bethany crossed her arms and looked Thom up and down. "What are you doing here?"

"Who is it?" someone called from the living room. Sarah Mazel.

But before Bethany could answer, Kathy came up behind her. For a second, Thom wondered what was going to happen. She geared herself up for something bad. The girls would eye each other. Laugh at Thom with ill-hidden malice. Kathy had been nice to her when they were alone sometimes, but in front of her friends, she had always treated Thom as if she wasn't worth it.

Weeks ago, the idea of their bullying might have frightened

her, made her withdraw into herself. But now she knew she was made of stronger stuff. She had defeated demons and battled the most powerful one of them all. She had faced off with the Jade Emperor and stood up for herself. She had challenged the heavens and asked them to change.

She could handle a couple of middle school girls.

To her surprise, Kathy grinned and waved at her. "Thom! You're back!" Kathy threw her arms around Thom's shoulders, and Thom froze, not expecting that, not knowing what to say. She patted Kathy's back awkwardly until Kathy pulled away.

"Yeah." Thom smiled, ignoring Bethany's stunned face. Sarah joined them at the door, mouth dropping open at the sight of Thom.

"I was really worried about you. Is everything okay? Where's Kha?" Kathy looked behind Thom.

"He . . . he moved," Thom said through a lump in her throat.

"What?" all three girls asked.

"Again?" Bethany asked. "Didn't he, like, just move here?"

"Yeah, it was really sudden, but . . ." Thom shrugged. "He decided to go back. To where he used to live. He's happier now."

"Seriously?" Kathy tucked her hair behind her ear. "That's a bummer. I really liked him."

"Yeah, I'm really going to miss him," Thom said. "But maybe he'll come visit."

"Let us know if he does, and we can all hang out," Kathy said. Bethany and Sarah looked at each other.

"Sure." Thom laughed, surprised but not sure how to react to Kathy being so nice to her. "Um, I came to get Mochi. Hope he didn't misbehave or anything."

"No way, he's like the best dog ever." Kathy opened the door wider. "I wish I could keep him forever."

Thom grinned. "You can come over and play with him anytime you want."

"Really? That's awesome." Kathy held on to the door. "Hey, want to come in? We're about to watch a movie."

Kathy was inviting Thom in. To hang out. With her. And her friends. Was this really happening? Thom had waited all school year for something like this. She looked at Bethany and Sarah for their reaction.

Bethany hesitated, but then shrugged. "Yeah, we haven't chosen, like, anything yet," she said.

Sarah still looked unsure, but Bethany nudged her. "I mean—yeah, you could be, like, the deciding vote."

It was exactly what Thom had hoped would happen when she'd joined the soccer team at DeMille Middle School. Friends. Someone to hang out with. Watch TV, have sleepovers, talk.

But the Monkey King was waiting for her nearby. And her dad was at home, finally, baking cookies. And her mom was no longer a cricket. There would be time for a social life later.

"I can't today," Thom said. "But maybe next time."

Kathy nodded understandingly. Bethany and Sarah looked indignant, as if no one had ever dared to turn them down before. But Thom didn't care. She followed Kathy into the house to collect Mochi. When he saw her, her dog wagged his tail so wildly that his back legs practically lifted. He jumped into her arms and licked her face. Kathy laughed, watching them, reaching out to scratch Mochi behind the ear.

Thom thanked Kathy and her parents for watching him, then headed out.

"You mean it, right?" Kathy called after her from the door. The other girls had gone back inside. "You'll come over another time?"

Thom nodded. "Yeah, definitely. Thanks again."

Kathy hesitated. "I'm really sorry," she blurted out, her face a bit scrunched up, as if it was hurting her to get the words out, but in a good way like when you finally had your stitches removed. "About . . . you know . . . before." She mumbled something else that Thom couldn't understand. But Thom was pretty sure she knew what Kathy meant.

"It's okay," Thom said, and she smiled to let Kathy know she meant it. Kathy let out a breath. "It really is. I'll . . . see you at practice."

"See you at school." Kathy waved.

Thom waved back and walked away with a lightness she hadn't felt for a long time, Mochi wiggling in her arms.

When she got back to the park, the Monkey King was waiting for her, perched on a branch, legs swinging.

"Ready?" he asked.

"Yeah."

He reached down and grabbed her hands, and together they went home.

ACKNOWLEDGMENTS

Thank you first to all the readers who made it this far! I'm so sorry about the cliffhanger ending in the first book, but I hope it was worth it.

I could never have gotten through this story without the work of my wonderful unicorn witch agent, Mary C. Moore. Thank you for your encouragement and support, believing in this story from the very beginning, and reminding me of all the reasons we started Thom's journey.

This adventure would not be the fun and magical ride that it is without the guidance and genius of my editor, Mekisha Telfer. Thank you for bringing Thom's story to life, the many hours you've poured into these books, and your steadfast work—all during a pandemic, too! To the rest of the team at Roaring Brook for championing this series and giving them a place in the world: Aurora Parlagreco, Allyson Floridia, Janet Renard, Melissa Croce, Mary Van Akin, Cynthia Lliguichuzhca, Kathryn Little, Celeste Cass, Connie Hsu, and Jennifer Besser. Thank you also to Phung Nguyen Quang and Huynh Kim Lien for yet another beautiful cover and more gorgeous illustrations.

To my agent-siblings for the boosts: Brandi Zeigler, Emi Watanabe Cohen, Rachelle E. Morrison, Alex Temblador, Donna Muñoz, Rati Mehrotra, and especially Kylie Lee Baker for being my DM buddy. And, of course, Amber Reed for your wonderful blurb and overall heartfelt support.

Thank you to my sister Vy Hoang for always checking up on me and for telling strangers about my books. To my mom, Tan Nguyen, for never once suggesting I become a doctor and my dad, Lon Hoang, for still, to this day, reminding me to do well in school. Con viết cuốn sách nữa!

To my bff4eva Susie Tae for <3-ing every one of my messages at all odd hours of the day and night, for your unwavering emotional support, for the surprise funnel cake and churros, our unboxing videos and vision board sessions, for obsessing with me over stickers and pens and markers and *goals*, and for reading all the books I recommend. To Adrian Garza for, um, the same. Just kidding—for your artistic critiques and questioning my understanding of the words *funnily* and *startled*. *Started?* To everyone else in our book club for never cringing whenever I talked about this book, especially Asia Evans for keeping us cool cool cool cool cool, Taona Haderlein for never saying no to shared appetizers, Janet Park for introducing me to charcoal soft-serve ice cream, and Valerie Worley for keeping me up-to-date on the latest YA.

I could not have gotten through the first draft without the overwhelming encouragement of the librarians, clerks, pages, volunteers, and staff at Huntington Beach Public Library. Thank you to all my work wives for the giggles and virtual hugs during the pandemic, especially to Melissa Ronning for always cheering me on, April Lammers for the constant support, Jessica Framson for being an all-around wonderful person, Laura Jenkins for adding so much beauty to the world, Abby Tapia for bringing an abundance of happiness and love to life, and everyone else who has been with me through this journey: Jessica Castro, Stephanie Beverage, Barbara Richardson, Claudia Locke, Lori Hellinger, Cynthia Flores, Steven Park, Christine Moore, Christany Edwards, Marissa Chamberlain, Maribel Fernandez, Lori Wright, Bonnie Novak, Andrea Sward, Mary Keeley, and Michele Gutierrez.

My friends deserve awards for hearing so much about these books and still being excited for me: Christine Truong for your lifelong friendship, Beverly Silvas and Maribeth Arriola for always being there, and Alex Lee for opening my eyes to the ideas that made this story possible.

And finally, thank you, thank you to my alpha reader, best friend, mischief-making husband for being the Tôn Ngộ Không in my life. I would never have made it this far without your guidance, research assistance, and supportive presence. Thank you also to our baby monkey demon for keeping me up at night so I could finish this book. As always, words will never be enough, so I'll end with this: heart, heart, kissy-winky face, huggy jazz hands, huggy jazz hands, huggy jazz hands, fireworks, monkey-see-no-evil, monkey cry-laughing, monkey smile, monkey sitting, cartwheel, cartwheel, cartwheel.